BAD BLOOD

In 1991 Dana Stabenow, born in Alaska and raised on a 75-foot fishing trawler, was offered a three-book deal for the first of her Kate Shugak mysteries. In 1992, the first in the series, *A Cold Day for Murder*, received an Edgar Award from the Crime Writers of America.

THE KATE SHUGAK SERIES

A Cold Day for Murder
A Fatal Thaw
Dead in the Water
A Cold Blooded Business
Play With Fire
Blood Will Tell
Breakup
Killing Grounds
Hunter's Moon
Midnight Come Again
The Singing of the Dead
A Fine and Bitter Snow
A Grave Denied
A Taint in the Blood
A Deeper Sleep
Whisper to the Blood
A Night Too Dark
Though Not Dead
Restless in the Grave
Bad Blood

DANA STABENOW

BAD BLOOD

First published in the United States of America in 2013 by
Minotaur Books, New York

This edition first published in the UK in 2013
by Head of Zeus Ltd

9 7 5 3 1 2 4 6 8

A CIP catalogue record for this book is available from the British Library.

ISBN (HB): 9781781851203
ISBN (XTPB): 9781781851210
ISBN (E): 9781781852897

Printed in Germany.

Head of Zeus Ltd
Clerkenwell House
45-47 Clerkenwell Green,
London EC1R 0HT

www.headofzeus.com

For Sharyn Wilson,
traveling companion extraordinaire.
China, Peru, Turkey—
where next?

BAD BLOOD

Prologue

One

TWO VILLAGES, WHERE TWO RIVERS MEET.

A geologic age before the runoff from Alaskan Glacier high up in the Quilak Mountains chewed through a granite ridge to form a narrow canyon fifteen miles long.

A millennium before, a massive earthquake exacerbated a fault in the ridge. Half of it cracked and slid off to the southwest. It left behind a V-shaped wedge between the confluence of two watercourses, which would one day be named Gruening River on the south side and Cataract Creek on the north.

The tip of the vee pointed due west. The surface of the wedge was flat and topped with a thick slice of verdant soil raised a hundred feet in the air by the earthquake. That earthquake had also fractured a way to the surface through the granite uplift for an underground spring. The spring's outflow trickled down the south face of the wedge, over time carving a channel for a little stream too steep to support a salmon run and too shallow to be good for anything but watering the blueberry bushes that grew thickly along its sides. In spring, this slope was first to thaw, snow and ice giving way to a fairyland of wildflowers, the brash orange and yellow florets of western columbine, the shy blue of forget-me-nots, the noxious brown blooms of chocolate lilies, the elegant pink paintbrush, and the dignified purple monkshood.

By luck of the geologic draw, the land across the river remained largely undisturbed by the earthquake, remaining a flat marsh covered in thick grass, cattails, and Alaska cotton. Over time glacial silt carried downriver filled in the marsh, and alder, diamond willow, and cottonwood grew out to the water's edge. The force and flow of the combined currents of river and stream undercut the banks to provide habitat for river otters, mink, and marten, and carved tiny tributaries to be dammed by beavers and colonized by salmon.

Two hundred winters before, the Mack family walked up the frozen river. It was a wide river, not too deep, with a good gravel bottom. When it thawed that spring, even on a cloudy day an endless silver horde was visible through the peaty water, a solidly packed, seemingly inexhaustible mixture of king and red and silver salmon moving inexorably upstream. Tobold Mack, the little clan's patriarch, had led them south from the Interior, where a wasting disease had affected the moose population. A decade of famine had led to inter-tribal competition among the local Athabascans over the remaining food sources, and to a disastrous decline in population of man and beast alike.

That summer, Tobold looked long on where the white water rushed to join the brown, at the arrows in both left by the dorsal fins of the struggling salmon, the birch stumps left by the beavers and the willow stands gnawed down by the moose. He looked up at the mountains that cut into the eastern horizon, beautiful and terrible, and yet comforting all the same in their solid impenetrability. With mountains like those at his back, a man felt safe.

"We have walked far enough," he said.

They built a weir and a snug dugout on the south shore of the river. Drying racks were next, for fish in summer and moose meat in winter, and caribou when the Quilak herds came down to the river to calve in spring. Babies were born and lived, and elders survived long enough to contribute their accumulated wisdom to the tribe, and for everyone in between there was enough food easily available that there was time to sing and dance and play and laugh. Time to not only make a birchwood bowl for eating, and time to carve decorations around its edge. Time not only to make a parka from beaver skins warm enough to withstand the worst winter could throw at them, and time to embroider the parka with trade beads and dentalium shells.

This village they named Kushtaka.

Seventy winters before the present day, Walter Estes and Percy Christianson came up the river, trappers looking for beaver. They were new to the country but not to Alaska, being Aleuts displaced from the island of Anua by the war the Japanese had brought to the great land. Walter and Percy had fought together in the islands and knew firsthand how little there was to go back to. Now they looked for a new place to call home.

The Macks, like any Alaskans happy to see a new face in the long dark doldrums of winter, made them welcome. Estes was half Italian and Christianson was half Norwegian but they both comported themselves as men should, sharing the game and the fish they took in equal measure with their hosts. There was still more than enough for all, then.

Five years later, Walter and Percy moved across the river and built their homes on top of the big wedge of rock rising in the vee between the creek and the river.

The Macks approved. Ownership of any part of river and creek and its adjacent lands was not a concept the people of Kushtaka understood. They hunted the moose that browsed through the willow and the caribou that calved on the riverbanks, they trapped the beaver and the river otter and the muskrat, they gathered the crowberries and the blueberries that grew on the south-facing slope of the wedge, and they cut the wood of the spruce and birch and alder for fuel. They took enough, never too much, because there was always next season, and they knew from hard experience handed down from Tobold Mack himself that there was always the chance that the next season could be a bad one, with the long cold returning, scarce game, and too many mouths to feed. In this vast land, there was still plenty of room for all, and a good neighbor was always welcome in hard times.

Percy sent for his bride, Balasha, who was half Russian, a plump, lively woman who settled down to smoke salmon, weave grass baskets in the fashion of the Aleuts, and pop out healthy children at the rate of one every two years. Walter married Nancy Mack, who joined him up on the wedge, in the log cabin he built for her.

They called their village Kuskulana. It was not as conveniently placed as Kushtaka, being a hard slog uphill from the salmon-rich waters of river and creek, and a longer, harder slog uphill when burdened with the hindquarter of a moose. But the spring that bubbled up provided much better drinking water than the Kushtaka wells, which were brown and brackish, and its sharp point hid a good-sized plateau that widened to the east, a good site for an airstrip. Walter, inspired by the sight of the fighters and bombers who had filled the air over the skies of the

Aleutians during the war, was determined to learn to fly and promptly hacked an airstrip out of the alders, tied a red flannel shirt on a pole at one end for a wind sock, and bought one of the first Piper Super Cubs.

Twenty winters on, President Eisenhower signed Alaska's statehood act, and among other things, the federal government began to build post offices in the Bush. Air taxies all over Alaska got federal mail contracts. Kuskulana and Kushtaka both applied for the post office, which went to Kuskulana because they had the airstrip, and Walter's son, Walter, Jr., got the mail contract.

And because the post office was in Kuskulana, a Christianson got the postmaster's job, a rare prize in Bush Alaska, full-time federal employment with a steady paycheck and benefits.

Twelve years after statehood, President Nixon signed the Alaska Native Claims Settlement Act, in which Alaskan tribes gave the federal government a right-of-way across aboriginal lands from Prudhoe Bay to Valdez for the Trans-Alaska Pipeline, built to bring North Slope oil to market. In exchange, the tribes received forty-four million acres and almost a billion dollars.

Some Alaska Natives claimed that, with the formation of tribes into corporations, their homes, their ways of life, their very cultures would be forfeit, requiring them to become white in an already too white world. But land and money, those two possessions by which white culture measured itself, were powerful inducements. As most tribes did after enduring three hundred years of forced secondary status, Kuskulana opted into the agreement.

Kushtaka was one of the handful of Alaskan villages that did not.

ANCSA money flowed into Kuskulana coffers, and the village blossomed out with new houses and the villagers with new skiffs and drifters and four-wheelers and snow machines.

Kushtaka rechinked the steadily increasing gaps between the logs on their fifty- and hundred-year-old cabin walls, and made do with boats and Snogos inherited from their fathers.

Kuskulana was given its pick of parcels of prime land in the area, and every Kuskulaner of any age from six months to sixty years became the proud owner of a five-acre lot, many of them on the Gruening River and several of which encroached on the land where Kushtaka's fish wheel had stood for generations. Roger Christianson, Sr., even tried to lay claim to the fish wheel site itself. Said claim was quickly quashed, but the Kushtakans didn't forget. It didn't help matters when Kuskulana built their new boat landing almost directly across the river from the Kushtaka fish wheel. The wash from the Kuskulana skiffs muddied the water near the fish wheel and frightened the salmon.

Dale and Mary Mack at Kushtaka opened a little store in their living room, stocking it with items they bought in bulk from Ahtna and Anchorage and selling them at a modest markup, dry and canned goods, cases of pop and potato chips, aspirin and Band-Aids.

And then Roger Christianson and Silvio Aguilar opened a full-service store in its own building in Kuskulana, with everything the Macks' store carried plus fresh fruit and vegetables and even fresh milk.

The Macks' store was out of business in three months. Dale Mack and Roger Christianson bumped into each other at Costco in Ahtna and had words that were witnessed by people from both villages, words that lost nothing in the retelling and only hardened the attitudes of everyone who heard it second- and thirdhand. You couldn't trust a Kuskulaner not to steal your idea and cheat you out of your business, the Kushtakans said. Those Kushtakers, said the Kuskulaners, they hadn't really made it into this century yet, you know? Probably wouldn't ever, the rate they were going. They hadn't even managed to muster the wherewithal to pay for a power line across the river, and there wasn't a flush toilet in the entire village.

Whereas every new house in Kuskulana had hot and cold running water.

Teenagers of both villages, quick to pick up the elder vibe, began a series of hormone-driven confrontations at various potlatches. Outnumbered five to one, the Kushtakers took home the majority of the bruises, but so long as the hostilities were confined to the occasional tribal celebration held far away from either village, the adults were inclined to look the other way.

Two years before, the world's second-largest gold deposit was found sixty miles north-northeast of where the creek and the river met.

Before the first backhoe was airlifted into the Suulutaq Mine, the population of Kuskulana climbed onto its many four-wheelers and beat down a serviceable trail between their village and the mine site. With ready access winter and summer, the trail made their people more attractive as employees to mine management. Given the working airstrip, Kuskulana became the designated alternative landing site in case Niniltna and Suulutaq were both socked in at the same time. Which made the Kuskulana strip eligible for federal funds for runway improvements, an electronic weather-reporting station, and the construction of a hangar.

Kuskulana was, therefore, enthusiastically pro-mine, and their people came home to spend their paychecks.

Kushtaka, on the wrong side of the river, sent fewer workers to the mine. Those who went seldom returned, preferring to resettle in Kuskulana and Niniltna and Ahtna and even Anchorage, where there was cable and Costco, and Beyoncé concerts only a 737 ride away. Kushtakans, fearing the drain on their population and resenting the ever-increasing wealth of their parvenu neighbors, came down hard against the mine, on the side of the fishermen and the environmentalists and the conservationists who were devoting their considerable resources to stop it.

That September, Zeke Mack was out moose-hunting on the south side of the river. Inexplicably, he missed the bull with the four brow tines on both sides and instead put a hole through the trailing edge of the right wing of Joe Estes's 172. Joe having just taken off from the south end of the Kuskulana airstrip and at that time 150 feet in the air.

Joe got back down in one piece, but it soon became known in both communities where the shot had come from, and there was some subsequent conversation about just how bad Zeke's eyesight was. A lot of laughter accompanied the conversation in Kushtaka. Laughter was conspicuous by its absence in Kuskulana, whose pilots started taking off to the north.

The following May, the state announced that it was closing the Kushtaka school because enrollment had fallen below ten students, and that Kushtaka students henceforth would attend the Kuskulana school. Truth to tell, Kushtaka had been fudging the numbers for years. Roger Christianson, Jr., in Kuskulana and Uncle Pat Mack in Kushtaka—on the whole, sensible men—did think privately that perhaps some of the hostility between the two villages might abate once the kids started having to sit next to one another in class.

That, of course, was before someone tried to set the Kuskulana Public School on fire with a five-gallon can of gasoline and a blowtorch.

And last September, Far North Communications built a cell

tower in Kuskulana. They dedicated one of the antennas on the tower to Kushtaka.

Geography informs who we are.

Kuskulana, flush with ANCSA, state, and federal dollars and land, a post office, an airstrip, a store, a school, a cell tower, on the same side of the river as a world-class industrial development and with a trail navigable by ATV and snow machine between the two, flourished.

Kushtaka . . . did not.

Act I

Two

TUESDAY, JULY 10

Kushtaka

TYLER MACK WAS AN EIGHTEEN-YEAR-OLD stick of postadolescent dynamite just waiting for the right match. He was smart in all the wrong ways, using his intelligence chiefly to conspire with Boris Balluta, his best friend and coconspirator since childhood, on ways and means to avoid manual labor.

Of medium height, built mostly of muscle and bone, Tyler had thick dark hair that flopped into dark brown eyes that always seemed to be more focused on his next deal than on the person he was talking to. He was a shirttail relative of Auntie Edna in Niniltna, which made the entire Shugak clan part of his extended family in Byzantine ways known only to its elders. Auntie Edna considered him a member of her personal tribe and was quick to grab him up by the ear when word of his activities came her way. Tyler, as quick as he was lazy, took good care to keep his ears out of her reach.

But this morning he hadn't been quick enough, his uncle Pat having dumped him out of bed at sunup, which in mid-July was 2 A.M., and booted him into his clothes and on his way upriver without so much as a mug of coffee to get his heart started.

It was a beautiful morning, clear and cool. Mist smoked up from the surface of the water, broken temporarily by the bow of the skiff moving upriver, closing in again behind its stern. Night, in summer only a suggestion of twilight between midnight and oh-dark-thirty, gave way to an intensifying rim of gold on that part of the horizon stretching from the northeast all the way around to the southwest. Uncle Pat's outboard was so finely tuned and so diligently maintained that its muted purr was barely audible above the rush of water beneath the skiff's hull. Eagles chittered from treetops. A moose cow and two leggy calves foraged for the tenderest shoots of willow on one bank. Around a bend, a grizzly bear sleeping peacefully on a gravel bar woke with a snort and glared around nearsightedly. He rolled to all four paws and gave himself a good shake, his thick golden pelt moving almost independently of the rich layer of fat beneath, and lumbered into the water to bat out a morning snack of red salmon.

Tyler noticed none of this. He hated working the fish wheel almost as much as he hated getting up before the crack of noon. Working the fish wheel was way too wet and entailed way too much heavy lifting for a man clearly meant for a cushier life. Uncle Pat was well able to tend to the fish wheel himself, eleven hundred years old or not. Tyler had had plans for today, plans that involved Boris and a scheme that was going to make them both rich enough to escape the influence of old farts like Uncle

Pat and Auntie Edna once and for all and set their feet on the path to riches and the high life. Park Strip condos in Anchorage, fitting themselves out in Armani at Nordstrom, parties at the Bush Company, weekends in Vegas. They'd be MVP Gold on Alaska Airlines before the year was out, and then everyone who'd ever shown Tyler Mack the back of their hand had better by god look out. Tyler was on his way to the big time, and no one and nothing was going to get in his way. He'd already proved that once, and he was ready to do it again, anyplace, anytime.

He imagined Uncle Pat coming to him for a loan for a new kicker or a new shotgun, and smiled to himself. Of course he would give him the money. Of course he would. He only hoped the old man would stroke out trying to say thank you.

Two miles above Kushtaka village, the river had carved a wide loop in the face of the landscape. Cottonwood grew in clumps on the curve, thick trunks covered with coarse bark looming thirty feet over the alder and diamond willow jostling for place below. The soft wood of the cottonwood tree made it prone to snap off in high winds. Cottonwood scrags formed bridges for the alder and willow to lean on and trail leafy fingers in the water beneath. Together they cast welcome shadows over the gravel shallows for weary salmon returning home to spawn.

The Mack family had had a fish wheel just below that gravel bar since 1901, when a stampeder, one Joshua Malachi Smith, had struck out panning for gold and got lost on his way to Valdez for a boat home. Daniel Mack found him trying to catch salmon with his bare hands, and the Kushtakans took him in before he starved to death or died of exposure, whichever came first. In return, he taught them how to build a fish wheel, a series of buckets on a wheel caused by the current of the river to rotate on an axle. The buckets scooped up the fish on their way upriver and dumped them into a chute that led to a holding pen. When the salmon were running, the holding pen had to be emptied two and three times a day. During a good run, sometimes more.

The first fish wheel was made of woven willow, which did not stand up well to a current made swift and strong by runoff from a winter's worth of snow, and had to be rebuilt every spring. Today, the Mack fish wheel was made of stainless steel and mesh, held together with nuts and bolts. It was indestructible as well as portable, designed to be removed from the water at the end of each season and rebuilt at the edge of the river again every spring.

A fat red jumped on Tyler's left, falling back against the water with a rich, full smack! The sun peeped over the Quilaks just in time to turn the resulting flash of droplets into liquid diamonds, suspending them momentarily in midair before they fell back into the river, itself a moving, jeweled surface pregnant with mystery and treasure.

None of which did Tyler take any notice of, and this in a year in which king salmon were scarce and cloudy, rainy days plentiful.

What he did see as he nosed the skiff into the bank next to the fish wheel, was Jennifer Mack in a skiff on the other side of the river. The wrong side of the river, which is what you might expect from a girl, who had no business anywhere near a fish wheel anyway.

He opened his mouth to ask her what the hell she thought she was doing—maybe he could blackmail her into working the wheel today while he was at it—when he caught sight of a second figure, a man standing in the alders at the foot of the set of stairs leading down to the gravel bar that served as Kuskulana's landing. The man stepped forward to catch the bowline she threw and hitched it to a tree branch.

It was Ryan Christianson, and the outraged yell died in the back of Tyler's throat, unuttered.

Pat Mack's outboard was so quiet that neither of them heard or saw Tyler, or maybe they were just too concentrated on each other to be aware of anything else. They vanished into the undergrowth as if they'd never been there. He would have doubted his own eyes were it not for the skiff, the name, *Jennifer M.*, painted plainly across the stern for all to see. Or rather, her father's skiff. Even without the name, Tyler would have recognized that elderly New England dory with the blue paint fading to white anywhere between here and Cordova.

He realized his own skiff was drifting out from shore and he gunned the outboard to nose it back in. The aluminum hull grated against the gravel and he hopped out and tugged it up out of the water close to the fish wheel, all the while his mind busy with speculation. What was his cousin, Jennifer, a Kushtaka Mack, doing meeting Ryan, a Kuskulana Christianson? And at this hour of the morning?

He pulled on rough rubber gloves that reached well past his elbows and hooked the suspenders of his hip waders over his shoulders. The water next to the fish wheel's bin was teeming with salmon, and he didn't even sigh at the sight.

Give him credit, he tried to be fair. He tried to think of all the reasons why Jennifer would be meeting Ryan on the wrong side of the river this early in the morning, and in the end could only come up with the obvious. If there had been any doubt, it would have been wiped clean by the way Jen's hand went into Ryan's—sure, easy, familiar. She'd put the boat in at his feet and he'd been standing in exactly the right spot to catch her bowline, too. It wasn't the first time they'd met there.

Tyler's eyes narrowed. So, he knew something he hadn't before. What was in it for him?

He'd have to talk it over with Boris. Boris always had all the best ideas.

He waded into the water and plunged his hands into the holding pen, grabbing the salmon by the gills and tossing them with a practiced throw so they thumped hard into the plastic tote sitting amidships of his uncle's skiff. He was good at it, because he hated it so much, he'd figured out the most economical way to get the job done as fast as possible. It was a good catch, maybe twenty-five reds weighing an average of eight pounds, and still pretty fat for having traveled all this way upstream.

He was so focused on getting the salmon out of the pen and into the tote that he didn't even hear the boots crunching into the gravel behind him.

Pat Mack was, indeed, eleven hundred years old, but there was nothing wrong with his eyesight, and when that worthless grandnephew of his hadn't shown up by four o'clock that afternoon, he went grumbling down to the beach and climbed into Tyler's tiny, trash-filled skiff, having sent Tyler upriver in Pat's own skiff because it was big enough hold a fish tote. The kicker, new when Eisenhower was invading Normandy, took a dozen tries before it caught and with a sound like a chain saw giving birth ripped a shrieking hole in the serenity of the afternoon. Tyler probably hadn't changed the oil since spring. Useless little fucker.

He pushed the kicker as hard as she'd go, which amounted to about half a knot per year. The sun had traveled to the other side of the sky and was making its usual empty threat to set by the time he got to the fish wheel. His mood, already bad, didn't improve when he saw that the fish wheel was jammed, the current battering it and rattling the above-water baskets in their brackets.

"Goddamn good-for-nothing little shit," he said, and beached the skiff.

His own skiff was there, drawn up on the gravel next to the fish wheel, tied off to a scrub spruce growing out of the edge of the bank.

Tyler wasn't, which only fueled his ire.

The tote held at least a dozen fish, red salmon, almost a hundred pounds of fish. Pat's temper spiked when he saw that they were all dead and had been sitting in the sun without ice. He poked at them. All day, by the look of them. It'd been a warm one, and they were starting to smell.

"Tyler, you useless little fucker, you'll be lucky if you're able to walk ever again when I get done with you!"

His bellow echoed across the water and startled a flock of pintail into the air. There was a rustle in the bushes across the river and he snapped his head around, one hand reached for his rifle. This time of year there was enough fish for everyone, but bears were not reasonable creatures.

It wasn't a bear; it was a man, ducking back into the alders behind the Kuskulana landing on the other side of the river. Pat squinted. Some Kuskulaner, most likely a Christianson, since most Kuskulaners were Christiansons, with a few Estes and Halvorsens and last he heard still one lone Romanoff thrown in. Might have been Roger's son. They all looked alike to Pat anyway. Although he had heard tell of a couple of new families totally unrelated to the existing population moving in. Which wasn't surprising. Kuskulana had everything Kushtaka did not and a functional airport besides, so you could get the hell outta town when you had to.

He saw them at their landing on the other side or driving by in a skiff from time to time. Sometimes they waved. Sometimes he waved back. Sometimes he even said hi. The longtime rivalry and resentment between the two villages was a lot of damn foolishness anyway, although he'd never be able to convince his nephew, Dale, of that. Or any of the other Kushtaka men, for that matter, young or old.

Sometimes Pat Mack thought of moving out of Kushtaka himself, by god, to Niniltna, maybe, or Ahtna, or all the way Outside. The Macks had family, albeit distant, in rural Oregon. Probably didn't snow as much there, and if there were family feuds, well, he didn't have to opt in to them. In the Park, birth, community, and history forced him down on the Kushtaka side of the fence whether it was the right side or not.

He stamped over to the fish wheel and looked into the holding pen. Still some fish in it, although not many. And where was that useless little fucker, Tyler? Nowhere to be found, as usual.

Muttering curses, Pat pulled on hip waders, sleeve protectors, and rubber gloves and waded in. The current wasn't as swift near the bank as it was center stream, but it had rained hard last week and the water was running high and dirty, so that he couldn't see beneath the surface. It was plenty fast enough to pull at his legs, which were not so young or so reliable beneath him as they used to be, and it was cold enough to instantly chill his flesh through multiple layers of protection. He took a minute to get and keep his balance, leaned against the current, and bent to run his hand along the curved edge of the wheel.

Two of the baskets were submerged, one partially, the other entirely. The partially submerged basket was clear of debris, although an eight-pound red that would have looked a lot better in the tote swam out and away as he was feeling around. The second basket was wedged firm.

"What the hell?"

There was something long and rigid thrust through the basket and into the riverbed, a branch or something. Probably a limb broken off a scrag. Although it felt awful solid and inflexible. It sure was stuck, good and hard. The current must have brought it downriver at a fast enough lick that it had somehow jammed itself through the open mesh of the basket and become wedged into the river bottom, bringing the entire fish wheel to a halt.

He heard the sound of an outboard engine and looked up to see a Kuskulaner idling by in his skiff, watching him with a curious look on his face. He looked back down and wrapped his hands around the branch and tugged. It didn't move. He wasn't altogether sure he had enough upper-body strength left to make it move, but Pat Mack never lacked for stubborn. He set his jaw, squared his shoulders, dug his heels more surely into the gravel, and tugged harder.

It came free with a whoosh of water. He dropped it and staggered back up the beach, sitting down hard half in and half out of the water, looking at what was in his hand. "How the hell—?"

The current pulled at the wheel. The freed basket scraped across the gravel, still not moving normally.

"Well, shit," Pat said, and pulled himself to his feet.

And then stood there, openmouthed, as the basket lifted free of the water to reveal the body of Tyler Mack crumbled inside it.

Three

TUESDAY, JULY 10, LATE EVENING

Kushtaka

THE OLD MAN WAS SITTING IN HIS SKIFF, his back to the fish wheel, puffing methodically through a pack of unfiltered Camels.

Jim picked up his evidence kit in one hand and used his other to vault over the side of Roger Christianson's skiff. His boots crunched when they landed in the gavel.

"Pat," he said.

"Got here quicker'n I thought," the old man said, lighting another Camel off the end of the last one.

"Chuck's call caught me at the post," Jim said.

The old man drew in hard on his cigarette. "That'd be Chuck Christianson, going by in his skiff? Yeah, I saw he had his cell phone out."

Chuck had, in fact, snapped a picture of Tyler Mack in the basket of the fish wheel and texted it to Jim, but Jim thought it tactless to mention that. "Anyway," he said, "I went straight up the hill, fired up the Cessna and flew to Kuskulana. Roger here was waiting on the strip. He brought me over."

The old man puffed out a cloud of smoke and peered through it. "Appreciate it, Roger."

Roger Christianson, staring with a sort of sick fascination at the body suspended in the fish wheel bucket above the swift-moving river, made a visible effort to pull himself together and said, "Glad I could be of help, Pat." And then, as if the words were wrenched out of him, "I'm sorry as hell about this."

"Yeah," Pat said.

Which exchange sort of surprised Jim, because until that moment, he would have taken bets on neither man knowing the other's name, let alone admitting to it out loud.

The body was mostly inside the basket, knees bent, arms tucked in, sightless eyes wide open and staring at the water hurrying swiftly south below it. The basket rocked a little, the river's current hitting the baskets still in the water. Jim spotted the line attached to the stump of a birch, holding the wheel steady against the push of the water.

Pat saw him looking. "Tied it off when I got here. Figured you'd want to see him as I found him."

Jim nodded. Everybody knew about *CSI*, even Kushtakans.

Water dripped from the body, making tiny circles on the silver surface of the river that quickly disappeared downstream.

Still in his skiff, Roger swallowed audibly. "That's really Tyler?" He was having the usual difficulty reconciling the sodden corpse with the living man.

The old man nodded, still without turning around. "That's him. Useless little fucker."

Shocked, Roger looked at Jim, who was making a bit of

a production of getting out his iPhone and turning on the camera.

"Couldn't never get him to come up here, and then when I finally threaten him into it, stupid bastard falls headfirst in and drowns." Pat inhaled, his cigarette burning down to his fingers. He lit another from the butt and flicked the butt over the side. A boil of water nearby indicated momentary interest on the part of something large with fins. Involuntarily, Pat thought of his dip net, Roger thought of his rod and reel, and Jim thought of Kate and the smoker she'd built from an old refrigerator out back of the house.

"Roger," Jim said, "could I ask you to stick around a little while longer? I'm going to take some photographs, and then I'm afraid I'm going to need some help getting Tyler out of that basket."

Roger swallowed hard and tore his eyes away from the body. "Sure, Jim. Whatever you need."

If he had cause to regret the offer, he didn't say so, even as he stood shivering uncontrollably on the river's edge. Like Jim, his hands were bruised and numb, and he was so cold, he thought he might break if he bumped against the side of his skiff one more time. There was no help from the sun, which by now was well behind the trees that lined the bank. Roger had spent his life manhandling gear into his gillnetter and salmon out of the gear, twelve- and twenty-four- and sometimes thirty-six-hour periods at a time, but none of it was any comparison to trying to get 130 pounds of previously healthy man out of a fish wheel bucket. It had taken a couple of tries, him on Pat's belaying line and Jim maneuvering the bucket to get it to a level where they could reach it from the skiff, which they had tied off to the fish wheel frame, and doing all this with the river pushing against them the whole time. It wasn't the steadiest platform from which to operate. Rigor had set in on the body, which made things even more awkward.

Pat didn't offer to help, but he didn't go anywhere, either. He sat in his skiff and watched them, his leathery, seamed face set, his eyes narrowed against the smoke from the Camels. A collection of ravens, crows, and magpies had gathered in the nearby treetops, not saying much, like Pat watchful, and waiting.

By the time they got Tyler's body out of the basket, Roger's skiff was nearly swamped and both Roger and Jim were soaking wet. They put the body on the beach so they could tip the water out of the skiff. While Roger, teeth chattering, bailed out the rest, Jim squatted over the contorted body to see what he could see. His hands were almost too cold to tap the button on the camera app.

The limbs were frozen in place, elbows bent, knees up, head bent far back, and unresponsive to pressure. Time of death was going to be a bitch, given the temperature of the river water, which rose in the Quilak Mountains and consisted for the most part of snow and glacier melt. The mesh of the basket had imprinted itself on Tyler's forehead.

In his pockets, Tyler had a cell phone that would not turn on—no surprise there—and a thick wad of twenties and fifties. That was all. Jim bagged them both and took a lot of photographs.

He stood up, stretching himself back into shape and trying not to groan out loud. His uniform was clammy against his skin. "What time did you say he came out here, Pat?"

Hiss of burning cigarette paper. "I booted his sorry ass out of bed at six A.M. He was on the river fifteen minutes later."

Jim rose to his feet and walked over to look into the square plastic tote in the aluminum skiff. It held about a dozen dead salmon. They had been there for long enough to begin to smell.

"You ever do any canning or smoking here on-site?" he said.

Pat Mack thought it over and decided it wasn't a trick question. "Sometimes."

"This year?"

The old man drew smoke deep into his lungs. "Don't think so. I haven't, anyway."

Jim looked into the pen attached to the fish wheel, again revolving with the passing river. The pen held more salmon, perhaps another dozen, these alive and well and whapping each other in the nose with their tails. Reds mostly, along with a few early silvers.

He looked up to find the old man watching him, the red glow of his cigarette the only warm thing on the river that evening. "How long would it take him to pick this many fish out of the pen and toss them into the skiff?"

Pat expelled a cloud of smoke with a snort. "Woulda took me about five minutes. With Tyler checking his text messages every thirty seconds, probably take him an hour."

So, Jim thought. On the water by six fifteen, twenty minutes, half an hour to get to the fish wheel. Pat's estimate on Tyler's fish-picking abilities could be taken with a grain of salt. Say thirty minutes. Jim checked his phone. It was now just after ten o'clock.

Rigor set in after three to four hours, held on for twelve. Fix a tentative time of death at, say, somewhere between 8:45 A.M. and 12:45 P.M. "What time did you find him, Pat?"

"Got here about five," Pat said. "Fish wheel was stuck. Took me a while to figure out why."

"How long is 'a while'?"

The old man's eyes narrowed. Jim met them with a steady gaze, refusing to apologize for the question.

Pat blinked first and looked away, across the river. "Maybe fifteen minutes."

"What had the basket stuck on?"

Pat shrugged again. "A stick."

"What stick? Where is it?"

Another shrug from Pat. "I must have tossed it. I got a little distracted there, what with trying to see if Tyler was still alive and all. Useless little fucker though he was, he's family, and he was my first concern." His cigarette had again burned all the way down to his fingers. His free hand searched for the packet. It was empty and he crumpled it up and threw it into the little skiff. Not into the water. Not on the beach. Not into his skiff. Into Tyler's skiff. It was a statement, Jim thought, although he didn't yet know exactly what statement that was.

The sun wouldn't go below the horizon again for another month, and then only for a few minutes, but when it got this low, the light was dim enough to reduce old men sitting in skiffs to grayish outlines.

Jim squatted again, this time to put his hand in the river.

If Tyler had died at 8:45 a.m., normally rigor would have set in by 12:45 p.m. If Tyler had screwed around, on his cell like the old man said or maybe just sacking out in the sun, and had not started picking fish until later, rigor would only now be coming on, or not coming on at all. In neither case should rigor be so fully involved as it was, but that discounted the effect of the body being immersed in the water from then to discovery. Temperature played hell with rigor, especially in the Arctic.

His hand was numb again. He pulled it out and dried it off,

and made a mental note to replace the thermometer to his evidence kit. The last one had disappeared at the last crime scene.

He pulled out a flashlight and walked up and down the gravel bank, peering into the shallows at the water's edge and into the shrubbery at the land's edge. He found an empty Coke can, a dozen empty Budweiser cans, some waterlogged cigarette butts that looked as if the fish or the ducks had been taking the occasional desultory nibble, a small pocketknife with just a blade and a nail file, an empty bag of Lay's potato chips, and a crumpled thermal receipt with the print so faded, it was unintelligible. He bagged them all.

Roger sat shivering in his skiff, Pat immobile in his. Roger's skiff was a large aluminum affair, free of rust and dents, a powerful new Mercury Marine on the back connected to a shiny red fuel tank by a clean black hose. A set of oars was run beneath the thwarts, and oarlocks dangled inside the skiff from their holes. A workmanlike tackle box sat next to the oars, and two fishing poles were locked into opposite sides below the oarlocks. A bought-new bailing can sat in the bow, with an aluminum body and a smooth wooden handle.

Pat's skiff was a lot older but much the same in its spare neatness.

Jim stepped over to look into the third skiff. "This Tyler's?"

"Yeah."

Tyler's skiff, on the other hand, was half the size of the other two, holding so much junk, Jim was surprised it was still floating. His bailing can was made from a sawed-off plastic gallon milk jug. His kicker looked like Ole Evinrude had put it together with his own hands, and his fuel tank looked like it was about to rust through from the inside. The bottom was covered with a collection of bits of two-by-four and a torn-off section of rain gutter and a piece of rebar and cogs and gearwheels and other unidentifiable machine parts, including a quart-size ziplock full of mismatched nuts and bolts. There was a twelve-pack carton of beer dissolving around the last can, the same brand as he'd found on the beach. Jim spotted a fishing reel—but no poles—and a ballpeen hammer and a couple of screwdrivers and a pair of needle-nosed pliers, but no toolbox. The tools looked as rusty as the fuel tank.

He looked up at Pat Mack, sitting in his own skiff, glowering. Jim didn't think Pat was glowering at him, specifically, but at the world in general, and more likely at his recently deceased nephew, without whose labor the old man would now have to get along. Such as it was. "Whose son was Tyler's, again?" he said.

Pat patted his pockets automatically, and stilled. "Piers'."

Jim thought. "I don't remember Piers."

"Died when his boat swamped on the Kanuyaq flats ten years ago. His wife died right after. I took on the boy."

Jim nodded. "The body has to go to the medical examiner in Anchorage, Pat."

"Why? Useless little fucker stumbled into the goddamn fish wheel. Ain't nobody's goddamn fault but his own."

"State law," Jim said. "Every accidental death requires an autopsy. I'm sorry." He moved to the body. "Roger, give me a hand here?"

Still shivering, Roger climbed out of his skiff and complied.

Act II

Four

WEDNESDAY, JULY 11

Kate's homestead

IT WAS THE SECOND WEEK OF JULY, AN UNusually fine day in the second month of a cool, rainy summer following a winter of record snowfall that had delayed the usual explosion of vegetative fecundity to the end of June. Only now could it be said that the deciduous trees were fully in leaf, rich shades of green in massed banks against a pale morning sky. Kate curled up on the couch, a mug of coffee in hand, and watched the light brighten in back of the Quilaks. Given birth by two tectonic plates pushing each other to the surface and nurtured on intermittent volcanic action and glacial wear and tear, the range of mountains forming the eastern border of the Park as well as the border between Alaska and Canada were in appearance simultaneously breathtaking in their beauty and terrifying in their menace. As the light of the rising sun crept westward, outlines changed and shadows grew and shrank, and if she watched for long enough without blinking, she could almost imagine the mountains marching in her direction.

Which Kate supposed they were. Kate had been born after the Great Alaska Earthquake of 1964, 9.2 on the Richter scale, but she'd heard about it often enough from Emaa and Old Sam and the aunties. Terra firma was an illusion. A quake a day was the norm in Alaska, where every day was a triumph of optimism over experience.

Kate never took the ground beneath her feet for granted.

Aboveground movement in the yard caught her eye, and she turned her head to see Mutt materializing out of the underbrush in what always seemed to be an act of teleportation. Even after a partnership moving into its tenth year, Kate still marveled at the ability of a 140-pound half wolf–half husky to vanish and reappear at will into the landscape.

Mutt gave an enthusiastic shake and trotted across the yard and up the steps. A moment later, Kate heard the latch click. Claws ticky-tacked across the wood floor. A cold nose shoved itself under her arm, sloshing the coffee in her mug. "Knock it off, monster," Kate said, giving Mutt's head a rough scratching. "Good hunting?"

"Wuff!" Mutt said, her yellow eyes bright, her tail a drumbeat against the side of the couch. She betook herself to the tumbled quilt in front of the fireplace, scraped it into a new pile, turned around three times, and subsided into a boneless, somnolent heap of gray fur. Kate, watching, thought it was like someone throwing a switch on a perpetual-motion machine.

She turned back to the windows that covered the southern wall of the house. The house, this two-story Lindal Cedar home that the Park rats built for her in three days three years before, was cool and quiet. Jim hadn't made it home last night—again—

and Johnny was working at the Suulutaq Mine, saving up for his freshman year of college at the University of Alaska in Anchorage. Van, his girlfriend, was attending UAA, too, and this fall they would both be living in the town house on Westchester Lagoon that Johnny had inherited from his father. Kate wasn't sure what she thought about any of that, in order high school sweethearts, going to the same college, and sharing living quarters. She wasn't going anywhere near the fact that after four years, Johnny was moving out of her house.

Not that she had any say in it. He was eighteen, a legal adult. He couldn't drink but he could vote, and the town house and the Subaru now belonged to him free and clear. Not to mention Jack's retirement, which Kate as executor had invested in a modest little investment fund recommended by Victoria Muravieff that had at least not lost any money during the recession.

Johnny was, she was glad to see, determined not to touch it unless and until he had to, which was why he was working his second summer two weeks on, two weeks off as a Suulutaq stickpicker. He'd sworn he wouldn't work during the semester, but she wasn't quite sure she believed him. A paycheck was a powerful stimulus. She'd managed to save some money toward his education herself, and she wondered now if she offered to pay him by the credit if he'd stick to his promise.

Johnny, she told herself firmly, would be fine. The question was, would Kate? For a kid who'd been with her for only four years, he had become a remarkably permanent fixture in her life. He was the best thing Jack had given her.

That big ugly man who knew all the lyrics to every Jimmy Buffett song ever recorded, who had been her boss in the Anchorage DA's investigative branch for five and a half years, who had been her lover for almost that long, and who had known her better than any man ever had before or since, would have been a constant presence in her life with or without his son. The son he had committed to her care a few seconds before he died of wounds sustained while saving her own life. The pain of his loss had been so great that she had abandoned everything and everyone she knew to hide out on the YK Delta in western Alaska. Where, of all the unlikely people, Sergeant Jim Chopin, Chopper Jim, the so-called Father of the Park, had found her, and shocked her back into some semblance of sanity, and harried her back to the Park, where she had found Johnny on her doorstep.

She came to herself with a start. Kate wasn't one to look back. There was nothing to be done about the past, and what happened next was always so much more interesting. But the nights of an Alaskan summer seemed to encourage introspection by virtue of their very length.

She grimaced. The only remedy to maudlin navel-gazing was to get in motion and stay in motion. She was good at both.

She went upstairs to shower and dress and came downstairs again clean and full of purpose, there to make an enormous breakfast of deer sausage and eggs and toast loaded with butter and nagoonberry jam, washed down by another cup of that fabulous Javaloha coffee that Brendan had sent her from Hawaii. Of course, he had also sent her a six-pack of Spam-flavored macadamia nuts, which did not accompany breakfast and, absent starvation, would very probably never make it out of the can. She drank this coffee standing up, allowing herself no time to brood over it, after which she washed the dishes and pattered briskly down the steps into the yard.

She wasn't on Alaganik Bay on a fishing boat or a tender for the second summer in a row. It might be a trend. Her bank balance was healthy, which also might be a trend. No one had tried to burn down her house or drop a jet engine through the roof of it, lately. Last night she'd finished up the paperwork and sent out the bills for her last two PI jobs—an employee background check and a lost husband, both of which had proved a lot more complicated and a lot more productive of revenue than first estimated. No one else had come knocking on her door to clear up a personal or professional mystery, and the State of Alaska and the federal government had been remarkably reticent since she'd neatened up that little matter of international gunrunning the previous January. Although both their checks had cleared the bank just fine.

She was faintly astonished to realize she was free to do whatever the hell she wanted. She stood in the middle of the clearing in front of her house, reveling in the clear, cool Park air, and thought about taking the summer off. A novel idea. She wasn't quite sure what that would entail.

The sun was well up in the sky by now, turning the Quilaks from their early-morning luminescent ghostliness into a solid dark blue fastness. If they did not quite lower, they definitely loomed, imposing, intimidating, impenetrable.

Although not quite. Old Sam had left her property deep in that fastness, a homestead he had staked as a young man. Canyon Hot Springs, a steep, narrow valley at the very edge of the border between Alaska and Canada, which included the remnants of the cabin Old Sam had built, and a hot springs that bubbled up out of the ground. He'd left her a few other surprises as well, farther up the canyon.

It was a heart-stoppingly beautiful place but difficult to access, a sweaty, bushwhacking journey on foot in the summer and a bewildering maze of dogleg turns by snowmobile in winter. She wondered how far the sun penetrated that narrow valley at this time of year. How long would it take, and how much effort, to get up there and see for herself?

Her gaze dropped to the nearer prospect.

She had inherited this homestead upon the death of her parents, which homestead had been grandfathered in when the twenty-million-acre national park had been created around it by the Alaska National Interest Lands Conservation Act in 1980. The Park, about the size of Oregon, encompassed the land up to and including most of the Quilak Mountains on the east, to the Glenn Highway in the north, in places to the Alaska Railroad on the west, and to Prince William Sound on the south. Kate's homestead was a little west of dead center, on Zoya Creek—named by her father for her mother—which fed into the Kanuyaq River. *Kanuyaq* was Aleut for "copper," which had been discovered in large quantity at the beginning of the previous century in the foothills of the Quilaks. Copper was the foundation of the Park's modern age, bringing in a railway from Cordova to the mine, the roadbed of which now served as the main access to the Park. Or it did when it was bladed by a state grader, which was twice a year, once in the spring and again in the fall.

Although that might be about to change. Kate scowled at a bald eagle sitting on a scrag, who, as usual, scowled back. Pissed off was any eagle's de facto demeanor. Probably why they felt like kin.

Two years before, discovery of another massive ore deposit, gold this time, had considerably livened up life in Niniltna, the Park's biggest village, as well as increased traffic on the road. Another unwelcome result was an increased clamor from industry—specifically Global Harvest Resource, Inc., the high bidders on the Suulutaq Mine leases—for the road to be improved. Another result was Park rats rising up in a body to say, "Just hold the fuck on."

Although that body was not so big as it might have been. The Suulutaq had put a lot of Park rats to work in numbers not seen since before the Depression, when the falling price of copper shut down the old Kanuyaq Copper Mine in 1936. Kate had even worked a case out at the Suulutaq, a murder, and been well paid for it, so the glass her house was made of was as transparent as anyone else's.

The environmental impact study was due out the following year, when the cost of the mine would be counted, in impacts on air and water quality, threatened or endangered species, historic and cultural sites, the social and economic effects on local communities, and finally in a cost–benefit analysis.

In the meantime, the price of gold kept going up, seventeen hundred dollars an ounce the last time Kate had checked. Which only guaranteed that someone, somehow was going to get the gold out, no matter what the EIS said.

Her eyes fell on the hammock, a new contribution from Jim, swinging gently between two trees at the edge of the clearing, the morning sun just hitting its surface to throw off sparkles from a layer of dew. A hammock, a jug of lemonade, and Reginald Hill's latest and sorrowfully last book, *The Stranger House,* beside her in the wilderness. "Get thee behind me, Satan," she said, and turned her back on seduction.

The homestead was the traditional 160 acres and, like the rest of any wilderness area in North America, had suffered cruelly over the past two decades from the spruce bark beetle. Kate had made a point of walking, snowshoeing, skiing, four-wheeling, and snow-machining every acre periodically, looking for the telltale rust, the little piles of sawdust and shed needles. Over the years, she had thinned out the spruce trees so there would be less competition for water and sunlight. The infected trees she had debarked, burning the bark to kill the beetles. The bad news was there were less than a third of the spruce trees on the property as there had been when her parents died. The good news was that now to the east she had a magnificent view of the Quilak Mountains from any part of the property. She swore to Ranger Dan that if she squinted, she could almost see the Park Service's headquarters on the Step. To the west she could see Mount Sanford and Mount Drum, and on very clear days she imagined that the Chugach Mountains etched a blue white line low on the horizon.

The shop door groaned when she pushed it back. She filled the chain saw with fuel and checked the oil. It started on the first pull. She changed her tennis shoes for insulated XtraTufs and found a pair of sturdy leather gloves. The four-wheeler, an ancient but thoroughly reliable Honda, also started at first touch. "If you take care of your tools, they'll take care of you," she said out loud, the ghosts of Abel Int-hout and Old Sam ranged approvingly at her back. The trailer was already hitched on behind. She put the chain saw in the trailer along with a jerry can full of extra gas, knotted a red bandanna around her forehead, and putted out of the garage.

She let up on the throttle and let the engine idle, waiting, but not for long.

The front door of the house crashed all the way back against the exterior wall, and Mutt took the steps from the deck to the ground in one leap. Another leap and she was on the seat in back of Kate, her muzzle thrust over Kate's shoulder, tail wagging hard enough to propel the ATV down the trail.

Kate laughed and pulled her ear. "What kept you?"

It was with a strong sense of virtue attained that she passed the hammock with no more than a longing look and entered the brush at the side of the clearing.

The granite uplift beneath Kate's homestead was the continuation of a long ridge that extended east and south from the Quilak Mountains, worn down in places by glaciers, recurring in humps and bumps here and there so that from the air it looked like Smaug had been buried on Kate's homestead beneath a barely decent layer of earth. Over the millennia, Zoya Creek had cut a deep channel through and between the granite. Around the creek, the land fell gradually from the northeast to the southeast, where it met the Park road.

Everything that grew in the Park grew on the homestead. While the black spruce and the white spruce had been thinned by two-thirds, the good news was that now light could get down to the quaking aspen and the paper birch. They had responded by leaps and bounds, forming large groves that turned a glorious gold in the fall. So prolific and determined were they that Kate had formed the habit of going out with a hatchet to hack them back enough so that the new spruce seedlings would have a chance. In another hundred years, the spruce would have reestablished themselves and the aspen and birch would die back to their previous levels, but Kate wasn't sorry she'd been here to see the transformation. Captain Cook had seen it, too, when he had sailed up Cook Inlet that May 230 or so years before. She'd read it in his log, an old leatherbound three-book edition of which she had inherited from Old Sam, along with all the rest of his books. Reading matter even more hammock-worthy than Reginald Hill, heresy though that might be.

The trail was one hacked out of the brush by Stephan long

ago, but in spite of its years of establishment, Kate felt like she ought to take a whip and a chair with her every time she traveled it. The undergrowth felt like a tiger waiting to spring, and she knew if she didn't maintain it that the forest would gobble it up between one year and the next. It was just wide enough for the four-wheeler, and it meandered, never taking a straight line when it could possibly avoid it, following the path of least resistance, around high knobs topped with erratics, gigantic boulders shrugged off by a passing glacier millennia before, and through sunken bogs lush with lowbush cranberry where ptarmigan hens and their chicks skittered frantically from in front of the ATV's wheels. Ranger Dan swore there was kinnikinnick tucked into the corner of one bald rocky top, although he didn't know what the hell it was doing below a thousand feet, and other gardeners pro and am had found every species of moss, fern, berry, and wildflower on the Park plant list within the borders of Kate's realm.

She had helped the plant life along, every fall beginning when she was a child planting half a dozen raspberry bushes somewhere along the trail, on the theory that if there were hundreds, the moose had to miss at least a few of them. She planted other things, too, salting the landscape with blueberry and salmonberry and Siberian larch and mountain ash, even honeysuckle and lilac. In a few south-facing hollows she tucked bulbs for tulips and daffodils, and sometimes they even survived the depredations of winter and fauna to bloom brightly in the spring. Half the time she forgot where she'd put them and in late spring it was always a glorious surprise to stumble across a bright patch of sunshine yellow or lipstick red.

Ahead she saw a broad brown back vanish into the brush, followed by two smaller ones. The cow moose had probably found that stand of diamond willow that edged the lower cranberry bog and staked it out for herself and her two calves. Kate welcomed the company, and hoped that at least one of the calves was a male. The cow hadn't moved like she was in a hurry, which told Kate that the local two-year-old grizzly, recently booted out by his mother in favor of her new twins, had abandoned his pursuit of the calves and moved down to the river, where the salmon were now migrating upstream in enough abundance that he didn't have to work too hard to fill his belly. In the distance, a goshawk plummeted down to disappear behind the trees, to reappear moments later with something mammalian wriggling uselessly in its talons. Closer inspection proved it to be an arctic hare, fat and brown and now lunchmeat for the baby goshawks back home. "Good on you," Kate told the goshawk. The hares were currently in their high cycle and had proved every bit as devastating to the shrubs and trees as had the spruce bark beetle. On the upside, Kate had seen seven different lynxes on her homestead alone that winter. She had a fondness for the cats with the tufted ears and the enormous paws, and for that alone she found she could forgive the hares much.

At her most recent windfall site, she fired up the boom box. Wearing earphones in the woods was way too risky, even with Mutt as an early warning system, and bears tended not to like loud noises, unless they were making them. By noon, with the aid of Adele, Brad Paisley, Cee Lo Green, Jimmy Buffett, the Steve Miller Band, and Dion, among others, she had sliced five felled, limbed, debarked spruce trees into neat three-foot rounds and made the trip to the woodpile in the clearing a dozen times with a loaded trailer, stacking the rounds next to the woodpile. The house had a Monitor, by now the Alaska state stove, that burned furnace oil very efficiently to heat the entire house, both floors. But she'd always liked a wood fire, the look of the bright, leaping flames, the sound of knots cracking and sap popping, the faint smell of woodsmoke it left on her clothes and in her hair. And a job done well was always satisfying in and of itself.

Sweaty, filthy, covered with scratches and needles and sap, she decided getting out the splitter could wait for another day. She washed down the ATV and the trailer and put them back into the garage, and as she came outside again, she saw that she had company.

A middle-aged couple stood at the edge of the clearing, holding an unfolded map between them as they gawked around with their eyes squinted against the sun, surrounded by a general air of bewilderment.

"Oh hell," Kate said, "not again." She walked forward, stripping off her gloves. "May I help you?"

They turned their heads. The woman took a step back, and it looked as if her man refrained from doing so only by exercising a strong effort of will. They were middle-aged, overweight, and blatantly Outsiders, with that unmistakably eager air of venturing into a wild frontier known to them previously only through the Discovery Channel.

"May I help you?" Kate said again.

This time her words penetrated, and they both visibly relaxed. "Oh, you speak English," the man said, sounding relieved.

"You're lost, I take it," Kate said, and tried hard not to make it sound like an accusation.

"We're looking for the gold mine," the woman said.

Which one? Kate almost said, and stopped herself in time.

"You turned too soon," she said. "Get back on the road and keep going about fifty miles until you come to a village."

The man nodded. "Ninilchik."

"Niniltna," Kate said. "The mine is on the other side of the village."

"Is the road not paved the whole way?" the woman asked, looking over Kate's shoulder at the house, and then looking back at Kate like she couldn't see Kate in it. That was okay. Sometimes Kate couldn't see herself in it, either.

"Yes, it's unpaved all the way," Kate said, and stepped forward, spreading her hands a little, just enough to give the impression she was shooing them back up the trail.

"Oh, Paul," said the woman, not budging. "My back's killing me."

"We're already halfway there, Alice," Paul said, still trying to locate them on the map. "We might as well keep going." He looked back at Kate. "Is there an RV park in this Nenana, do you know?"

Mutt reappeared at that moment, translating from dark green brush to iron gray wolf in a single step. She gave herself a vigorous shake and trotted forward, very businesslike. Alice squeaked. Mutt looked up at Kate and gave an inquiring yip.

Alice answered with another squeak and plucked imploringly at Paul's sleeve.

"In a minute, Alice," he said testily, and then looked up. "Oh. Ah. Jesus." He cleared his throat, and Kate had to give him points for standing his ground. "Is that a wolf?"

"Only half," Kate said, dropping a casual hand to scratch behind Mutt's ears. Mutt let her jaw fall open and her tongue loll out past canines Dracula would have envied.

"How many does that make," Kate said to Mutt as they watched Alice and Paul scuttle up the trail to the road. "Four? Five?"

"Wuff," Mutt said with a hearty sneeze.

"You're right, might be six."

The world's second-largest gold mine, which might yet turn out to be the world's largest gold mine, had been discovered in the southeast corner of the Park two years before. The first to appear on scene after the geologists were the resource corporations. After them came the journalists, followed by people looking for jobs, and then, inevitably, came the tourists. Had the Park been a normal remote Alaskan location, access would have been limited to airplane. But no, the Park had a road, and said road was pleased to deliver random tourists to the Park's doorstep, for which Kate's homestead was sometimes mistaken.

She had a momentary vision of herself at the controls of a Caterpillar D9 tractor, big shiny blade pushing up a mound of earth taller than herself to block the trail into her homestead.

Lunch was a thick slice of last night's moose meat loaf and a big red apple, astonishingly juicy and crisp, always a rarity in produce shipped to Alaska. With some of Corinna Chapman's lemon cordial, she made a pitcher of sweet, tart lemonade and took it and *The Stranger House* out to the hammock. It was warm from the sun, and molded around her body as if it had been made for that purpose. A light breeze kept off the bugs.

One of Jim's better ideas, she thought, the hammock swinging gently from side to side, and that was the last she knew until her cell phone dinged against her hip and she came to with the open book across her face. It startled her enough that she nearly dumped herself out of the hammock. She moved the book out of the way and fished out her phone and looked at the screen.

You home?

She texted back.

Yes. Where are you?

Reply:

Kushtaka.

Her:

What's going on?

Him:

Maybe an accident.

Her:

Maybe?

Jim didn't reply immediately.

Maybe not?

Maddeningly, no response again. She wondered if his phone had dropped its connection. While the cell phone towers had gone up with an almost miraculous rapidity over the last year, the system still had a few kinks, and their putative range held more than a few dead spots. Not that Jim would know, since the Park rats had taken to dialing 911 with a heady, entitled abandon for everything from noisy neighbors (the Bingleys had fallen out of love again) to bloody riot (Suulutaq miners whooping it up at Bernie's Roadhouse). Previously, Kate would have been called out to quell the former and Bernie would have quelled the latter with the baseball bat behind the bar, but having an Alaska state trooper on your speed dial seemed to bring out the previously unsuspected needy in the most self-sufficient Park rat. Very odd.

Kate rolled out of the hammock, collected book and glass, and headed back to the house. It was four o'clock. She hadn't checked the mail in a week, or maybe two, and she ought to be able to make it into town just before the post office closed so she could pick up any packages without standing in line. "Want to go to town?" she said.

Mutt was out the door and across the deck and down the steps and dancing impatiently next to the battered red pickup before Kate could grab her wallet.

Five

WEDNESDAY, JULY 11

Kushtaka

THE SOUND OF THE ENGINE ON THE SKIFF carrying Tyler Mack away from his native side of the river had barely faded out of earshot when they gathered at the chief's house in Kushtaka. His wife and daughter were sent next door. This was talk for men.

Pat Mack described what he had seen. The object was produced and passed hand to hand. Returned to him, he set it on the floor, in the middle of the circle of men.

There was a long, deliberative silence, broken first by Pat Mack. "He was my great-nephew."

Dale Mack looked up. "He was my nephew, too."

"He was ours," said the eldest, and the others were silenced.

"Who did this thing?" the eldest said.

"I don't know," Pat said. He said it without hesitation and with perfect truth. He didn't know whom he'd seen at Kuskulana landing when he arrived at the fish wheel. He couldn't be sure it was Roger's son, and when he'd seen him, it had been hours after Tyler was killed. He would not accuse unless he was sure. A name would be spark to Kushtaka timber and the resulting blaze could burn down both villages.

Others with less cause were less hesitant. "I can make a pretty good guess," one of the younger men said, his eyes hot. "Someone from across the river."

"Ya think?" Rick Estes said. He was the youngest man there, and he bit back what else he might have said when the eldest raised his hand for silence.

"Talk to his friend," the eldest said.

"Boris?" Rick said, looking at Dale, who nodded.

"See what he says," the eldest said.

Dale Mack's face was red, and it was obvious he was laboring under a great need to speak his mind. "Uncle, there is no need. We know who did this."

"Speak to his friend," the eldest said. His voice quavered, but there was no gainsaying that tone, not if you'd been born and raised in Kushtaka, and not if you wanted to go on living there. "We must know more before we act."

When the others left, Rick Estes stayed behind. "What do we do?"

Dale Mack's jaw was tight. "Talk to Boris. See what he says. Ask him who Tyler had pissed off recently."

Patrick Estes, Rick for short, was in his early twenties, with black hair and eyes and smooth brown skin tanned a permanent chestnut from spending all his time on the water. His hands were strong from working the fish wheel and the drift net from the front of his bowpicker in Alaganik Bay. He didn't talk much, or smile, but he was the best of his small generation: a hunter, a trapper, and a fisherman in the traditional mold that went all the way back to Tobold Mack.

Dale Mack thought again how much he would have loved to have Rick Estes as his son, and how perverse a world it was that put a Tyler Mack ahead of a Rick Estes by blood and tribal precedence and tradition. "That way," he said deliberately, "we can tell the eldest that we did what he said."

Their eyes met, and Dale Mack saw understanding dawn in Rick's eyes.

The door opened, and his wife and daughter came inside, followed by a third figure, short and plump, with a round, foolish face beneath a fringe of graying hair she was continually shaking out of bright, inquisitive eyes. His wife, even more monosyllabic than Rick Estes, went immediately to the stove to check the fish head stew.

"Big powwow all done?" Auntie Nan said.

Auntie Nan, his wife's cousin somewhere on her mother's side, had moved in with the Macks when her husband died. That was eighteen years ago, just before Jennifer had been born. After a prolonged and difficult labor that had proved to be her last and only, his wife welcomed the extra pair of hands. Her husband had not welcomed the extra mouth to feed but never had the courage to ask Auntie Nan to move on, and eventually she had become a fixture in their home.

Auntie Nan, dim though she might be, had an instinctive sense of self-preservation and scurried to the counter without waiting for an answer, there to throw flour and sugar and milk and yeast into a bowl with so much energy that much of it spilled on the counter and more of it onto the floor. She uttered a distressed sound and snatched up a broom and dustpan to sweep it up, leaving a large smear of white behind. His wife's shoulders raised and fell in a sigh she would never allow to become audible in front of her husband, and she cleaned up the smear with a damp sponge.

Dale Mack watched as Rick's eyes were drawn irresistibly to Jennifer's face and stayed there.

"Hi, Jennifer."

The older man stopped himself from cringing, barely, at the open note of adoration in the younger man's voice. Servility would never get Rick Estes anywhere with Dale Mack's daughter.

"Hey, Rick." Her smile was perfunctory, and she was looking at her father. "What was all that about?"

"None of your business," Dale Mack said, wishing, not for the first time, that his daughter looked upon Rick Estes with half as much interest as Rick Estes looked upon her. A great deal of trouble would have been saved thereby, beginning with her, him, and the entire village of Kushtaka.

It would have helped, too, if she hadn't been so goddamned beautiful. Sometimes he felt his own eyes straying to that cape of shining black hair, the proportionately long legs, the hourglass figure, the clear olive skin, partly in a kind of dumb admiration but mostly in bewilderment that a child so striking had sprung from his own loins. When she hit fourteen, the boys had shown up in what seemed to Dale Mack like herds. He didn't begin to know how to handle it, other than with rough oaths and dire threats and sometimes simply forbidding Jennifer to leave the house. An edict she managed to flout with contemptuous ease whenever she wanted to.

"Is it true?" Jennifer said, her glowing presence a living flame in the dark environs of the little cabin. "Is Tyler Mack dead?"

Dale Mack hesitated. This wasn't the kind of thing one spoke of with women. "Yes," he said at last.

"And that he was murdered?"

Her father's mouth tightened. "Yes," he said.

She ignored the accompanying glare. "Do they know who did it?"

If he'd been less concerned with his own affairs and the affairs of the village of Kushtaka, he would have heard the undertone of anxiety warning of problems closer to home.

But he'd already caught seventeen different kinds of grief from the village elders for teaching Jennifer to work the fish wheel. Especially from the women, whom one would have thought might have been on Jennifer's side. From there, things seemed to progress exponentially, until somehow he was taking her with him when he was running his traplines. She learned, quickly, just by watching, how to set traps, how to skin and tan hides.

Her mother had tried to teach her how to smoke fish, but here, too, Jennifer nagged Dale until he took her out on the Sound and taught her how to gillnet. The whole village heard what the elders had thought about that. Girls didn't fish, either. At least Kushtaka girls didn't.

Resentful of the criticism, despairing because he had no son, he bought her a rifle and taught her to shoot. It didn't help that she turned out to be the best shot in the village, taking down a bull moose the previous fall so big, it had taken two days to pack out. There was plenty of grumbling over this blatant flouting of tradition, too, but Dale hadn't seen any of the elders turning up their noses at Jennifer's mom's moose stew at the Christmas party at the gym.

She'd always been smart, and quick to learn. She should have been a boy.

Jennifer, of course, had ignored the whispers behind her back and the scolding to her face with equal disregard. Perhaps that kind and quality of beauty bred its own indifference to authority.

Suddenly, Dale Mack was afraid for his daughter, afraid for his family, for his village, a nameless, inchoate fear that threatened to well up and choke him where he sat.

He looked at Rick. "Want to stay for supper, Rick?"

The younger man brightened. "Sure."

And Dale Mack cravenly ignored the dark fury in the glance directed his way by his only child, and said, "Set an extra place, Jennifer."

Six

WEDNESDAY, JULY 11

Niniltna

THE CELL TOWER ON THE HILL IN BACK of the school was the first thing to be seen driving into Niniltna, a village built along one street that paralleled the river. Houses varied in construction from one-year-old split-level ranch homes to hundred-year-old log cabins, with a few tar paper shacks thrown in just to keep the place humble. The school's gymnasium was the largest building in town and where every event of any significance was held, from the Kanuyaq Kings basketball team's annual grudge match with the Cordova Wolverines to Niniltna Native Association annual board meetings to potlatches for any event, birth, death, wedding, or old-fashioned ego trip for the host. *See how rich I am? See what good food I serve? See how many rifles and blankets I can give away? You should vote for me next time, for NNA board or CEO or state senator.*

There was a single grocery store, a restaurant, and a fuel

dealer with a lone gas pump out front, $7.40 a gallon today, Kate saw. Which was why everyone who could afford to bought their gas in fifty-five-gallon drums trucked in from Ahtna, or in bulk delivered to personal fuel tanks by the tanker truck that made the trip into the Park once a month during the summer. Which wasn't much cheaper, but every little bit helped, especially before the fish started running.

The Kanuyaq River at Niniltna was deep enough along its eastern edge to bring smaller fishing boats in to the many docks attached to the houses built along the bank. The southern side of the river was less populated, mostly by log cabins that predated the Park, every second one of which was abandoned, tumbledown, and covered with moss.

Kate stopped at the Riverside Cafe for one of Laurel's Americanos, heavy on the half-and-half, and spent a few moments catching up on the local gossip. Kushtaka did not figure in it, so the news had not percolated this far north. Cindy and Ben Bingley did. "Is the store closed?" Kate said, thinking of the shopping list she had in the pocket of her jeans.

A Meganack, the apple hadn't fallen that far from the familial tree in that Laurel owned and operated the Riverside Cafe, one of Niniltna's newer and healthier commercial concerns. The mine had helped, of course, since the café was the only place a Suulutaq miner could buy a burger and at the same time eye up the local talent, of which Laurel was certainly a member. In her twenties, long dark hair pulled into a loose ponytail, big dark eyes framed with thick lashes, an hourglass figure showcased in tight jeans and tighter T-shirts, even if Laurel had been the worst cook between Niniltna and Anchorage, she could still have packed them in just by bending over the counter to refill mugs. She knew she wasn't only selling espresso.

Laurel stripped a piece of beef jerky out of cellophane and offered it to Mutt, who took it delicately between her front teeth and then suffered her head to be scratched with a kind of weary stoicism. Mutt wasn't a misogynist, precisely, but with a few rare exceptions, Kate fortunately among them, she did vastly prefer men to women. "No," Laurel said, answering Kate's question, "Annie took care of it."

"What'd she do?"

Laurel smiled. "She sent Auntie Vi over to the Bingleys."

Kate laughed. "Auntie Vi drop-kick Cindy back to the store?"

"No," Laurel said. "She demanded the keys. Said if Cindy and Ben couldn't get enough of their shit together to sell milk to the Park rats, she'd do it for them."

Kate's eyebrows went up. "Auntie Vi's running the store?"

"She is," Laurel said gravely, but with a twinkle in her eye, "and it's my understanding that about five minutes after she did, Howie and Willard had to find somewhere else to conduct business."

Kate made an effort to keep her grin tacked in place, but on her way up to the post office she did wonder where Howie and Willard had moved their operation. Bootlegging was one industry that never went out of business in the Park.

The old-fashioned brass bell above the door jingled when she pushed it open. The Niniltna post office had been built on the side of the airstrip, the easier to transfer mailbags and packages from the plane they rode in on. Inside there was a Dutch door opposite, top half open, next to a wall of post office boxes. One corner held a shelf with a selection of USPS shipping boxes, Bubble Wrap, and strapping tape; another, a tall brass étagère with glass shelves. The étagère held a selection of Bonnie Jeppsen's beadwork—headbands, eyeglass holders, earrings, bracelets, and bookmarks—all tastefully displayed with discreet price tags attached. "What's this?" Kate said, examining one such object. "It looks like a rock. With beads on it."

The postmistress was a large, zaftig woman with long, grayish blond hair and a floating, floral style of dress. "They are rocks, Kate. With beads on them."

Kate picked one up, fascinated by the incorporation of tiny snail, mussel, and clam shells among the green and gray and brown beads. "Did you glue them on?"

"No, I sewed them on."

"You're kidding."

"Nope," Bonnie said. "Needle and thread. A skinny needle and a special kind of thread."

"Wow. Must have taken a while."

"I went to Anchorage and took a couple of classes."

Kate put the rock down and turned. Bonnie was in her fifties, with an air of incorporeality that might have been studied or might have been natural, Kate could never tell. It was relatively new, dating from her leaving her sister Cheryl and Cheryl's abusive husband and the rest of the born-again Jeppsens up on their homestead and moving into town. That was, what, five years ago now? At any rate, Bonnie had switched allegiance to Wicca and was now into homeopathy, healing crystals, herbal tinctures, and for all Kate knew, dancing naked under a solstice moon.

"Gorgeous," she said, putting the rock back on the shelf without looking at the tag on the bottom. However tempted, she would rather wash dishes for three days in a row than try to dust that rock after it had been sitting on a shelf in her house for more than a week.

She felt to see if the ivory otter was still in her left-hand pocket. It was, as it had been for the last six years, and it would never need dusting so long as she carried it around with her.

"Want your mail?" Cheryl said.

Kate took a step toward her mailbox and Bonnie said, "Don't bother, I've got it in overflow." She disappeared and reappeared with a plastic bin filled to the brim with envelopes white and manila, magazines, catalogs, half a dozen book-shaped packages from Amazon, and a glossy color brochure. The brochure's logo was a circular figure of a woman with long swirling dark hair cradling Planet Earth in her arms.

"Gaea still in business, I see," Kate said.

"That one's four weeks old," Bonnie said. "You might like to check your mail more than once a month."

"Has it been a month?" Kate said, trying not to sound guilty. "I thought it was only a couple of weeks."

Bonnie gave her a stern look. "What if there's an overdue bill somewhere in there?"

Kate didn't have that many bills, but she took Bonnie's point and hauled the bin out to her pickup and spent half an hour sorting the wheat from the chaff. Direct mail advertising and catalogs were fast-forwarded to the trash. Neither was she interested in solicitations from the AARP, the NRA, the AFL–CIO, the United Fund, the Republican Party, the Democratic Party, the Libertarian Party, the Secessionist Party, or the Tea Party. Likewise, she tossed missives from Doctors Without Borders and Heifer International, both of which organizations she sent a check to every Christmas already. Why was it that the instant you sent someone a check, no matter how worthy the organization, the first thing they did was ask you for more? Irritating, and a waste of the money she had just sent them.

There were, miraculously, some items meriting a forty-six-cent stamp. She smiled over a postcard from Andy Pence, which read, "You don't call, you don't write, you couldn't stop off in Dutch on your way to Adak?" She wondered how he had found out about her overnighter to Adak in January, though not for long. Fishermen were worse gossips than any auntie she had ever met.

There was a rare letter from Stephanie Chevak in Bering. Stephanie was, what, fifteen now? But she wrote with all the formality of a Victorian great-aunt. She was well and in good health, as Kate knew she would be graduating early from high school and she was already preparing to submit college applications. Would Kate be willing to write her a letter of recommendation?

Kate would indeed, since she was already convinced that little Stephanie Chevak of Bering was well on her way to becoming the Carl Sagan of her generation. Fifteen seemed to be a little early to be thinking of graduation, even for Stephanie, and then Kate remembered that her middle school teachers had jumped her a grade. Or was it two? Past time Kate went out to Bering for a visit. She set the letter aside with Andy's postcard.

Another envelope from Pletnikof Investigations, Ltd., held a deposit slip to her account in the Last Frontier Bank. Kate paid her respects to the amount of numbers in front of the decimal point with a reverent whistle. A scribbled sticky note read, "Business is good. Kurt."

From bear-poaching Park rat to Alaska's Allan Pinkerton in three years, courtesy in part because Kate had bankrolled Kurt Pletnikof as a silent partner. One of her better investments.

She looked over at Stephanie's letter. Stephanie would undoubtedly be offered a full ride at whatever institute of higher learning was lucky enough to get her, but just in case, it was good to know Kate had her financial back.

There was a separate communication from Kurt's executive assistant, a flat manila envelope postmarked the previous month, which contained an update on the activities of one Erland Bannister, owner and proprietor of Arctic Investments, an Alaska venture capital firm that was a recent minority shareholder in the Suulutaq Mine. She'd put Kurt on retainer to keep an eye on him. This month's report included a few clippings from the *Journal of the Alaska Chamber of Commerce, Alaska Business Monthly*, and a highlighted paragraph in a *Wall Street Journal* story on the Suulutaq Mine, in which Erland declared himself delighted at being a stakeholder in the mine, a project with an extremely beneficial effect on the long-term economy of the state of Alaska.

The fact that he'd been jailed for attempted murder until a smart—read expensive—lawyer got him out on a technicality involving alleged prosecutorial misconduct appeared to have escaped the reporter's notice. Lips pressed together in a straight line, Kate stuffed the clippings back in the envelope without reading the rest of them and set it aside. She leaned back against her seat and stared out the open window of her pickup.

Traffic at the Niniltna airstrip was certainly more active than at this time two years before. One of George Perry's Single Otter turbos touched down at the end of the 4,800-foot runway, paved only last year, and taxied briskly up to the Chugach Air Taxi hangar to disgorge a load of Suulutaq workers, hungover from their weeks off. They were bundled into two Beavers, which whisked them into the air on a south-southeast heading for the mine. Meanwhile, the Otter loaded the mine workers headed for town. Some of the outgoing miners didn't look to be in much better shape than the incoming ones, and Kate wondered what Vern Truax, the mine's superintendent, was doing about substance abuse on the job. She also wondered who was bringing said substances in. There were over a hundred workers out at Suulutaq, last time she checked. Howie and Willard at their most efficient couldn't have supplied a tenth that many without tripping over their own dicks in front of Jim, or her.

Two of the outgoing miners, both skinny young men in worn jeans, scuffed boots, and plaid jackets, got into a fistfight over who got to board first. A third, in line behind them and older and much larger, raised two hands the size of baseball gloves and smacked their heads together, once. Once was enough. The two younger miners went rubber-legged up the airstairs with an inexorable assist from their disciplinarian and a round of applause from the miners behind him.

George, observing from a distance, saw Kate on the other side of the runway and waved in the middle of his preflight. In very few moments, the Otter was but a memory on the horizon. "You fine," Kate said to its rapidly disappearing rudder. The Otter turbos were new, and very fine, indeed.

Demetri Totemoff drove up to meet a Cessna 180 with a pilot and five passengers on board. Demetri loaded them into his brand-new Dodge Durango Citadel (the one with all the options, including the fold-down captain's chairs in the second row and the DVD entertainment section; Kate had already had the tour), and he, too, waved without stopping. Kate wondered where he was taking them, because there wasn't a road to his high-end hunting and fishing lodge. It was located south of the Suulutaq, almost as close to the Canadian border as Canyon Hot Springs, and with a lot better view of Mount Saint Elias.

Well, she thought, there hadn't been a road last time she'd checked.

A yellow and white Piper Tri-Pacer set itself down with circumspection at the end of the runway and taxied decorously to a parking spot on the post office side of the runway. When the pilot got out, Kate could hardly believe her eyes.

"Anne! Anne Flanagan!" She got out of her truck.

The pilot shaded her eyes with one hand. "Kate? Kate Shugak?"

She was of medium height and sturdily built, with blond hair cut short and blue eyes that crinkled when she smiled. She was smiling now, and she took Kate's hand in both of her own.

"What are you doing in Niniltna?" Kate said.

"I'm on my way downriver. Hoping Bonnie will let me use her bathroom."

Kate nodded at the Tri-Pacer. "Since when are you a pilot?"

Anne's smile was proud. "And thereby hangs a tale."

⁂

This time when Kate walked into the Riverside Cafe, a young miner who was either drunk or high or both was behind the counter making an inept attempt at opening the cash register. Laurel kept slapping his hands away, and looked to be rapidly losing her patience. "Knock it off," she said as they walked in, but the miner either ignored her or was so under the influence that his ears had stopped working.

Kate walked up behind him and tapped on his shoulder. She had to do it twice before he turned around. His pupils were the size of Lincoln pennies, and the whites were a streaky red. He scratched first beneath his left arm, moved up to the back of his neck, and then reached for his crotch, stepping from one foot to the other. "Hey," he said to Kate, without much interest, "you're hot." He looked at Anne. "You wanna dance? There should be music." He looked up at the ceiling and shouted, "I need me some Linkin Park! Building it up to burn it down! Whoa."

He closed his eyes and put out his arms for balance. "The room's going around. I hate that."

When he opened his eyes again, they fell on the cash register and he reached for it again. Laurel slapped his hands away. He burst into tears.

Laurel looked at Kate. "Five minutes ago, we were having a perfectly rational conversation about whether Justin Bieber was the Antichrist."

The young miner stopped crying as if he had turned off a faucet and said, "Do you have any eggs? I've got a recipe for a killer cheese souffle." He made for the kitchen, only to be thwarted again by Laurel.

Before he could burst into tears a second time, Kate said to Anne, "Be right back," got the miner by one arm and a handful of hair, and frog-marched him out the door and up the street, to scattered applause and a few honks from Peter Grosdidier's passing pickup. Around the corner and up the hill to the trooper's post they went, where with Maggie's blessing, Kate tucked him into one of the cells and left him to dry out or come down.

It was the only one of the cells that was empty, and the smell of vomit lingered unpleasantly on the air. She went back out to the office and tossed a small, clear plastic bag full of white powder on Maggie's desk. "Found it in the pocket of his jeans."

"Another one?" Maggie sighed and got out an evidence bag.

"Is that what the other three are in for?"

Maggie nodded, her face grim. "And those are only the ones we caught."

"I haven't been in town for a while," Kate said. "This happening a lot lately?"

Maggie pushed back from her desk and scrubbed her hands over her face. She looked tired and exasperated. "Since May, it's been like someone has been parachuting the stuff in. The cells have been full since June, and as soon as we ship the miscreants off to Judge Singh in Ahtna, they're full up again."

"Any ideas on who's bringing it in?"

"The usual suspects deal retail, not wholesale."

"So, somebody new."

"Somebody new to the business," Maggie said. "Not someone new to the Park. Moving that much product requires resources. Staff. Storage. Transportation."

"Oh," Kate said. "So not just cocaine."

"No, indeed," Maggie said, "booze, too. A lot of booze." Her gaze went past Kate to the map on the wall. It was a large-scale topographical map of the Park, every physical detail faithfully rendered and including every village of one or more people and every known airstrip. "Sooner or later, someone will talk, or someone unexpected will flash out with a lot of money. We'll get them, Kate."

Eventually, Kate thought. In the meantime, the Niniltna trooper post was running a B and B for drug users. It was only a matter of time before one of the dealers got greedy and started cutting the cocaine with Alka-Seltzer Plus or some equally ostensibly harmless over-the-counter drug and Park rats started stroking out.

⁂

Back at the Riverside Cafe, Laurel said, "You know, I never made all that much money before the mine went in, and I love what it did for my bank balance, I really do, but I'm beginning to wonder if the trade-off in drunks and highs are worth it. When you get a chance, tell Jim I said so, would you?"

Kate said she would, not that Jim had a magic wand to make everything all better, and she and Anne settled into a booth. During Kate's absence, Paul and Alice had also found their way to the Riverside. Paul was still studying his map with a frown of concentration, and Alice was looking at the cappuccino in her hand with an expression of outright incredulity.

"When was the last time I saw you?" Kate said.

"Three years," Anne said promptly. "I was spackling your Sheetrock. Is the house still standing?"

Kate smiled. "It is, and I love it even more now than I did when you built it for me." Anne had responded to Dinah Clark's call to action when Kate's cabin was torched and she and Johnny had been left with shop, outhouse, greenhouse, and cache, but no beds. Park rats current and former, friends of Kate going all the way back to college, ex-clients, and people she had met during some of her cases in Anchorage had rallied with tools, supplies, transportation, heavy equipment, and sweat equity to effect a house-raising in three days.

"You were still grieving over your cabin then," Anne said.

"That pretty much went down the flush toilet the first week," Kate said.

Anne laughed. Her skin had a healthy tan, her eyes were bright, her hair gleamed.

"You look," Kate said, "terrific. Are you in love, or what?"

Anne laughed again. "No. I mean, yes, I guess." She took a big bite of one of Laurel's plain cake doughnuts. "Yumm," she said thickly.

"I know," Kate said. "Best cake doughnuts this side of the

Girdwood Y bakery. Well, don't leave me hanging. Do the girls like him?"

The girls being Anne's twin daughters, who had to be, what, fourteen years old now.

"It's not a guy," Anne said, swallowing. "I guess . . . I guess it's flying."

"You're in love with the Tri-Pacer?"

Anne chuckled. "I just might be, at that." She brushed crumbs from the front of her denim shirt and straightened her shoulders. "Allow me to introduce you to the new flying pastor for the Park."

"Well." Kate sat back in her seat and thought about it. "Been a while since the Park had a flying pastor."

"About fifteen years," Anne said, "since Father Frank pranged the parish Beaver down at Chulyin."

"Yeah," Kate said, remembering. "I'd forgotten about that. Didn't I hear he'd been drinking?"

"He was always drinking," Anne said. "Nobody minded that so much, because he was a damn good shepherd to his flock. But they were really annoyed with him when he totaled their aircraft." She smiled. "Why they're making me buy mine."

"Seriously?"

She nodded. "They fronted the purchase price, I'm buying it back out of my salary. Okay by me, I'd rather be flying—and maintaining—my own plane."

The smile spread across her face, and Kate saw again how, well, happy the Presbyterian minister looked. "I never knew you wanted to learn how to fly," she said.

"Oh yeah," Anne said, "like only since the first time I ever got on a small plane. There was no point in talking about it, because I figured I could never afford it."

An old story, although Kate had noticed that Alaskans who wanted to learn to fly usually found a way. It was an instantaneous and lifelong addiction. Before long, when people asked Anne Flanagan what she did, she'd answer, "I'm a pilot." *Minister* would be just an addendum.

Kate did not say that, however. "What's the actual job like?" she said instead, curious. "Do you fly and preach every day? Do you get days off? How many people do there have to be assembled before it's worth it for you to fly in?"

Anne drained her mug and Laurel brought a refill just so she could loiter around to hear the answer. She might even be a potential member of the congregation, although Kate knew enough about Laurel's personal history that she took leave to doubt the possibility. "One person who needs me is enough for me to stop. One or a dozen or a hundred, it's all the same. No flyover country in the Park, not for me. The circuit can last anywhere from a week to ten days, then I fly back to Cordova for a week."

"So week on, week off," Kate said. "More or less."

"Like working at Suulutaq," Laurel said.

"It can be," Anne said. "This time of year especially. There's almost no one left in the villages, they're all out fishing. I'm guessing winter will be a lot busier."

"Where do you meet?" Laurel said. "Somebody's house?"

Anne nodded. "If they don't have a gym."

"Do you preach every time?"

"Sometimes they don't need a sermon," Anne said. "Sometimes they need some family counseling. Sometimes they just want to talk about faith, and life, and . . ."

"And if God sees the little sparrow fall," Kate said.

Anne grinned, remembering, like Kate, the first time they had met. It had been, Kate thought, a total-immersion experience.

Anne's grin faded. "I was so sorry to hear about Old Sam."

It was going on a year, and the words still put a lump in Kate's throat. "He is missed," she said softly.

Anne reached across the table and touched her hand briefly. Kate wasn't much for outward shows of affection, but this, from this woman, she would take as Old Sam's due. "He liked you, a lot," she said.

"I know," Anne said. "I was proud he did. He didn't like everybody."

The remark surprised a laugh out of Kate. "He sure didn't." She willed the tears from her eyes. Laurel watched, fascinated, until Kate glared at her and she remembered that there was something she had to check in the kitchen. "The girls okay with this?" Kate said. "How are they, anyway? What are they now, fourteen?"

"Lauren and Caitlin? Fifteen. They're good. They stay in Cordova with their grandmother while I fly the circuit."

"They still packing lightsabers?"

Anne laughed. "I'm either happy or sad to report that they've graduated to phasers and photon torpedos. They've been watching all the *Star Trek* series on DVD. Lauren keeps running into doors. I don't know if she really expects them to slide open, so much as she thinks they ought to in a better organized universe."

"Ah," Kate said. "*TOS* or *TNG*?"

Anne laughed again. "They love *Voyager* for Janeway and Nine, but they were both *DS9* girls from the first year. Everyone's using iPads in *DS9*. I think they're both geeks for life." She looked at her watch. "I've got to go. I'm due in Double Eagle this evening for a christening, and then Kushtaka tomorrow."

"Kushtaka?"

"Yeah. Why?"

"Jim's down there. Been an accident of some kind."

"Somebody hurt?"

"He wasn't specific," Kate said, crossing her fingers beneath the table. "But there is trouble."

Anne frowned. "Good thing I'm already scheduled there, then."

She said it utterly without ego or vanity. Anne Flanagan was in service to the community and it wasn't about her; it was about the people on her pastoral circuit. Kate had to admire that, even if she was never going to attend one of Anne's services. Although she might do that one day, too, because what Anne said about faith would be a lot different from what Pastor Seabolt in Chistona said about faith. Kate was certain any god Anne paid homage to would be a lot more accepting of the various, beautiful, and new flavors of people. She might even have a sense of humor, too.

She drove Anne back to the airport. As the minister preflighted and did the walkaround, one of George's Single Otter turbos took off for the mine and a small white private jet touched down and rolled to a stop in front of his hangar.

Anne paused, following Kate's gaze. "What is that, a G2?"

"Beats me," Kate said.

Her clipped tone made Anne give her a quizzical glance, which narrowed when a tall man with thick white hair and jeans that looked tailored to fit disembarked from the jet. He caught sight of them, waved, and jogged across the airstrip.

In the cab of Kate's pickup, Mutt sat up, ears cocked and yellow eyes fixed on the oncoming figure.

"Stay, Mutt," Kate said.

"Kate?" Anne said in a low voice.

"Kate," the man said jovially, coming to a stop in front of them, hands in the pockets of an elegant olive green safari jacket that

Anne estimated probably cost as much as her Tri-Pacer. "And this is?" He smiled at Anne, and she had to admit it was a very nice smile, white even teeth in a tanned face filled with interesting lines. He walked like a much younger man, but up close she could see he was older than she'd first thought.

"Anne Flanagan," she said, and wondered at the faint sense of uneasiness she felt in his presence.

"Ah yes," he said, holding out his hand, "the new flying pastor?"

"Why, yes," she said. His grip was hard and firm and meant to leave an impression. "I'm sorry, we haven't met, have we?"

"Erland Bannister," he said, and the faint sense of uneasiness jolted into full-blown alarm. She recovered almost immediately but he had seen, and his smile widened. "I see you've heard all about me, Reverend Flanagan." He turned that smile on Kate. "Yes, well, you might like to consider your source."

Kate's expression didn't change. She didn't offer her hand, and she didn't say anything, but something in the steady gaze of those hard hazel eyes caused some of the self-satisfied assurance to fade from Erland Bannister's smile. Anne, watching, had the breathless feeling of sharpened weapons ready to be drawn on a moment's notice, with no quarter asked for or given.

She knew the story, of course. Everyone did, or a version thereof. Some years before, Kate had hired on to look into a suspicious death in Erland Bannister's family, which had resulted in a nearly successful attempt on Kate's own life and in Erland's incarceration at the maximum security facility in Spring Creek. Owing to Erland's seemingly limitless resources, he'd stayed there for only two years before the courts set aside the verdict on grounds of prosecutorial misconduct. He was released and the district attorney's office, seeing the writing on the judicial wall, had declined to prosecute the case a second time. About the only consolation the friends of Kate Shugak could take was that declining to prosecute was not the same as being released without a stain upon his character.

In other words, if it looked like a skunk, if it smelled like a skunk, if it walked like a skunk, it probably was a skunk. Anne wondered what said skunk was doing in Niniltna. She also wondered why he was so au courant with Park affairs that he knew who she was.

A question for another day. She said briskly, "Well, I've got to hit the road."

Erland broke off the staring match first and said courteously, "Certainly, Reverend." He raised two fingers in a salute. "Kate," he said, and turned and walked back across the airstrip.

"What the hell was that?" Anne said in a low voice.

"Well," Kate said, "it wasn't Justin Bieber."

Both women started to giggle, more from a relaxation from tension than out of mirth, but Erland heard them. He didn't look around or pause in his stride, but even at that distance, Kate could see his neck reddening. Erland Bannister enjoyed a joke as much as anyone, just so long as the joke was never on him.

Anne looked at Kate and raised an eyebrow. "Anything you want to tell me?"

Kate watched Erland walk around his jet. "You already know everything there is to know."

Anne snorted. "Sure I do."

She climbed into the Tri-Pacer without further conversation. The engine twitched into life, and the nose pulled down as the prop accelerated into a blur. Anne waved at Kate, pulled the little aircraft around, lifted off neatly on a southeasterly heading.

Kate climbed into her pickup and stared at Erland's jet.

She liked Anne Flanagan fine, but Niniltna and the Park had been blessedly—she smiled at her choice of adverb—blessedly free of the taint of religious controversy for most of her life. Niniltna had to be the only village of its size in Alaska without its very own Russian Orthodox, Pentecostal, and Catholic churches. Ahtna was a big enough town that it had at least a minimum complement of every denomination from atheism to Zoroastrianism, but in Niniltna, the one organized congregation met at the Roadhouse, and not too regularly, mostly because of simple logistics. The Roadhouse had begun life a century ago as an actual roadhouse, a waypoint on the stampeders' trail between the Port of Cordova and Interior Alaska. It was fifty miles from Niniltna, the road was not maintained, in winter it was virtually impassable until the snow machines had beaten it into at least a semblance of flat, and lately falling spruce trees were a real hazard at any time of year. It didn't make for regular meetings of the congregation.

Ulanie Anahonak, the token right-wing nut on the Niniltna Native Association board, had been bemoaning the lack since she'd been sworn in, so far without much success. Most Park rats operated under the theory that if it ain't broke, don't fix it. Maybe bringing back the flying pastor was the thin end of the wedge.

Kate stared at Erland's jet as if trying to see through the fuselage, and wondered who had really bankrolled Anne Flanagan's Tri-Pacer.

Act III

Seven

THURSDAY, JULY 12

Anchorage

AT THE SAME MOMENT ANNE FLANAGAN'S Aviating Evangelist Piper Tri-Pacer was taking off from Niniltna, Jim Chopin was landing his Alaska Department of Public Safety Cessna 180 in Anchorage, where he unloaded Tyler's body into the back of an ambulance. He spent the night at the Merrill Field Inn, had pie for breakfast at Peggy's Airport Cafe, called the ME to make sure the body had arrived at the right lab, and was leveling off on a northeasterly heading, adjusting for drift under the influence of a twelve-knot tailwind, when his cell phone played a short burst from Lenny Kravitz's "Lady."

Where are you?

He texted back.

Ten minutes out of Anchorage. OTG Niniltna in a couple of hours. You?

Her:

Home. Who died?

He was only surprised she hadn't heard yet.

Tyler Mack.

Seconds passed.

Accident or on purpose?

On purpose.

Sure?

Pretty sure. Waiting on the ME.

Coming home?

Going straight back to Kuskulana.

Crap. Later then. Horny.

He laughed.

Me, too.

He was in a much better mood when he landed in Kuskulana than when he had departed the day before. It didn't last long.

Kuskulana was a lot like Niniltna in structure, albeit higher in elevation. There was, incredibly at any time of year but particularly in summer, an air of bustle about it, two new houses going up at opposite ends of the village, an extension going onto the two-year-old store that would double its size. It didn't have a hotel yet, but Jim saw five B and B signs between the airstrip and the creek landing, and Kuskulana hosted one of the brand-new cell towers that had sprung up overnight like mushrooms between Ahtna and Cordova.

The landing, at one time nothing more than a wide spot on the river, now boasted a mooring slip, a twenty-five-foot wooden float topped with open metal grating. Pilings had been driven through open squares in the four corners so that the slip would rise and fall with the rise and fall of the water on the river. It sat lengthwise against the bank and was reached by a metal gangplank, attached to a flight of wide, sturdy stairs made of treated wood posts and more metal grating, attached to more pilings that climbed the cliff to the plateau. The wood of the pilings gleaming with tar that had yet to turn brown from time and weather, and a pile of construction material, two-by-fours, twelve-by-twelves, angle iron, rebar, a couple of leftover Permafloats, some broken concrete blocks, were piled neatly beneath the gangplank out of the reach of the river. This far upstream, the Gruening River was too shallow for fishing boats, but every second Kuskulaner had his own skiff, and that de facto presupposed the existence of the upriver equivalent of a small boat harbor.

There was a cluster of young men at the landing when Jim stepped off the gangplank. In their late teens, dressed in T-shirts and jeans, most of them looked familiar enough that Jim knew he'd seen them in aggregate at a basketball game or a potlatch in the Niniltna gym, but none of them were so familiar that he'd ever arrested them for vandalism or underage drinking.

They were piling backpacks, folded tents, sleeping bags, and cardboard cartons into two big skiffs. They paused when they saw him. The tallest stepped forward. "Sergeant Chopin?"

"That'd be me," Jim said, pulling off his ball cap and pushing his fingers through his hair to let the breeze dry off his scalp. It was a warm day, welcome after all the rain. "And you are?"

"Ryan Christianson."

Roger's son. They both had the sharp Kuskulana cheekbones, although Ryan was whipcord lean in comparison to Roger's comfortably padded frame, and his son was maybe two inches taller. His brown hair was a little lighter in color, but he had the same deep-set eyes and the same firm jaw. There was a little acne left over from adolescence but on the whole a handsome boy with the promise of character in his steady gaze and firm chin.

"Dad said you're to have the use of the skiff for as long as you need it," Ryan said.

Jim resettled his cap on his head. "He going to be home this afternoon?" Ryan nodded. "Tell him I'll stop in on my way back."

"Will do." Ryan hesitated, then said, "Is it true? Is Tyler Mack dead?"

"Yes," Jim said.

The emotion that flitted across the boy's face was fleeting and hard to identify. It might have been fear, or it might have been something else entirely. Jim looked across the river at the Kushtaka fish wheel, sitting just above the first bend south of the Kuskulana landing. Take all of five minutes to get there from where he was standing. "You know him?" he said.

Ryan followed his gaze, and then looked back at Jim. "Everybody knows everybody around here," he said.

Jim was very conscious of the other boys standing in back of Ryan, their attention a palpable weight. When he looked over at them, inspecting every face one at a time, they met his eyes readily enough, perhaps even with a trace of challenge in their collective gaze. They were united in the way most teenage packs were united, either against his age or his profession or both. "True enough," he said peaceably, and this time there was no mistaking the relief on Ryan's face.

"Maybe not by name," Ryan said.

"But you can tell a Kushtakan from a Kuskulaner," Jim said.

The pack huddled up and stared out at him from the same inimical face.

"Any of you down here at the landing Tuesday morning? See anything or anyone over at the Kushtaka fish wheel?"

Sidelong glances, followed by a mass shrug. "Any of the rest of you know Tyler?"

"We don't hang with Kushtakans," one of the other boys said.

"He was your age. Did he come to school on this side of the river when their school closed?" Silence. "Did you have him in your English class? Pass him a basketball during an away game? I hear you guys have a pretty good men's team."

More silence. Officer Friendly wasn't working.

"The skiff's rafted third out." Ryan pointed, all business now. "There."

He recognized it from the day before. "Thanks."

The cardboard cartons stacked among the boys' supplies might not bear close examination, but murder outranked underage drinking every time. He had to climb over two skiffs to get to Roger's, but at least there wasn't another rafted off on the other side, so all he had to do was free the lines and go. The 250 hp Mercury Marine seemed like overkill for a river the size of the Gruening, but it, too, was new and started at a touch.

The pack stood watching until he was around the first bend.

The Mercury made short work of the two miles between the Kuskulana and Kushtaka landings. The Kushtaka landing consisted of a small, unimproved gravel bar with half a dozen beat-up skiffs sitting on it, bows in the bushes.

Jim nosed in Roger's skiff, hopped out, and dragged it up onshore, between two skiffs he recognized as belonging to Pat Mack and Tyler Mack. He fastened the bowline to a convenient bush, taking his time while reinventorying the contents of both skiffs, and then followed the path, littered with garbage, through the clump of willow trees that crowded the edge of the bank. He emerged almost immediately onto a dusty path, wide enough in most places for an ATV in the summer and in winter for a snow machine. Main Street, Kushtaka, Alaska, only titularly USA.

The dozen cabins on either side of the path were small, most of them listing in one direction or another, and none had seen fresh paint in a generation. He wasn't entirely sure they were all occupied. There were a couple of ATVs that looked as worn out as the houses they were parked in front of. There were no utility lines. The spaces between the cabins were filled with lean-tos and drying racks displaying filets of salmon hung on split tails, exposed flesh glowing like faceted carnelian. It was the most colorful thing in the drab little village.

Barring the small prefab school, standing on pilings at one end of the village, doors and windows covered with sheets of plywood, there were no public buildings, and no commercial buildings, either. In Kushtaka if you wanted five pounds of flour, you got in your skiff and went down the Gruening and then up the Kanuyaq to Niniltna, or downriver and west on Prince William Sound to Cordova. More like, you waited until the fall Costco run to Ahtna.

The Kuskulana store was not an option, not if you lived in Kushtaka.

A very few kids of widely varying ages and heights were shooting free throws through a netless hoop nailed to a wall of the school, on a basketball court consisting of faded lines painted on cracked pavement. A yellowing lace curtain moved but when Jim looked, it had already fallen back over the window.

An old man sat on a straight-backed chair leaned up against the wall of another cabin, smoking. Jim walked over to him. "Uncle."

The old man exhaled and narrowed his eyes against the smoke.

"I'm Sergeant Jim Chopin of the Alaska State Troopers," Jim said, pulling off his ball cap. "I helped Pat with Tyler's body. I'm very sorry for the trouble that has come to your village."

The surest way to get people to clam up on you in the traditional villages was to ask questions. Jim didn't say anything more, just stood where he was, hat in hand, nose into the breeze coming up the river. It brought with it a mixed aroma of diesel exhaust, woodsmoke, and decaying salmon. A dog barked and a gray-striped cat, hair sticking straight out all over its body, galloped around a cabin and disappeared into the grass. A family of goldeneyes made a strafing run over the rooftops and landed somewhere out of sight, setting up a furious quacking. An eagle soaring above provided the reason. From inside the cabin, Jim heard the muted sound of a radio and what might have been Bobby Clark's voice. Park Air was probably the only contact Kushtaka had with the outside world.

After a while, the old man got up, knees popping, and hobbled into the cabin. Presently he came out carrying another chair and two boat mugs by a finger hooked through their handles. Jim sat in the chair and accepted the mug. "Thank you, Uncle." Manners were manners, and Jim was experienced enough not to mistake mandatory Bush hospitality for an offer of friendship. It would not do to presume.

They drank. The coffee tasted like it had first been brewed during the Kennedy administration, with more grounds and water added every morning ever since. Jim could feel the old man's attention, and took another big gulp, suppressing the resulting gag reflex without so much as a single betraying quiver. Not for nothing did they call Alaska State Troopers the toughest of frontier lawmakers.

After a while, a younger man came out of the house opposite and started doing something to the Honda four-wheeler parked outside, which looked like it needed the encouragement. They watched him in silence. Ten minutes later, he got on the ATV and pushed the starter. With reluctance, the four-wheeler allowed itself to be coaxed into life. The man revved it a few times and turned it off. He wiped his hands on a rag and seemed to notice the two of them for the first time. He walked across the road. "Uncle."

The old man nodded. Maybe he was mute.

The younger man looked at Jim.

"I'm—"

"I know who you are," the younger man said. "I'm Dale Mack. I'm the chief here."

If Jim stood up, he would tower over the other man. But if he didn't stand up, it could be regarded as a sign of disrespect not only of the chief but of his entire tribe as well. He put down his mug and stood up. "Any relation to Tyler?"

The other man gave a short laugh. "We were all related to Tyler." He ran a hand through a crop of shaggy hair. He was medium height and built like a wrestler without being muscle-bound. There was a sureness when he was in motion that was not quite grace. That certainty reminded Jim a little of Kate.

"You take his body to Anchorage?"

Jim nodded.

"We'll want it back." Dale Mack nodded toward the back of the little town, where Jim had seen Kushtaka cemetery from the air. "He'll rest here with his family."

"Of course."

"Don't know why you had to do an autopsy. Uncle Pat said Tyler tripped over his own damn feet and fell in and got stuck under the fish wheel." He met Jim's eyes steadily.

"It's state law in the case of every accidental death," Jim said. "And until we get the medical examiner's report, we won't know exactly how he died."

Dale Mack scowled.

"Where is Pat?" Jim said. "I'd like to talk to him."

"What do you need to know?"

Jim allowed himself to be diverted, for the moment. "More about Tyler, for starters. Did he have a job? Friends? A wife or girlfriend, maybe?"

Dale Mack looked at the old man sitting at Jim's side. The old man gazed into the distance with a bland expression. "I knew him about as well as anyone in Kushtaka. His only job that I know of here was to clean out the fish wheel holding pen, and half the time he couldn't be bothered to do that. I hear tell he was working up at the Suulutaq Mine now and then. He hung out a lot with Boris Balluta up in Niniltna."

Freely translated, *Why don't you go talk to Boris and leave us alone?* Jim nodded at the village. "He have a cabin here?"

Dale Mack hesitated, and then gave a surly nod. He led the way to the end of the street and pointed. It was less a cabin than a shed, a lean-to without another structure to lean against. The slanted roof was covered with asphalt shingles themselves covered with moss, and the exterior was T1-11 that had never been painted and was now weathered to a lifeless gray. The homemade door was reinforced with chicken wire and fastened with a hasp and a brass padlock that dangled open. Jim contemplated the padlock for a moment, before removing it and opening the door.

Very little light was admitted through the single very small window on the back wall. Jim pushed the door wide and ducked his head to step inside.

He was surprised at how neat it was. A single bunk carefully made with army surplus blankets on the left. On the opposite wall, a counter made of two-by-fours and a slab of plywood, topped with a sheet of Formica in a faded green pattern. On it sat a Coleman two-burner propane stove and a square blue plastic washbasin. On the shelf beneath, canned goods were stacked with labels facing out. Jim looked, and looked again. Also sorted by kind, peaches, pears, and cherries, green and black and pinto and kidney beans, tomato sauce and tomato paste. Next to them dishes, glasses, flatware, utensils, a cast iron frying pan and a saucepan, all scoured clean.

There was a recliner of venerable vintage against the back wall. Next to it a Coleman lantern hung from a stand handmade from a piece of angle iron welded to what looked like an old brake shoe for a base and what might have been a wrought iron plant hanger welded to the top. A plastic bucket on the floor next to the chair was filled with *Playboy*s, *Penthouse*s, and *Hustler*s. Jim flipped through them and found an ad torn from a month-old Anchorage paper for the Brown Jug Warehouse in Anchorage.

Behind him Dale Mack sighed and shifted from one foot to the other. Jim ignored him.

Several items on the ad were heavily circled in pencil—whiskey, bourbon, tequila, all hard liquor. Evidently Tyler hadn't been into beer or wine.

Two plastic bins with snap-on lids under the bed held clothes, most notable of which were a pair of Guess jeans and a couple of Ralph Lauren knockoff shirts. They had been very carefully folded. A third plastic bin contained paperwork. Jim leafed through it. A birth certificate. A high school diploma. A bill of sale for a twenty-two-year-old Dodge Ram pickup. There were some photographs, school photos of Tyler through the years and a couple of him and his extended family, all of them on the river in various skiffs. There was one of Tyler at around age fourteen working the fish wheel. He didn't look happy.

"Find anything?" Dale Mack said from the door, voice brusque.

Jim sat back on his heels. "Not much. Never find very many real docs and photos anymore, everyone's gone digital." Proving his point, he got out his phone and took careful photos of the birth certificate, the diploma, and the bill of sale, and with a mental shrug the few photos as well. He tucked everything back into the bin, replaced the cover, and got to his feet. "Did he have a bank account, do you know?"

Dale Mack snorted. "Might have. So far as I know, he didn't have anything to put in it."

Jim thought of the roll of sodden cash he'd found in Tyler's pocket. "To your knowledge, had Tyler been in a fight recently?"

Dale Mack snorted again. "Tyler wouldn't have risked bruising that pretty face."

The other man's attitude got Jim's goat, and he spoke a lot more bluntly than was his wont at these kinds of scenes. "Someone took one hell of a whack at the back of his head. The ME will be able to determine a time when Tyler received that wound. I'm not calling it a homicide yet, but you should know it's a possibility."

Was it Jim's imagination, or did Dale Mack's skin pale beneath its olive tint? Certainly, the scowl that Jim was tending to think was habitual was replaced with something close to apprehension.

A girl appeared behind Dale Mack in the doorway, a slender figure outlined against the sun, a shiny cape of long black hair lifting in the breeze. "Dad?"

Dale Mack turned. "What?"

"Mom says is the trooper coming for lunch?"

"No."

"Dad."

"Get on home, Jennifer, tell your mother I'll be right there." He turned back to Jim. "You about done here?"

Jim walked outside, pushing Dale Mack out of the lean-to doorway by the sheer mass of his six-foot-four-inch, blue-and-gold-clad presence, and pulled the door of Tyler Mack's cabin shut behind him. He turned to replace the padlock, after a moment's inner debate leaving it unlocked, as he had found it. The place could have been ransacked twenty times in the last twenty-four hours, and he'd seen everything there was to see that remained.

He turned and looked a foot down at Dale Mack's glowering countenance, giving his weapons belt a tug as he did so. "I'm going to talk to a few more people first, I think, Dale," he said, his voice pleasant, his tone inexorable. "A man is dead. State law requires I investigate the matter fully. I'm sure you understand."

His manner, while respectful, indicated that he didn't care if Dale Mack understood or not. Dale Mack hesitated, swore without bothering to lower his voice, turned on his heel, and walked away.

It took a pitifully short time to knock on every door in Kushtaka. The story he met with was everywhere so similar, he could be forgiven for imagining it had been rehearsed by the entire village the day before. Tyler had been dangerously charming and incurably lazy, not a combination guaranteed to make a mother proud, according to one elderly auntie with an acid tongue. He worked at the Suulutaq Mine, except when he didn't, which was most of the time. His best friend had been Boris Balluta, a childhood relationship and one that the village as a whole considered to have done Tyler no good. "He was such a sweet baby," one middle-aged woman said, wringing a dishcloth between her hands, and then someone hidden in the dark reaches of the cabin behind her cleared his throat and she paled and with a mumbled apology closed the door in Jim's face.

It was with a feeling of the ranks closing in behind him that he climbed back into Roger's skiff and headed upriver.

Or he would have, if Roger's skiff hadn't started to sink out from under him.

Eight

THURSDAY, JULY 12

Farther down the river

THE YOUNG MEN HAD SET OUT DOWNRIVER in two skiffs loaded to the gunnels with all the essentials. Their plan was to take four days to travel to the mouth of the Kanuyaq, camping nights along the way, drinking, swapping stories, maybe scope out where the moose were congregating in anticipation of the hunting season opening next month. They would arrive in time to work the Monday opener in Alaganik, if there was one.

At least that was what they had told their parents. It was the truth, mostly.

But only mostly.

They left Kuskulana shortly after the trooper departed, the skiffs traveling side by side. Somebody had his iPhone hooked up to battery-powered speakers, and they shouted the lyrics to Maroon 5 and Flo Rida and Neon Trees and Fun from boat to boat. A "Call Me Maybe" cover (Get this net a rollin' / Reds schooling up the ocean / High boat is what we're wanting / Where you think you're going, salmon?) ended in mild hysteria and a near-grounding of one of the skiffs, but by then they were at their first stop and no harm done. The tiny gravel beach was overhung with willow and alder and cottonwood and thickly lined with beach grass. Camouflage from land and river both.

It was also on the wrong side of the river but they pulled in anyway. All the boys but Ryan got into the bigger skiff, taking everything except a single tent, two sleeping bags, and two days' worth of food and water for two people, plus Ryan's duffel.

They stood around in awkward silence afterwards. "You sure about this, Ryan?" one of them said in a low voice.

"Never been so sure about anything in my life," Ryan said.

The note of deep certainty in his voice opened their eyes a little, but the other boy only nodded. "All right, then. We got your back."

Ryan shook hands with all of them. "Thanks. Have a good time on the river."

They laughed. "You should talk."

They pushed off and he stood watching as they started the outboard. Ten minutes later, he raised a hand in farewell as they went around the next bend and out of his sight, probably for the last time. He pulled his skiff up under cover of the trees and settled in to wait.

The first time he'd seen her, they would have been about ten, him on his side of the river scraping the bottom of his father's skiff, her on her side helping her father on the fish wheel. Their eyes had met, holding, until her father spoke sharply, drawing her attention away, and Ryan had gone back to scraping the hull, although all he could see was her face.

There had been other glimpses over the years, at potlatches up and down the river, at Costco in Ahtna, at the Park Basketball Tournament in Niniltna. He could walk into a room and know if she was in it before he saw her. Always there would be that first, long glance, always interrupted by her father or mother or a friend, turning her attention elsewhere. Nothing else, no lingering glances, not a word spoken between the two of them.

And then the Kushtaka school closed, and her parents moved her to the Kuskulana school. Her beauty garnered its share of attention from the boys, but she favored none of them, at least so far as he could tell. She did her work, an A student who answered when called on by the teacher but who didn't volunteer. She played guard on the women's basketball team, with fast hands, quick feet, and an ability to score three-pointers when they were really needed. She was pleasant but made no friends. Her confidence and self-possession kept her apart. Sometimes he thought the other students were a little afraid of her.

He wasn't, but he wasn't going to be so stupid as to alert anyone in either village to his interest. And then came that away game last October. Men's and women's teams both to Ahtna, playing in the regional tournament on the Ahtna high school gym floor by day and sleeping on it by night. Even then it didn't seem as if there would be any chance to talk to her. Late the second night, burningly aware that she was in her own sleeping bag on the other side of the gym, he sneaked out alone, only to find her sneaking out right behind him.

He smiled.

That was the beginning.

If nothing went wrong, she should have heard his message this morning, and they would be away before anyone knew. A few hours' head start was all he asked.

His smile faded. The death of Tyler Mack was going to complicate things. He thought back to Tuesday morning on the river, and shuddered, remembering the meaty thunk of metal hitting flesh. A horrible sound.

He remembered, too, Chopper Jim's eyes fixed steadily on his face at Kuskulana landing before he and his posse had left. But what could the trooper know? Only what everyone did, that Kuskulana and Kushtaka were at each other's throats and had been for years. He couldn't know anything else, because no one on the Kuskulana side of the river would ever tell him anything.

Especially not Ryan.

Nine

THURSDAY, JULY 12, EARLIER

Niniltna

KATE LEFT HER PHONE IN THE HOUSE AND worked off frustrated sexual tension by a morning spent splitting wood. After lunch, the hammock and Peter Lovesay's latest beckoned, but she was still restless. She and Mutt drove back into Niniltna, through it, and five miles down the older and even less well maintained Roadhouse road. There she turned left on the track that led to the one-lane wooden bridge over Squaw Candy Creek, pausing to give prior right of passage to two young bull moose whose half-grown racks were covered in rich velvet and who had their eye on a stand of young alder they had somehow previously overlooked, stopped again on the other side of the bridge for a big fat bristly porcupine who was superbly indifferent to Kate, Mutt, the moose, fire, famine, or flood, and continued up to the A-frame with the

212-foot steel communications tower looming up behind it. The yard was covered in shorn green velvet and western columbines, and rugosa roses bloomed promiscuously everywhere Dinah had fought the brush to a standstill and freed up a small patch of ground.

Kate parked and got out to hold the door for Mutt, who brushed past her without so much as a backward glance. "Faithless bitch," Kate said in her wake, and followed her to the A-frame's front door at a far more leisurely pace.

The spruce bark beetle had visited Bobby's property, too, so that for the first time in the decade she'd been visiting him here, Kate could see the blue flash of a few mountains between the few still-standing trees. As on her homestead, as all over the Park, there seemed to be even more light than usual everywhere she looked, and during an Alaskan summer when there was already enough light to keep everyone up all night, the result was almost blinding.

The door stood wide open to the second warm day in a row, and Kate abandoned the busy hum of happy bees for the cool of the relative darkness inside.

Bobby was sitting at the center console of the A-frame, back to the door, when Kate walked in. His wife, Dinah, was nowhere to be seen, nor was the ball of fire also known as his daughter, Katya. Kate's namesake and goddaughter, Kate had also delivered her one memorable August day five years before, about an hour after she had acted as best woman and officiator at her parents' marriage. A fraught occasion.

She admired his broad shoulders with appreciation. Long before Dinah came into his life, back when Kate herself was in the middle of a long, painful recovery from five and a half years working the front lines of sex crimes in Anchorage, she had cause to know those shoulders and everything affiliated with them in intimate and delicious detail.

His back was bare and muscled, a trim waist disappearing into a pair of cutoff jeans, from which two legs emerged, both truncated at slightly differing lengths just below the knee, the missing pieces having been left behind in a rice paddy in Vietnam. A wheelchair with the parking brake on put him within easy reach of every knob and switch of the custom-made electronic Frankenstein sitting on the custom-made table that circled the twelve-by-twelve beam running straight up to the ridgepole of the roof. Wire and cable snaked up all four sides of the beam, connecting Frankenstein with the antennas and dishes on the tower out back.

All to support the NOAA observer in the Park. Allegedly. It was not the done thing to inquire too closely into how Bobby really supported himself and his lifestyle, which included a hefty portion of alcoholic refreshment imported by the case direct from Tennessee, his once and never again home state. Kate could make a good guess, but she didn't. Dinah probably knew, but she wasn't talking. Nobody else, if they knew what was good for them, was prepared even to speculate out loud, and Jim didn't care so long as Bobby was retired. Which he appeared to be.

Headphones were balanced precariously one ear on and one off, and he was speaking into a microphone dangling from a segmented metal pole. "Yeah, been a long cold one, but the sun's finally out and so am I, Bobby Clark, your very own silver-tongued Bard of the Big Bump and all we survey, coming to you live from—never mind."

Sometimes Bobby broadcast for four hours every night, usually during an election year, and sometimes for fifteen minutes once a week in the morning, usually during fishing season. Park rats had to divine the correct frequency pretty much telepathically because it changed every day and sometimes twice a day. Park Air was, unsurprisingly, FCC-unapproved and certainly unlicensed.

"Got a couple of screaming deals for you today, fellow rats," said that basso profundo, which registered on a visceral level with everyone in the Park with an X on both chromosomes, and not a few with XY, too. "A PSA before we get to them. Listen up. Red Run wants their safe back. They know who took it, they know you can't open it, just bring it back and no questions asked. No reward, either, and no whining about it or they call in Chopper Jim. You know how he gets when he has to fill out all that paperwork. And won't you just love being on the inside during the first above-sixty days we've seen this year. Sober up, morons, and get that safe back in the Red Run city hall offices pronto."

Bobby had a tendency to editorialize his public service announcements, but the entertainment value was worth the risk to most Park rats who wanted them broadcast. It certainly ensured that everyone would be listening.

Bobby adjusted a knob. "Scott Ukatish is dragging up, which is not surprising, considering he'll probably be the last one left to turn out the lights when he leaves the ghost town of Potlatch, for what I understand is a nice little one-bedroom condo in Sag Harbor, corner unit, top floor, good bar on the ground floor, frequented by a lotta local talent." A verse from "Looking for Love" rose and fell briefly in the background. "Scott says he's outta here September first, as he don't want to hit any snow on the Alcan going south. Between now and then, everything he can't fit into the back of his pickup is for sale, list price the day you show up or best offer by August fifteenth and it goes without saying you haul it away yourself. There's a list of the stuff he's got for sale on parkair-dot-radio, and it also goes without saying that you'll be bidding against me for the vintage collection of *Playboys*, which Scott tells me goes all the way back to the December 1953 first edition, yeah, the one with Marilyn Monroe on the cover, the one every guy my age remembers locking himself in the bathroom with."

If possible, his voice dropped even lower. "Just don't tell Dinah."

Bobby let Elton John's "A Candle in the Wind" drown him out while he shuffled bits of lined notebook paper, most of them scribbled in his own hand in scrawling black Sharpie. Elton muted, Bobby back at full volume. "Herbie Topkok needs a mechanic. Someone versed in the mysteries of everything from Evinrude to Honda to Ski-Doo to Fix Or Repair Daily. Full-time, hourly wage to be negotiated, and if you're any good, that includes straight through the winter, Herbie's word on it. Method of payment also negotiable, cash, check, or money order." Bobby laughed, a laugh that lived up in every timbre to the bass profundo voice. Kate was sure she would have heard it in the fillings in her teeth, if she'd had any fillings.

"Apply in person, preferably not loaded, last house on the left but one on your way to Ahtna.

"Okay," he said, looking down and shuffling more paper, "Boris Balluta wants to sell his Honda Rancher ATV. Four years old, been to the river and back a few times but in good shape overall. Yeah, I've see Boris running that four-wheeler hell-for-leather through town. She does look rode hard and put away wet, but she sounds sweet, and while Boris may always be looking for the easiest out in a room filled with bill collectors, he knows his way around an engine. He should be banging down

Herbie's front door, and if he didn't mind getting his hands dirty with actual work, he would be, but we all know that's not happening, don't we?

"Ruthe Bauman is looking for a print of Machetanz's *Eighty Winters*. A print, she says, not the original, doesn't have to be matted and framed, but she'll pay more if it is, save her doing it herself. Leave a message for her at the Roadhouse."

He pushed a slider over an inch, pulled another one back two inches. "Couple of personals now."

This was what the Park rats really tuned in for, or did before cell phones. Kate wondered how many were listening now.

"'Carol Sweeney, we're in Anchorage, due in on George tomorrow on the nine A.M. flight. Love you, see you soon.' Ha. Must be Carol's folks in from West Virginia. Welcome almost back, Sadie and Bert. Showing me something, coming back after last time and that whole moose collision incident.

"'J, I'll be at the usual place this afternoon and I'll wait.' Hmm. Short, to the point, sure hope J knows where 'the usual place' is." Bobby sat up, his back still to Kate, and popped his neck. "Okay, going out on a piece of big juicy gossip. Kermit the Clark here, with Park Air News, deet-te-deet-deet-deet. Listen up, folks." The sound of typewriter keys clicked and clacked over the speakers. Kate wondered how many of Bobby's listeners even knew what a typewriter was. "You know that new film incentive law they wished on us down in Juneau? Well, your intrepid reporter has heard a rumor that the Park—yes, our very own Park—is being scouted as a film location."

Kate's heart skipped a beat.

"No, no names, we don't know yet if it's Robert Downey, Jr., Hugh Jackman, or Gabe McGuire who will be starring in our very own personal Park epic, but I'm holding out for Denzel to play me, and I'm kinda hoping Zoe Saldana plays the love interest." He dropped his voice. "Just don't tell Dinah."

He reached for a knob. "Okay, that's it for now. Might be back on tonight, might not, but right now let's go out on somebody who knew their way around a song."

He flipped a switch, turned another knob, ran some sliders in opposite directions, and the first bars of the Beatles' "Please Mr. Postman" rocked out of the speakers.

Mutt couldn't stand it one minute longer and took the intervening space between the door and the man in one smooth leap and reared up to rest her paws lightly on the back of the wheelchair and swipe a long, agile tongue right up Bobby's bare spine, ending with a loving tickle behind his right ear that took the headphones the rest of the way off. Bobby jumped so violently that he knocked the brakes loose on his wheelchair. The wheels rolled forward and he rolled backwards, right out of the chair to land on his back on the floor. Where Mutt took merciless advantage.

"God *damn*!" The roar went right out over Park Air, west to Ahtna and all the way down to Cordova when the skip was good, or it would have if the mike had still been hot. "Fucking *wolves* in the fucking *house* again! Shugak! Get this beast off me! Goddammit, Shugak, I know you're there!"

Kate, hands in her pockets, strolled over to grin at him upside down, where he was feebly trying to stave off Mutt's efforts to remove the skin from his face with her tongue. "You rang?"

"*Get* this fucking wolf *off* me!"

"Only half," Kate said.

"*Shugak!*"

Kate gave an elaborate sigh. "Mutt?" she said, but really it was only a suggestion, and all three of them knew it.

Mutt moved back maybe an inch and laughed down at Bobby, a lupine laugh, tongue lolling out of her mouth.

"Shugak! Goddammit, call her off!"

Kate sighed. "Well, okay. If you insist."

"Shugak!"

Kate signaled Mutt, and Mutt gave Bobby one last, loving swipe, shook her coat into elegant layers, and trotted over to the wood box, where she knew Bobby stored the occasional mammoth clavicle to stave off marauding wolves.

"God *damn*," Bobby said, wiping the face in the crook of his arm and blinking up at Kate. "How many times have I told you about fucking *wolves* in the fucking *house*, Shugak?"

"Lots and lots of times, Clark," she said, giving him a hand up.

Slyly, he took that hand and held on while using the other to right his chair and slip into it, managing in the same motion to yank her into his lap and give her a lavish kiss.

She gave as good as she got, and when he pulled back she smiled up at him, a siren's seduction in her eyes, and said in a come-hither voice, "Where's your wife?"

He boomed out a laugh and dumped her on her feet. "She left me. Her and the kid both. Abandoned. Bereft." He waggled lascivious eyebrows. "All by myself."

"Uh-huh," she said.

"I'd put on some Eric Carmen to prove it if I could stand to listen to the fucker." He rolled over to the kitchen to put on the kettle. "They're in Anchorage. Eye doctor, dentist, shots, like that. Dinah wants to get a jump on the paperwork for school this year."

"Right, first grade," Kate said. "You, uh, volunteering at the school again?"

"Damn right I am."

She sighed. "You're going to give the kid a complex before she's ten."

"Then she has a complex. Nobody messes with the kid, Shugak."

"Understood, Clark. But really, who would dare?"

"Exactly," he said smugly. He opened the bag of coffee—Kaladi Brothers French Roast, not bad—and poured it into the filter without measuring. "What're you doing in town?"

"You know. This and that. Checking the mail. Buying some groceries. Visiting my best bud."

He glanced at her over his shoulder and grinned. "Where's Jim?"

"Up yours," she said, annoyed.

He laughed. The kettle whistled and he poured the water through the filter, doctored a mug with cream and sugar just the way she liked it, and they moved to the long couches in the living room, where Mutt was gnawing on a monster bone that looked fresh out of a Jack Horner dig with an expression of pure bliss.

"Did you ever meet Anne Flanagan?" she said after a moment to properly appreciate the magic elixir in her mug.

He cocked his head. "Minister? Down Cordova way?"

She nodded. "Ran into her outside the post office yesterday, we went for coffee. She's the new flying pastor for the Park."

"Yeah? A woman pastor?" He snorted. "I wonder how some of the old farts in the villages are gonna take to that."

"Old Sam liked her."

"Old Sam is no longer here to run interference for her," Bobby said, and added, "Sorry," when Kate didn't quite wince.

She waved off the apology. "She's excited. They fronted her the money for a Piper Tri-Pacer. Said she's always wanted to fly."

"Good on her," he said, nodding. He had a specially modified, exquisitely maintained Piper Super Cub on call on his own strip behind the tower in back of the A-frame. She'd known it well, at one time, and they smiled at each other in mutual remembrance of a certain sunny day beside a certain sparkling stream with a conveniently placed dirt strip nearby.

"I've been thinking about Canyon Hot Springs," she said.

"What to do with it, you mean?"

She nodded. "It's just sitting up there, falling down. Dan wants me to deed it over to the Park."

"I'll bet he does," Bobby said. "Ranger Dan would like every breathing Park rat to deed every piece of real Park property we own to the Park Service. Not happening."

She ignored the gibe, which was mostly bluster anyway. Chief Park Ranger Dan O'Brian had the distinction of being one of the few rangers in the entire National Park system who got along with the people whose property had been grandfathered in at the time of the creation of the Park around them. Or at least none of them had ever taken a shot at him, which amounted to the same thing. "Yeah, but maybe he has a point."

Bobby leveled an admonitory finger. "It hasn't even been a year, Shugak. Don't do anything in a hurry." He paused. "And think first about what Old Sam would have wanted. And . . ."

It was irresistible. "And?"

"And," he said slowly, "about what you really want, but hold that thought. I'm remembering I wanted to talk to you about something. A coupla things."

"What?"

"Somebody's running booze and drugs to the McMiners out at the Suulutaq."

She looked at him.

He looked back.

She rolled her eyes. "That's news?"

"You knew about it?"

"I knew it was inevitable," she said. "Young men plus too much money equals booze and drugs. It's like a natural law or something. Definitely a mathematical certainty."

"Does Jim know?"

"Of course he does." She told him about the McMiner at the Riverside the day before, and her subsequent conversation with Maggie.

"So we're talking commercial quantities here," he said thoughtfully.

You would know, she thought but didn't say.

"Does Jim know who?"

Her gaze sharpened. "Do you?"

He wasn't ready to share. "Just rumors."

"When you hear a name, let us know."

He cocked his head. "Us? Not just you? Not just Jim?"

She flipped him off, and he laughed. "Where is Jim, anyway? Haven't seen him around in a while."

"Kushtaka," she said. "Tyler Mack was murdered."

"Ah, shit," Bobby said.

"Probably," Kate said. "Jim's waiting on the ME to say one way or the other."

"Man, I hope it's the other. I thought we got over our Hatfield-and-McCoy phase when you settled things between the Kreugers and the Jeppsens with a D6 Cat."

Kate let her head fall back against the couch. "We don't know what this is yet."

"Yeah," Bobby said, "we do." He paused. "You ever told Jim—?"

"No," Kate said.

"Maybe—"

"No."

He held up a hand, palm out. "Whatever. I'm all for a quiet life." They sat for a few moments, listening to the sounds of the birds and the bees coming through the open door. "We ought to legalize and tax all drugs," Bobby said. "Treat 'em like booze and smokes. If somebody wants to stick a needle in their arm or powder up their nose, that's their business. Keep 'em out of the hands of children and people who operate heavy equipment."

"No argument here," Kate said. "I'm all for treating people like grown-ups."

"You've never had a drink, Kate," Bobby said. "I'm not sure you get a say."

"No," Kate said, "but I'm alive and I've got eyes and I've read a little history. The last time we tried prohibition, it didn't work out for us all that well. Forbidding something just makes it that much more attractive, especially to teenagers."

"They say it's a disease."

"It isn't one we have to contract, not with some positive reinforcement and responsible parenting." She picked at a piece of lint on her jeans, feeling his eyes on her. When she spoke again her voice was quiet. "Both my parents were alcoholics. Which means I've got the gene. Alcohol killed them both, one way or another. It's not getting a shot at me. Legal or not."

"You didn't feel so relaxed about alcohol in the Park, once."

She gave a short laugh and drank coffee. "I was a lot more pissed off, once." She changed the subject. "I saw a private jet land yesterday while I was checking my mail."

He raised an eyebrow.

She nodded. "He came over to say hi. My, he was friendly. It's like he didn't kidnap me or try to kill me or anything."

"He's really cozying up," Bobby said.

"He's trying," Kate said.

"You hear he bought into the Suulutaq?"

She nodded.

"Doesn't bother you?"

"Bothers the hell out of me," Kate said, "but I don't know what I can do about it."

"Gaea might," he said.

She laughed out loud this time, with genuine amusement. "What, you think I should join?"

Gaea being the environmental organization of the glossy brochure in her mail the previous day. It had sprung into being full grown with the discovery of the Suulutaq Mine. They were headquartered in Anchorage, and Kate had had the personal dollar-and-a-quarter tour from its executive director. Thinking of that tour now, of how well funded the organization had appeared, she said, "I don't think they need my money."

He shrugged. "Might be a way to stick it back to that fucker Erland. Seems like he's had it all his own way for a while now."

"Tell me about it," she said. "It's what we do."

"What is?"

She looked up. "Alaska. We pull stuff out. We pull stuff out of the water, and we pull stuff out of the ground. If we could figure out a way to pull stuff out of the air, we would. It's who we are. It's what we do. We don't know how to do anything else." A note of acid crept into her voice. "We certainly don't know how to do anything else in Juneau."

"So?"

"So, have you seen the price of gold lately?"

"The mine's going in no matter what, is that what you're saying?"

She leaned forward. "Look down the road a little, Bobby, even just a few years. The mine is up and running. They're a fact of life. Hell, they're a neighbor. How much time do you think they're going to have for neighbors who have been drawing horns and tails on their pictures for three solid years?"

She sat back again. "If it was me, zero."

He thought about it. "Yeah, well, you've always been an unforgiving bitch."

She laughed again. "True." She drained her mug. "The EIS isn't even done, Bobby. Let science have its say. And then we'll see."

He looked at her, openly speculative.

"What?"

"What if they'd found the gold at Canyon Hot Springs?"

She stared at him, her mug stopped halfway to her mouth.

He smiled. "What I thought. And in the meantime?"

Kate recovered herself with an effort. "We wait. We're always waiting. It's like Potlatch."

"Potlatch?" He looked surprised. "You mean Scott dragging up?"

"I mean everybody dragging up because they're tired of waiting. That is also who we are. Seward's Folly, until for a while we aren't. The Klondike Gold Rush. Those farmers who settled in the Matsu during the Depression. World War Two and Lend-Lease. The Swanson River oil field. Prudhoe Bay.

"People have always followed the money north. They stick it out for long enough to make their pile, and drag up south again." Even as she said the words, she felt more tired than indignant. "We're a transient community, the people who stay being way in the minority. Nobody new to the state is going to vote for more taxes to build more roads or schools or put in more sewers. So villages like Potlatch are dying because they're leaving, too, for the bigger communities like Bering and Barrow and Newenham and Juneau, Fairbanks and Anchorage. Kushtaka, they just lost their school because they ran out of kids. Cheryl Moonin, one of Auntie Balasha's nieces, Cheryl moved out to Wisconsin with her husband and three daughters. They'll grow up there, they'll go to school there, they'll probably marry there. For sure they won't be coming back to the Park." She raised a hand, palm up. "Easy equation. No jobs, no people. No people, no kids. No kids, no schools. No schools, no community. No community, no jobs, and the snake eats its tail and consumes itself."

His smile was crooked. "Adapt to the Suulutaq Mine or die?"

"Maybe that is what I mean," she said, her voice rueful.

"You do know," he said, "that some people would rather die."

"I know," she said, and thought again of Canyon Hot Springs.

She got up and refilled the kettle. With her back to him, she said, "That true, what you heard about somebody making a movie in the Park?"

"Who knows?" he said. "But we've already had Drew Barrymore and John Cusack making movies in Anchorage. Probably just a matter of time before some Hollywood honcho discovers just how photogenic we are by comparison."

She sincerely hoped not.

Ten

THURSDAY, JULY 12

Kuskulana

THE SKIFF SWAMPED TEN FEET SHORT OF the bank, and Jim pulled his phone out, grabbed the bowline, and went over the side, holding the hand with the phone in it over his head. The water was up to his shoulders and so cold, he felt like an instant Creamsicle. The current, swollen with snowmelt after two warm days, was running strongly downriver.

He turned his body sideways to it to reduce drag and fought the current to shore, where he stumbled out and fumbled with numb hands to fasten the bowline to a convenient willow branch. He looked back in time to see Roger Christianson's beautiful skiff and brand-new outboard sink beneath the surface of the river with a long, slow death gurgle.

His hair and hat and his phone and the bottom half of his left sleeve were still dry, but he was freezing cold and starting to shiver. He thought briefly about starting a fire, but there wasn't an app for that and rubbing two sticks together seemed like a lot more trouble than getting to his feet and starting to walk.

In the very little time allotted to him to think when the skiff had begun to fill with water, he'd thrown the kicker hard over and headed straight for the Kushtaka side of the river. Not only was it closer, but if he had to walk out, the Kushtaka side was a better bet. The Kuskulana side dead-ended in the confluence of Cataract Creek and the Gruening River, and he would have had to wade across, which given the force of the creek's current (not for nothing had it come by its name) was to say the least inadvisable.

The Kushtaka side of the creek, on the other hand, had Kushtaka village south and the Kushtaka fish wheel north of where he'd put to shore. The fish wheel was across the river from Kuskulana and his aircraft, but it was at least within shouting distance of Kuskulana landing.

The traffic on the Gruening was nowhere near what it was on the Kanuyaq, so his chances of thumbing a ride were not good. He thought of heading back to Kushtaka, but empirical evidence recently acquired advised him to head north instead.

The next two hours were among the longest he ever recalled living. Apart from a few game trails that meandered off into the woods too soon, the brush next to the river was so thick as to be nearly impenetrable, and it became immediately obvious that the reason Kushtaka's fish wheel was two miles upriver from the village was that it was on the first stretch of open gravel above water between there and Kushtaka.

It was a long, slow slog. His clothes stayed wet and his boots squelched with every step and the trees were almost malevolent in their attempts to blind him and the mosquitoes swarmed around him like starlets around a Hollywood producer. He did his best to ignore current conditions and tried instead to concentrate on how he got there. He was pretty sure he knew.

While he'd been busy interviewing people in Kushtaka, someone had unsnapped the drain plug.

All skiffs had drains, a small hole beneath the outboard that drained the bottom of the skiff when it was hauled out of the water. When the skiff was in use, as in on the water, the drains were plugged with a drain plug that usually had some kind of simple locking mechanism.

Someone had unlocked the drain plug on Roger's skiff while Jim was in Kushtaka. They'd probably loosened it, too, just enough so that the forward motion of the water beneath the hull would tug out the plug when he got well and truly up to speed on the river. The results were always fairly spectacularly fast, so he could rule out someone from Kuskulana having done it or he would have sunk on the way to Kushtaka.

His first year in the Park, he had responded to what was eventually called an accidental drowning when the same thing happened downriver from Niniltna. In that case, it was an old skiff with an older plug and an even older boat driver, who had drowned before he could make it to shore. Alaskan fishermen were notorious for not knowing how to swim, general opinion holding that you'd be dead from hypothermia before you figured which way was up, so why bother?

Jim could have been dead of hypothermia himself, and in a little while he was going to be warm and dry enough to be well and truly pissed off about that. There was zero chance of finding out who had pulled the plug, and he wondered if the guilty party had done it on his own or if it was a joint decision by the entire village of Kushtaka. The message was equally clear either way: *Keep your nose out of our business, Trooper.*

Except that he couldn't, and wouldn't anyway, if what he suspected was true about Tyler Mack's death.

He blundered through a stand of diamond willow, stepped into a saltwater marsh up to his knee, and swore, loudly and profanely, offending the delicate sensibilities of a cow moose who had until that moment been indulging in a peaceful nibble at some tender new willow shoots. She gave Jim an indignant look and turned to depart with dignity, shepherding her calf before her in an effort to shield her innocent offspring from the bad, bad man.

"Yeah, you're just lucky I'm a law enforcement professional," he said to her retreating back, and bushwhacked on. Twenty minutes later, he muscled through the thick underbrush out onto the beach where the Kushtaka fish wheel had returned to its stately circle, dripping water and the occasional fish down the chute into the holding pen.

He had his first bit of real luck of the day when he saw a skiff passing downriver. He staggered down to the edge of the water and waved his arms like semaphores. "Hey! Hey!"

The skiff driver, by a miracle from neither Kuskulana nor Kushtaka but a sports fisherman from Eagle River, gaped at him for thirty seconds before recovering enough to put the kicker over to the right and come to the rescue of the bedraggled trooper. Safely ashore on the right side of the river, Jim said thanks and offered him a sodden twenty-dollar bill peeled out of his wallet. The Good Samaritan took it gingerly by one corner and said, "Really, Sergeant, you shouldn't have," without conviction. Jim knew the day he'd picked up the soaking wet Park trooper off the side of the Gruening River was about to enter into Park, if not Alaska, legend and lose nothing in the telling, either.

He shook his sodden uniform into some semblance of order and hoped he had no cause to draw his weapon anytime soon. He stared across the river at the Kushtaka fish wheel.

Kuskulana didn't have a fish wheel. Kuskulanans fished for salmon in Alaganik Bay from fishing boats they owned. He wondered if it was partly because the Kushtakers were originally Athabascan in ancestry, Interior dwellers with an innate distrust of salt water. Although it was probably more due to the difference in their median income.

He wondered, too, what someone standing where he was right now might have seen across the river early Tuesday morning.

Carol Christianson invited him in with exclamations of concern, relieved him of jacket, shirt, boots, and socks and sat him down at the kitchen table, and offered him his choice of coffee, tea, or cold beer. He was greatly tempted by the beer. "Better be coffee," he said regretfully. "I'm flying."

"Then how about a latte?" she said, and demonstrated on a big cube of stainless steel, with spouts, that she said was from Switzerland. While the drink was creating itself, she produced half of a coffee cake that smelled of lemon and proved to be frosted with cream cheese icing. Jim hadn't had anything since pie for breakfast, and he dug in. The cake was moist and chewy and tasted of fresh lemons, and the latte was a perfect brew, hot and aromatic and revivifying.

Roger, next to him, was similarly occupied, and Carol pulled up a chair and observed them both with satisfaction. "Love me a man who likes to eat," she said.

"Marry me," Jim said, spluttering crumbs.

"Hey," Roger said, spluttering his own crumbs, "I'm sitting right here."

Carol laughed, a mellow sound full of good humor. "It's okay," she said. "I think Kate Shugak got in there ahead of me."

"At least give me the recipe," Jim said, and Carol wrote it out on a three-by-five index card forthwith. He tucked it carefully away and sat back looking around him with new eyes. The sugar and the caffeine together produced a low-level simmer just beneath the surface of his skin. "I might live," he said, as if it were a new idea.

Carol regarded him anxiously. "Are you sure you don't want some dry clothes, Jim? I'm sure I can find something of Roger's to fit." She eyed their respective sizes. "Or maybe Ryan's."

"Hey," Roger said, indignant, and Carol laughed again.

"I'm sorry about the skiff, Roger." Jim had already said it once, but, considering the lemon coffee cake, he felt that it bore repeating.

"Not your fault, Jim," Roger said, all trace of humor vanishing. "Wouldn't be the first time someone from Kushtaka took their mad out on someone from Kuskulana."

Which was the first time Jim considered that pulling the drain plug on Roger Christianson's skiff might be regarded as a twofer in Kushtaka.

The kitchen was painted white with sunny yellow accents in the backsplash and curtains, and the floor was white and black tiles. The appliances were white, a six-burner propane stove, a massive refrigerator, they even had a dishwasher. He felt warmer and drier just looking around the room.

The white-framed sash-weight windows opened into a yard planted with pale pink Sitka roses and midnight blue delphiniums onto a street that appeared to be bustling with traffic—pickup, four-wheeler, and foot. Through a doorway, he could see a living room with a rock fireplace and an enormous flat-screen TV where an ordinary mantel would have been, and a brown leather couch that looked long enough for even Jim to stretch out on, flanked by a love seat and two recliners.

It was a comfortable home by anyone's standards, whether you were in Kuskulana, Anchorage, or Des Moines. The difference between Kuskulana and Kushtaka could not have been made more manifest. The fact that Roger had stayed for coffee and cake instead of rushing immediately down to pull his skiff out of the river told its own tale.

Roger polished off the last piece of cake and got up to refill everyone's mugs. He brought them back to the table and sat down. "Other than trying to drown you, how are the Kushtakers holding up?"

Jim thought of Dale Mack's glowering presence. "Angry, mostly."

Roger nodded. "Understandable. I don't think they've got thirty people left in Kushtaka. Losing even one has got to be hard."

Remembering the general attitude in response to his questions, Jim didn't think "hard" was exactly the right word. Or "loss," for that matter. "Did you know him?" he said. "Tyler?"

Roger looked at Carol "There aren't many people in Kuskulana who can say they know many in Kushtaka," he said.

His answer felt deliberately evasive to Jim. "You seemed to know Pat."

"To wave to, sure." Roger shrugged. "We don't socialize."

"I thought when the state closed the Kushtaka school after their enrollment dropped below nine students that their kids came to yours."

The couple looked uncomfortable. "Some of them did," Roger said. "The ones whose parents didn't decide to home-school them so they could keep 'em on their side of the river, well away from our pernicious influence."

Carol put a hand over his, and Roger looked a little embarrassed. "Sorry. I think one or two got sent to the boarding school in Ahtna, too."

"Was Tyler one of the ones who attended Kuskulana?"

Roger nodded. "I think so. Ryan would know."

Interesting, Jim thought, considering Ryan's misdirected answers to Jim's questions that morning. "Is he here?"

"No, he's not. Him and a bunch of his buddies are camping their way downriver to Alaganik, on the off chance there will ever be another opener." He looked momentarily envious.

Jim remembered those anonymous cardboard cartons and felt a little envious himself. Being a teenager didn't totally bite, not in the Park. "Anyone else here you can think of who might have known Tyler?"

He was aware that something had changed in the way both of the Christiansons were looking at him. "You're asking an awful lot of questions about a boy who tripped and fell into a fish wheel," Carol said.

"Yeah," Roger said, "what's going on here, Jim?"

Jim gave a mental sigh. He had already aired his suspicions to Dale Mack, which meant everyone in Kushtaka knew by now. "Until the medical examiner says different, Tyler might have been murdered."

The ticking of the kitchen clock was very loud in the silence that fell. Outside, an ATV roared down the road, followed in more stately fashion by a pickup truck. A bird twittered. A fly buzzed.

A glance exchanged between host and hostess acknowledged that the silence had gone on too long. Roger raised his mug, took a long, deliberate pull, and set it down, centering it precisely on the table in front of him. "What makes you say that?"

"Somebody took a comprehensive whack at the back of his head. Also, as you saw yourself, he was seriously stuck into that basket. I have a hard time believing anyone could just fall into a fish wheel basket, first, and second, get so stuck, he couldn't get out again. Seems more likely he was put there, unconscious, and left to drown."

"That's awful, Jim," Carol said. "That's—that's just awful."

She rose abruptly and left the room, returning shortly with his shirt and socks. "Do you have any idea who might have done it?"

He understood and even appreciated the strategic change of subject. "So far?" he said, shrugging into his shirt. "Not a clue." He sat down to pull on his socks. They were wonderfully warm from the dryer. "Who's the chief here?"

"Good question," Roger said, looking at Carol.

"I suppose I am," Carol said, pulling a wry mouth. "I'm not elected, but if we're counting old blood, I've probably got more of it than anyone else in town. We never applied for status individually. As a federally recognized tribe," she added when she saw Jim's blank look. "We're all Niniltna Native Association shareholders in Kuskulana."

Jim hadn't known that, but then he tried to keep his distance from Native politics in the Park. He was white and he was a cop, which made two strikes against him already, and some people would say sleeping with Kate Shugak made three. "How'd that happen?" he said, his voice carefully incurious.

"After ANCSA, everyone in town with Native blood took a vote and signed up with the NNA," Carol said. "Why?"

Jim stood up and reached for the damp jacket hanging over a chair. "Because," he said, "if the autopsy shows that Tyler was murdered, I'll be back here, and in Kushtaka, as many times as I have to be to find out who did it." He pulled his ball cap on tight. "I'd like to think that I had the support of the local authorities."

Carol stood up and extended her hand. "I'll do my best to see that you do."

She had to say that, of course. Nevertheless, he shook her hand, then Roger's. "I appreciate it. Thanks for the coffee and cake. You saved my life."

He left without further comment, and was aware as he walked down the street that they both watched him from the doorway until he turned the corner to the airstrip.

He preflighted the Cessna with obsessive intensity, going so far as to get the laminated preflight checklist out of the cabin and going down the items one by one. Fuel tanks, filler caps, windshield, ignition and master switches, leading and trailing edges of both wings, flaps, ailerons, rudder, vent openings, tires, brakes, fuel sumps, cabin air intakes, he went right down the list like he was still wearing his checkride shirt. Whoever had pulled the drain plug on the skiff had had plenty of time to get to the Kuskulana airstrip while Jim was bushwhacking his way upriver.

A little yellow and white Piper Tri-Pacer was on approach and he watched it touch down at the end of the gravel strip and taxi to the side. A couple of ATVs with plastic bins bungeed to the back took off on the trail that led from the airstrip on a direct heading for the Suulutaq Mine. He only hoped that he would not be called upon to find out what was in those bins in any official capacity.

"Sergeant Chopin?"

He turned to see a plump woman of medium height and graying blond hair. Her blue eyes were narrowed against the sun. "Reverend Flanagan?"

She smiled. "Please, it's Anne."

They shook hands. "Been a while."

"When we built Kate's house." She cocked her head. "Which I understand you're a lot more familiar with nowadays."

He felt an unaccustomed flush creep up the back of his neck. "Yeah, well."

She smiled. "Relax. I didn't come over to harangue you about living in sin."

"What are you doing here?" he said, relieved.

"I'm the Park's new flying pastor."

He raised his eyebrows. "Congratulations. Or commiserations. When did you get your license?"

"Last year."

He smiled.

She smiled.

He said, "Good job to build your hours."

She said, "Lots of weather and different terrain."

"Some interesting airstrips." He grinned. "And you're doing good work as well."

Her turn to flush, and then she laughed. "True enough." She seemed to become aware of his damp state and gave him a quizzical once-over. "What did you fall into?"

"The river," he said. "Don't ask."

"Okay," she said. "I ran into Kate in Niniltna yesterday."

"You've seen her more recently than I have," Jim said, and for the life of him wasn't able to keep himself from sounding disgruntled.

The Right Reverend Anne Flanagan looked as if she might be struggling to hold back another laugh, but mercifully decided to refrain. "What brings you here?" she said instead.

Jim pulled off his ball cap and examined the seal of the Alaska State Troopers on the crown. "Tyler Mack. He tripped and fell into the village's fish wheel and drowned."

The lines of her face settled into what Jim could only think of as ministerial lines. "Yes. I was in Double Eagle. Dale Mack came upriver and asked me to officiate at Tyler's memorial service."

"His body's still in Anchorage."

"I know. When will it be returned?"

"I don't know. The backlog at the medical examiner's is pretty long, but I have a feeling they'll bump this to the top of their list."

Her gaze sharpened. "Why?"

He looked up to meet her eyes. "Because it may be that Tyler didn't trip."

A pause. "Do you mean he was murdered?"

"I don't know yet. I won't know for sure until the ME's report comes in, and maybe not even then. He had suffered a blow to the back of his head very recently. He was in the water long enough so that the wound was washed clean, but the blow was hard enough to break the skin of his scalp. If he were leaning over the holding pen, pulling fish out, it would have been easy enough for someone to come up behind him with a rock, a chunk of wood, a rifle butt."

"I truly hope that is not the case," she said gravely. "Not only for Tyler Mack, but his family and his community as well." She glanced at her watch. "I'm afraid I have to go."

"Anne," he said as she turned to leave. "The Kushtakers have closed ranks. They're telling me nothing. I'd be grateful if you passed on anything you heard."

Her mouth tightened. "I'm their spiritual adviser, Sergeant, not your spy."

He felt the color run up his neck again, but this time he was angry. "A man is dead. A kid, really, the ink barely dry on his high school diploma. Forgive me if my first concern is not the spiritual well-being of a group of people who may include the person who murdered him."

She frowned at him, frowned at the ground, frowned at his Cessna, frowned at her Piper, and frowned at some random Kuskulaner when he rode his ATV out onto the apron. He quailed beneath that forbidding look and turned his ATV around and went back the way he came a little faster than he had arrived.

"All right," she said. "I'll keep my ears open." She looked up. "I'm not saying I'm going to report back to you on every single thing I hear. But if I hear anything about Tyler's death, I'll find a way to pass it on."

He figured he'd pushed her as far as he could. "I'd appreciate it."

"Now," she said, "if you'll excuse me, I have to get to Kushtaka."

"Nothing spiritual going on in Kuskulana?"

She damned him with a glare. "Kuskulana has given me to

understand that my services are required at Easter and Christmas Eve. Period."

"Pagans," he said.

She struggled for a moment between rage and laughter. Laughter won. Excommunication averted, he helped her tie down her plane and then let her help him untie his. "Anne?" he said as she turned to go.

She looked back at him.

"Be careful." He thought of how cold the river had been that morning, what a shock it had been when the water engulfed the skiff and washed up his body. "Be really careful. They're pretty upset, and they know a lot more than they're telling, and they don't take kindly to interference. And one of them might be a murderer."

She made him wait, before nodding, once, solemnly, as if she was taking a vow.

As the Cessna rose from the runway, he noticed again the two new houses going up at opposite ends of the town, at the traffic in the few streets, at people gardening and hanging out washing and working on engines. Again, he couldn't help contrasting the hustle and bustle of Kuskulana with the decay and desolation of Kushtaka. Two villages, one river, and no comparison.

As he banked left to roll out, he saw Anne heading up the little road that led into town, there probably to buttonhole the first person she saw and commandeer a ride to Kushtaka.

He could only hope the Kushtakers would be more forthcoming with her than they had been with him.

And that the Right Reverend Anne Flanagan would see fit to share.

Eleven

THURSDAY, JULY 12

Kushtaka

THE STOLE WAS FOUR INCHES WIDE AND nine feet long and made from a heavy cream silk. It was heavily fringed and embroidered at both ends with a Celtic cross, or what was meant to be. Anne Flanagan thought privately that one looked more like a basket of snakes and the other a little too much like a swastika, but they had been painstakingly picked out in contrasting green and gold silk by the hands of her daughters, one to each end, and she would officiate wearing it until either she or the stole disintegrated.

The distance an airplane went on a single load of fuel was measured in proportion to how much freight it carried. Fuel was expensive; therefore, Anne traveled light. Her only badge of office was the stole, and she kissed and draped it around her neck now, and opened her Bible and looked at the group gathered in

Dale Mack's house. Sadly, it was big enough to contain all the people in Kushtaka who wished to attend.

She kept it simple, first the Twenty-third Psalm.

"The Lord is my Shepherd; I shall not want. . . ."

It had the comfort of familiarity, and of company on that long, last road.

"Yea, though I walk through the valley of the shadow of death, I will fear no evil: For thou art with me. . . ."

By the end, people were speaking the lines along with her in soft cadences. She let her voice fall on the last words, and allowed the silence to gather.

"Pat wants to say a few words," she said, closing the Bible and holding it to her chest, trying to make a little space for the grieving uncle in that crowded room.

The old man rose to his feet, staying where he was. He was freshly showered, what little hair he had left slicked back, shirt and jeans scrupulously clean, if heavily wrinkled from being folded away since May. Park rats tended to wear the same two sets of clothes straight through the summer and then, when they were stiff with salmon scales and gurry, toss them, usually just before the AFN convention in October, an event always bookended by shopping and doctor's appointments.

Everyone in the room was dressed the same way, although Jennifer Mack and her mother had donned long-sleeved black T-shirts. Auntie Nan, too, although hers was covered in a voluminous stained apron, over which her large-knuckled, floury hands were clasped. She looked up suddenly to meet Anne's eyes, and flushed and looked away again immediately. Jennifer's face was expressionless, containing a quality of immobility that did not go well with her youth. Her mother, as usual, looked tired, but there was a faded copy of her daughter's beauty still there for those with the eye to see it. Anne wasn't at all sure that Dale Mack could be included in that number.

The few elders were seated in front, close to Anne. Everyone else remained standing. The curtains were drawn back on all the windows and the door had been propped open but it still seemed dark inside. That might have been due to the occasion.

"Tyler wasn't worth much as a human being," Pat said.

Anne looked at Pat, startled, but the Kushtaka congregation took it without a blink.

"We all know that," Pat said. "Always looking for the quick buck, never willing to put any shoulder into a job, hell—pardon me, Reverend—he ran the other way when he saw a job coming. Not much respect for his elders, that's for damn—pardon me, Reverend—but that's just for damn sure. His last day on this earth, I had to boot his ass—pardon me, Reverend—out of bed to get on up the river."

Pat paused. "But he was ours," he said firmly, looking up and around the room, lingering on a face here, a face there. "Ours. Our blood. Our bones. Our son. He wasn't married, and so far as I know he had no children. Me and Dale are his closest living relatives. He was prepared to leave us behind once he shook Kushtaka dust from his shoes, but he still woulda been ours. As he still is, even now that's he's no longer with us."

He took another look around the room. "So what happens next is up to us, too."

Anne gave him a sharp look.

Pat either didn't see it or ignored it. "In the meantime, mourn the loss of someone barely more than a boy, robbed of his future. He coulda changed. We don't know. Now we never will. So mourn his loss."

Pat sat down again. Dale Mack, standing behind him, put a hand on his shoulder.

There passed a few moments of silence, as Anne thought hard and fast, reviewing biblical verses on vengeance. *Leave it to the wrath of God, vengeance is mine, I will repay.* Which could and was frequently replied to with, *An eye for an eye, hand for hand, burning for burning.* But didn't Matthew say in reply to that, *If anyone slaps you on the right cheek, turn to him the other also*?

Saying anything about vengeance would only draw more attention to what any fool could imagine was meant from the old man's words.

At this uncomfortable moment she remembered what Jim Chopin had said not two hours before. *They're pretty upset, and they know a lot more than they're telling, and they don't take kindly to interference.*

She went with what she had planned in the first place—a slow, measured recitation of the Lord's Prayer—inviting everyone to say it with her.

"Our father, who art in heaven, hallowed be thy name. . . ."

It was the one prayer everyone always knew all the words to, even people who never stepped inside a church except for weddings, funerals, and baptisms, and again, it conveyed comfort by its very familiarity. If her voice got a little louder when they came to ". . . forgive us our trespasses, as we forgive them that trespass against us . . . ," no one betrayed awareness by so much as a raised eyebrow.

They ended by singing "Amazing Grace," a hymn pitched for every voice, a song always improved by the number of voices singing it, and a first verse everyone knew the words to thanks to Joan Baez. They sang the first verse through twice, and Anne ended with a soft-voiced "Amen," answered by the people gathered there in even softer voices, hands clasped, heads bent, as one repeating the word after her.

To Anne's ears, their "Amen" had an ominous ring to it, a vow taken by everyone present except her. She turned so they wouldn't see the dismay she was sure showed on her face, and busied herself by replacing the Bible in her bag. She removed the stole, kissed it, folded it carefully, and tucked it in next to the Bible.

When she turned again, Jennifer, her mother, and her aunt had whipped towels from the dishes loading down the kitchen table. "Reverend?" Jennifer's mother said.

Anne, appreciative of the honor but knowing what was due, heaped a paper plate high with fried salmon, sticky rice, and macaroni and cheese and presented it along with a plastic fork to Pat Mack. He accepted it with a faint smile. As she turned back to the table, she saw approving looks from other elders and was thankful she hadn't stepped in it during her first memorial service as the flying pastor.

She deliberately scored more points by smilingly refusing to accept a plate for herself until the rest of the elders had been served, which was when she realized that the number of elders in the village was totally out of proportion to its population. Of the thirty or so people there, more than half of them looked to be in their sixties and seventies and in Pat's case, in his eighties. Dale Mack was one of only two men in their forties, and Jennifer's mother only one of three women who were. Anne counted four grade-school children, no babies and no toddlers, and Jennifer the only teenage girl. There was a young man Anne was introduced to as Rick Estes by Dale Mack, who kept a fatherly hand on his shoulder as he did so. Rick was polite and nice-looking and couldn't keep his eyes from straying in whatever direction

Dale's daughter, Jennifer, was moving. He was of course not alone in that, but besides Rick, there were only three other men of his age.

From what Anne could tell, Jennifer was superbly indifferent to them all. She moved through the crowd dispensing napkins and refills of water and pop with friendly smiles, and then with a nod at her mother was out the door. Rick Estes almost rose to his feet to follow her, but Dale Mack, unattending, put a hand on his arm and drew him into a conversation with a couple of elders.

Anne only hoped her own daughters would be able to handle that much attention that well when they were her age. Of course, if Jean-Luc Picard showed up, all bets were off.

She turned her thoughts back to the room. A depleted population was a sight she found all too familiar in the downriver villages. There were no jobs, and the subsistence lifestyle receded farther into the past every time someone of the next generation turned on a television with a satellite feed and saw all the wonders of the world available to them if only they lived in Fairbanks or Anchorage.

Everyone was speaking English, either out of respect for the Anglo flying pastor's presence or because their ancestral Athabascan had been lost to them over the years. Probably a combination of both. She smiled and nodded and praised the food and listened to stories of Tyler Mack as a little boy, although these were few in number and most of them rendered almost incomprehensible by the mouths full of missing teeth that were relating them. She kept an attentive smile fixed to her face and an ear tuned for other stories beyond the ones being told to her face, and caught a few snippets that tantalized in their brevity and provocation. Most were spoken by the younger men.

"I don't see why we have to wait on what Rick finds out from Boris."

"Yeah. Not like we don't know who."

"Rose, I think her heart broken by that overriver boy."

"Alacka. The young heart all the time broken."

"Catch is way down compared to last year. I don't know how we're going to pay for fuel come winter."

"Still got plenty of trees."

"I hear Viola Shugak is running the Niniltna store now."

"Still going to be cheaper than shopping in Kuskulana. You know they double the prices the minute we walk in the door."

"Think the trooper made it?"

This speaker was immediately hushed, and Anne remembered the damp and wrinkled state of Jim Chopin's uniform.

Someone plucked at her sleeve, and she turned her head to see the round, foolish face of Jennifer Mack's auntie Nan standing at her elbow. "Missus Priest, can I see you outside? Just for a minute?" She spoke barely above a whisper, her head turned as if to hide what she was saying from whoever might be watching.

"Of course." Anne, oppressed by the dimness of the room and the weight of old resentments and secrets, could do with some fresh air. She made as if to put her plate down.

Nan clutched at her arm. "No, no. I go away. You wait, Missus Priest, you wait. A little while goes by and then you come outside. No one come with you. Please?"

The urgency in Auntie Nan's voice was obvious and compelling. Instead of putting her plate down, Anne turned the movement into another forkful of mac and cheese, and bent her head to listen to an old woman tell a story in English so heavily accented, she couldn't make out any word except "raven." She laughed when everyone else did, and when she stopped found Jennifer's mother at her side. For the life of her, she could not remember her hostess's name, and eating her food under her roof was not the time to ask. "Would you like some more, Reverend?"

"No, no, thank you, I've had too much as it is. It was all so wonderful, though, thank you so much."

The other woman took her plate, and Anne said, "Is there a—?"

Mrs. Mack flushed. "I'm afraid it's outside."

"Not a problem," Anne said. "Where—?"

Mrs. Mack pointed, and Anne escaped.

Outside she stood blinking in the bright sunlight. The air was made sweet by the scents of cottonwood and alder, while birdsong came at her in surround sound. The voices in the cabin continued in their steady, somehow vaguely sinister hum. Auntie Nan was nowhere to be seen, and thinking she might as well avail herself of the premises, such as they were, she went around behind the cabin.

When she came out again, Auntie Nan was waiting for her. "You come now, Missus Priest," she whispered, looking over her shoulder at Dale Mack's cabin.

Anne, still a little dazed from the brilliant sunshine, went without asking why.

Nan led the way, down a narrow almost invisible path that began where the village met the woods. After a while Anne noticed that Nan was carrying a rectangular black bag with a headset peeking out of it.

Anne's bag, in fact.

Fifteen minutes later, they were in a little clearing.

Two people waited there. One was Jennifer Mack. The other was a young man Anne did not know.

When they told her what they wanted, she said, "No. Absolutely not. Out of the question."

They explained further, and she said, "But—"

More talk, and she said, "If you're underage—"

They talked for a while longer, and she said, "Without a license—"

When the time came, Auntie Nan was at her elbow, waiting, Anne's stole in one hand and Anne's Bible in the other.

When it was done, the other three vanished into the trees, Auntie Nan and Jennifer down the trail to the village and the young man in the opposite direction. Anne was left standing alone in the little clearing, wondering if she had just dreamed it all.

She repacked the stole and the Bible, picked up her bag, and found the path. It felt narrower, somehow, and darker, as if the sun-dappled woodland she had passed through not half an hour before had transformed itself into a threat to take back the townsite of Kushtaka one leaf, one branch, one root at a time. And maybe anyone it found wandering on the path while it was at it.

She burst out of the trees and into the village, panting, sweat beading her forehead. *What have I done?* she thought, panicking.

She said the words out loud. "God in heaven, what have I done?"

The murmur of voices inside the Macks' cabin had risen since she left it. People were yelling at one another, men and women both, and as Anne stood there, there was a sudden sound of flesh on flesh. One of the young men staggered backwards out of the open door, followed by another ready to take another swing. They weren't drunk. They were angry, and they were taking it out on each other with their fists.

The rest of the village's population poured out of the Mack house, looking more like a mob than like a civilizing force. Then

Pat Mack saw Anne standing there and nudged someone else. Everyone who wasn't fighting waded in and took an arm or a leg and it was over.

Dale's wife came over and, red-faced, apologized. "Please don't think we're like this," she said. "This isn't us. Usually."

Over her shoulder, Anne caught a glimpse of Jennifer, standing in the doorway of the cabin with her arms folded across her breast. She looked at Anne over her mother's shoulder, her eyes dark and proud and unyielding, before she vanished back inside.

Later, sitting in the skiff carrying her back to the Kuskulana landing, Anne thought again, *What have I done?*

It was an unwritten law. Like a doctor's obligation to his patient, a pastor's first duty to her flock was to first do no harm.

But if she had helped put out the fire before it started? she thought, almost despairingly.

Surely that was a good thing?

Twelve

THURSDAY, JULY 12, AN HOUR LATER

Kuskulana

WHAT MEMBERS OF THE KUSKULANA VILlage council weren't fishing somewhere in Prince William Sound met at the chief's house. The tale was quickly told.

"Jesus," somebody said, "they coulda killed the trooper."

"They don't care," someone else said. "Those Kushtakers still think it's 1777, when Alaska wasn't even a twinkle in Captain Cook's eye."

"Let it be a lesson to him not to interfere in their affairs," said the first man, "is the way they'd think of it."

"True," Roger said. "But now I've got to go get my skiff off the bottom of the Gruening River. Along with everything else, it's a fucking hazard to navigation."

"See what being a good citizen gets you?" the second man said.

The laughter that followed was grim and soon silenced. Still, after some discussion, the consensus was that it was Kushtaka's problem. A Kushtaka boy was dead, which was sad, but he wasn't a Kuskulana boy, which would have been a lot more sad and might have required action on their part, and summer was a busy enough time already without dealing with a cross-river feud that had been ongoing since before statehood.

At this inopportune moment, there was a knock on the door. Roger opened it and found Kenny Halvorsen standing on the other side. He was in his mid-twenties, of medium height and build, with dishwater blond hair unevenly cut and brown eyes. He wore frayed jeans with a faded Raven, Inc., sweatshirt and a pair of XtraTufs rolled down. He was unshaven and gaunt and his eyes were red, as if he were hungover. Or, unthinkably, had been crying. "Mitch is dead," he said.

Roger blinked at him. "What?"

"Mitch," Kenny said, "Mitchell Halvorsen, my brother, is dead. Something wrong with your hearing? Or you high muckety-mucks just don't want to remember there are Halvorsens living in your village, too?"

Roger bristled, but Carol appeared next to him and laid a calming hand on his arm. "What's this all about, Kenny? Did I hear you say something about Mitch?"

Kenny's voice rose. "He's dead, goddammit, dead! Those fucking Kushtakers killed him, and I want to know what you're going to do about it!"

⁂

"Have you heard from Ryan?" Roger said when they were home again.

Carol looked surprised. "No. Have you?"

Roger felt a sick feeling somewhere behind his breastbone, and did his best not to let it show. "I tried calling him on his cell," he said, trying for offhand. "He didn't pick up."

But they'd been married too long. "They're probably halfway down the Kanuyaq by now," Carol said, as if willing both of them to believe it, "camped out on purpose in some dead spot so they can party without their parents calling them every five minutes."

He didn't say anything, and her eyes narrowed. "Ryan didn't have anything to do with this, Roger."

He waved a hand. "No, no, of course not." He hesitated. "If he knew about Mitch—"

"He didn't," Carol said in her chief's voice.

Roger didn't reply, but the crease between his brows deepened.

Thirteen

THURSDAY, JULY 12

Kuskulana

JIM WAS STARTING TO FEEL AS IF HE COULD find his way from Niniltna to Kuskulana blindfolded. "Roger," he said as he stepped from the Cessna.

"Jim," Roger said.

He looked unhappy, and Jim couldn't tell if it was because he was entertaining the state trooper unawares for the second time that day or just because of the general situation. There was plenty to be unhappy about, all right. Jim reached into the plane for his crime scene bag and closed the Cessna's door. "Take me to him."

The body was in the crawl space of one of the two houses under construction that Jim had noticed the last time he was in Kuskulana. As he clocked it, all of two hours before. It seemed a lot closer to town from the air than it did on the ground. It was situated south and east, half a mile from the village down a rudimentary road a pickup truck wide with a couple of serious bends in it.

The crawl space beneath the unfinished house was four inches short of allowing him to stand upright, and his back protested at the necessary stoop. He ignored it, and continued to play the beam of his flashlight around the dark subterranean space, made more claustrophobic by the boxes of various sizes and shapes stacked around it. Above his head was the only light source, an open hatch through which the sunshine streamed, where it wasn't blocked by the half dozen heads peering down, Roger and others of his village cohorts who had been summoned to the scene.

"Get out of the light, guys?" Jim said.

Not one of them moved.

Squarely in the patch of interrupted light lay the body. This was Mitchell Halvorsen, although Jim would have to take the Kuskulanans' word for it until the ME made a positive, because the body had decayed to the point of unrecognizability. The smell was pretty bad.

A rough but sturdy ladder built of two-by-fours led from the floor above to the crawl space. The body lay next to it, on its left side, knees bent, as if it had been sitting, back to the ladder, and then fallen over. As his flashlight moved up the torso, the face seemed to move.

The flashlight jerked in his hand. It took all of his considerable self-control not to leap for the ladder. Big tough Alaska State Trooper.

"Jesus!" someone said above him, a different voice this time.

Swallowing hard, he bent forward to look at the face more closely. "It's just bugs, eating on him."

"'Just,'" the voice said weakly. "Jesus."

"I think I'm gonna hurl," a third voice said.

"Not into the crawl space," Jim said, pitching his voice to be heard, and was rewarded by a scramble of feet and legs, rapid footsteps, and the distant sound of retching.

Maybe his reputation for sangfroid was safe after all. He bent over the corpse, but didn't see anything new. He took a long last look around the crawl space. Now that his eyes had become more accustomed to the dark, he saw that the boxes were mostly cardboard with the names of the contents scrawled on the sides, DISHES, TOWELS, SILVERWARE, SHEETS. They lined the four walls of the space, leaving the area in the center, where the ladder led down from the hatch, free. The floor of the crawl space was packed ground covered in sheets of clear, heavy-duty plastic, which so far as Jim could tell, ran up all four sides of the space. There was no kiss of moisture on his cheek. He couldn't smell so much as a single spore of mildew. Good construction job. Hermetically sealed, practically.

He looked at the body at his feet.

Tomblike, even.

The dust lay thick on the plastic underfoot, scuffed by innumerable footprints. It also showed the markings of many more boxes than currently present.

He got out his phone and switched on the camera, with flash.

Ten minutes later, he was back in the waning sunlight of his second evening on the Gruening River in three days, the body in a bag on the unfinished floor of the house next to him. Roger and four of the other Kuskulanans watched him with much the same appalled expression. The sixth man, younger, red-eyed and wild-haired, was staring at Kate.

She'd been coming out of the post office when he'd touched

down in Niniltna, and had ridden shotgun back to Kuskulana. Now she stood to one side, meditating on a fine old paper birch growing at the edge of the clearing, hands in her pockets. The hatch to the crawl space was in front of her. One toe was tapping it thoughtfully, as if keeping time to some song only she could hear. Mutt was standing next to her, alert and watchful.

Jim slotted his flashlight back into his belt and pulled off his cap to wipe a clammy forehead on his uniform sleeve, taking a couple of steps forward to stand beside her, ostensibly to clear out his lungs. Almost as an afterthought, he bent over to look at the hatch, both sides, very slowly and very carefully indeed.

Her toe stilled.

The hatch was made of a double layer of three-quarter-inch plywood. There was a large metal ring set into the top that when released tucked back into a groove on the surface. The edges of the bottom had been routered to fit into the hatch. He tried it to be sure, and noticed something he hadn't seen at first. There were jagged, nail-sized holes, a dozen of them, equally spaced around the top edge of the hatch cover.

The hair rose on the back of his neck.

He wiped out the sweatband of his cap and pulled it back on, turning to walk back to look at the open hatch. There were a dozen corresponding holes in the edge of it.

He looked around and spotted a sturdy red toolbox sitting next to a pile of short ends of lumber of various sizes, and walked over to open it. Screwdrivers, wrenches, a hammer, a box of bright ten-penny nails.

"Whose house is this?" he said, pleased to hear that his voice sounded calm and pleasant. Or maybe not so much, because even Roger took an involuntary step back.

Kenny Halvorsen, the younger man who was still staring at

Kate, said, "It's Mitch's. My brother, Mitch Halvorsen's. Recognize the name?"

Kate turned her head to meet his eyes without flinching. Halvorsen's face reddened.

"You found the body," Jim said. "You called 911."

"Yeah," Kenny said, breaking off the staring match with Kate and looking at Jim.

"He's been down there awhile," Jim said, an understatement that would have done the Queen of England proud. "Did no one miss him? Wife? Kids?" He looked at Kenny. "His brother?"

"He's divorced, no kids," Roger said. "His ex lives Outside. Nevada, I think." He looked around. "I figured he was out fishing." Everyone nodded, Kenny a little belatedly. "Last time I saw him was in May, waiting on George for a flight to Anchorage so he could catch a plane to Chignik for herring. He doesn't usually come back to the Park during the summer."

"Who was building his house?"

"He was," Kenny said.

"Only him?"

"I did the dirt work," Roger said, "and put in the foundation. Quad-Lock."

"Not for love," Kenny said.

Roger looked at him. "None of my family eats air, Kenny."

Kenny's face was a mess of tears and snot, which made his sneer even more fearsome. "Neither does mine, Roger. Fortunately, we didn't have to, lately."

"Kenny." Roger's voice was a single warning note.

"What," Kenny said, "you gonna sic Ryan on me the way you did on Mitch?"

"I didn't sic him on you," Roger said, angry but controlled.

"Mitch said some unacceptable things in Ryan's hearing. Ryan called him on it and Mitch swung first."

"Yeah," Kenny said, "and I'm sure everyone here will say the same thing."

"Because that's the way it happened," Roger said sharply.

They glared at each other. In spite of Kenny's rage and tears, the family resemblance was very strong, the height, the cheekbones, although Kenny's chin might have been a little weaker.

They both belatedly came to the realization that there were witnesses to their argument, one of them a very interested state trooper.

"Anyone else working on the house?" Jim said blandly.

Everyone shook their heads. Again, it was a communal gesture, damn near in unison. It reminded him only too well of the looks exchanged and the shaking of heads in Kushtaka. Or the boys on the landing. Same shit, same day.

Kenny wiped his nose on his sleeve and spoke brusquely. "He put on the roof and was just starting the framing before he left in the spring. He was planning to get the walls up and do the plumbing and electrical after fishing season."

"You said you found the body," Jim said.

Kenny nodded.

"What were you doing here?"

"He was letting me store some of my gear in his crawl space," Kenny said.

Jim noted Kenny's furtive look, the hunched shoulders, the fists jammed into his jeans, and knew Kenny was lying. He thought about impressions in the dust on the floor of the crawl space, but all he said was, "And?"

Kenny swallowed hard and looked around the circle. The

other men, Roger and what looked like three of Kenny's newest best friends, looked sympathetic but didn't say anything to help get him off the hook. "I opened up the hatch and he . . . he was at the bottom of the ladder."

There was a fine line between conducting an effective investigation and retaining one's humanity. Jim was only getting started, though, plenty of time to turn bad cop. However great the temptation. "How were you able to recognize him?" he said instead.

Kenny's eyes filled with tears again but he blinked furiously, desperate to keep them from falling. "That Gaga T-shirt. He hasn't had it off ever since he flew to San Diego for one of her concerts last year. I think he was even sleeping in it."

Jim nodded as if this all made perfect sense. Since he'd stopped listening to popular music when rap came in, he wasn't all that *au fait* with the current music scene. Lady Gaga he vaguely remembered as someone who wore couture breakfast meat. "Roger?" he said. "Have you got an electric saw I can borrow?"

Roger looked startled, but said, "Sure, Jim."

He headed off and Jim looked at Kenny. "I'm afraid I'm going to have to remove the hatch frame. It's evidence. You might want to find a tarp to cover the hole."

"Evidence?" Kenny looked bewildered, and might even have been sincere. "Evidence of what?"

"Murder," Jim said, and only then realized how angry he was. Everyone else realized it, too, again taking that group step backwards, one of them nearly stepping off the floor of the half-made house. Jim waited until, windmilling his arms and with an assist from one of his friends, he was upright again. He met each of their eyes with a long, hard, cold stare, one after the other. "Cold-blooded, premeditated murder."

The words had their effect, as he had meant them to, on most of his audience. Kenny, he saw, was looking at Kate again.

Kate was looking back, impassive, balanced over spread feet, knees slightly bent, hands curled loosely at her sides. Mutt stood at her side, ears up, tail still, yellow eyes fixed on Kenny Halvorsen's face. With a slight shock, Jim realized the two of them were prepared to be attacked, and preparing to attack back.

Back at the airstrip, Mitchell Halvorsen's body in the back of the Cessna, triple bagged because of the smell, Jim paused with his hands on the yoke. "Kate."

She looked at him. Mutt was being uncharacteristically unobtrusive behind them.

"Someone nailed that poor bastard into his own crawl space and left him there to die."

"I saw."

"If it turns out that someone was a Kushtaker, and if it turns out that Mitchell Halvorsen's death was why I pulled Tyler Mack's body out of a fish wheel basket yesterday, I will track down both sonsabitches and arrest their goddamn asses."

"I know."

"I don't care whose sons or nephews or cousins or brothers they are. They go down."

"I agree."

"I don't care what Annie Mike or Auntie Vi or Auntie Balasha or anyone on the NNA board or any of the shareholders say. This isn't family. This is murder, twice over, premeditated and loaded with malice aforethought."

"Yes."

"Neither of these men went down easy, and neither was anywhere near his time. Shit, Tyler was barely out of high school."

"At some point soon," Kate said, "you'll notice I'm not arguing with you."

He'd been speaking to the windshield through clenched teeth. At this, he turned to look at her.

Her face, that olive-skinned, high-cheekboned oval that haunted him waking and sleeping, was set like stone. The wide-spaced, changeable hazel eyes with that suspicion of an epicanthic fold were flat and hard, and the wide, full lips were pulled into a hard line. She thrust a hand into the short cap of thick, ink-black hair and held it off her brow, before turning in her seat to look at him straight on.

"We find who did this," she said, "and we kick their ass all the way down the road to Spring Creek."

He was pretty sure she meant it.

Pretty sure.

Fourteen

THURSDAY, JULY 12
FRIDAY, JULY 13

Anchorage

KATE AND JIM FLEW DIRECTLY FROM KUSkulana to Anchorage, accompanied by Mutt, a body bag, and the hatch cover—including the frame it was set into—inexpertly cut out of the floor by Jim with help from Roger Christianson's power saw. The hatch was two feet by two and a half, and Jim had been generous on the cut, which made the frame about four feet square. Or possibly rhomboidal, Kate thought.

Just getting it into the Cessna was awkward as hell, and into the trunk of a cab in Anchorage a virtual impossibility. Finally they paid off the cab with a ten-dollar bill and called Brillo at the crime lab. Twenty minutes later, a skinny lab assistant who was at a generous estimate eleven and a half years old showed up in a fire engine red GMC Sierra extended-cab pickup. For him, it was a long jump down from the cab. "Sergeant Chopin?" He gave Kate the once-over, and brightened from behind thick glasses with Buddy Holly rims. "And—?" Mutt stuck her head out from behind Kate, and he paled. "Is that a wolf?" he said in a faint voice.

"Only half," Kate said. By now the reply was ritual. Something bad might happen if she didn't give it.

"Just help me get this thing into the back of your truck," Jim said.

Kate, to make up for his lack of civilized manners, beamed one of her better smiles.

The lab assistant, who when he regained the vertical and got his tongue untied introduced himself as Steve, unhooked his tailgate and helped Jim maneuver the hatch and frame into the back of the Sierra. The body was placed on top of it with noticeably less care, having no sharp edges with which to threaten the finish on Steve's pickup.

They all climbed into the cab, including Mutt, after which there was still room for all of Annie Mike's kids plus a platoon of marines. Steve, whose feet barely reached the pedals, drove with a panache that, if Jim hadn't been riding with him, would have had him reaching for his ticket book.

At the lab, Brillo, the wiry black hair that had resulted in his nickname undiminished in either volume or exuberance, listened to what Jim wanted, objected as a matter of course, and dismissed him with an order to return the following day "but not before noon. I mean it, Chopin, goddammit!" He then turned his attention to Kate, who was hard-put to rebuff him since she was with Jim and Jim was asking him to shove all his current cases to one side in favor of producing a miracle of overnight deduction. As it was past ten o'clock, she might have thrown a little extra style into it, which made Brillo even more reluctant to give up her presence.

They escaped finally, and Jim prevailed upon a trooper passing through the front office to give the three of them a ride to the town house on Westchester Lagoon. The Subaru started with a turn of the key, and Kate went down to Safeway to lay in supplies, City Market being long since closed. She returned to the town house to find Jim in exactly the same position she had left him in, sitting at the kitchen table, staring at his clasped hands, a heavy frown on his face.

She put away the groceries and nudged him. "Change into civvies, and we can hit the trail."

He came out of it and blinked at her and then out the window. "It's past ten."

"So what? It's still light out."

It was, of course. They both kept a store of clothes at the town house. He came downstairs in jeans and sweatshirt and found his town sneakers next to the door.

The Chester Creek Trail ran along the edge of the lagoon until it passed through a tunnel beneath the railroad tracks where it ran along the edge of Knik Arm and became the Coastal Trail. It wasn't precisely crowded, but there was even this late still traffic, a mother jogging behind a racing stroller, a commuter carrying a briefcase, a blader, two boarders, and a slight, dark woman with a pixie haircut walking two black Labs and a golden Alaska husky with ice blue eyes, properly on leashes, although they strained so hard in Mutt's direction that Kate was of two minds who was doing the walking, the woman or the dogs. Next came a man with a golden retriever and a malamute, neither on leash. They came barreling up to investigate, where they ran into a

DEW Line of Mutt's bared teeth. They abased themselves immediately and let Mutt sniff them all over before sending them whimpering back to their master, tails tucked between their legs. Their master glared impartially at Kate and Jim and gathered his darlings to himself again, but not, Kate noticed, putting them on leashes. Audible threats of calling the pound trailed in his affronted wake.

"How to win friends and influence people," Jim said, still scowling.

After Lyn Aery, the traffic dwindled, mostly bicycles going too fast with riders that yelled "On your left!" whether Jim and Kate were on the right side of the trail or not.

"Ever want to be a Borg?" Kate said. "Just raise your big metal arm and clothesline one of those dorks?"

No reply. Four miles later, they reached Point Woronzof, where the trail ran along the end of Runway 32. An Alaska Airlines 737 was thundering into the air, followed shortly by a FedEx DC-11. Both banked left and headed south-southwest, the sun trailing an anticipatory toe into the horizon in preparation for its brief nightly dip.

"Bethel and, what do you think, Hong Kong?" Jim said.

The scowl on his face had finally faded. He was watching the DC-11 climb into the sky. His hair shone gold as the sunset, and his eyes had never seemed more blue.

"I ever tell you I'm scared on the big jets?" she said.

"You? Afraid of flying? Never."

"On the big jets, I'm always nervous."

He thought about it. "You don't know the pilots."

"Or the mechanics," she said, nodding.

He smiled. As always, it did nice things to an already very nice face.

"What?" he said.

Kate realized she was staring, and felt her own face heat. She only hoped it didn't show beneath her summer tan.

A hand slid around her waist and yanked her up close and personal. "What?" he said again. This time it was a murmur right against her lips, and he didn't give her time to answer.

Which was good, because she forgot the question, and was only recalled to the here and now when a biker's long, loud wolf whistle made a kind of Doppler effect as he passed by.

She pulled back and blinked up at him, her vision a little hazy. "If you're feeling like that, we should at least get the women and children off the streets first."

He laughed, low in his throat, and wouldn't let her step away. She wriggled against him, partly in earnest and partly to tease. "Keep that up, and you'll get yours up against the nearest tree."

She ran a hand up the nape of his neck to knot in his hair. "Mutt!"

Mutt came arrowing out of the brush at a dead run and knocked Jim on his keister a second after Kate managed to wrestle free.

"Tag-teaming me," Jim said, getting to his feet. "Okay, fine. Let it never be said that Jim Chopin was bested by a couple of girls."

The horseplay lasted all the way home, four interminable, exquisite miles of kisses and caresses and Mutt nipping at their heels. They were impervious to the looks they got, both envious and condemnatory, and by the time they got back to the town house, Jim had a hard time fitting the key in the door.

"Hope finding the right hole's not a chronic problem with you," Kate said.

The door opened finally and Jim took her by the arm and Mutt by the collar and yanked them both inside, letting the door slam behind them. He held one finger up in front of Kate. "Wait," he said, breathing hard, "wait right here." The finger traced a line over her lips, down her throat, between her breasts, around her belly button to the crotch seam of her jeans.

She stayed where she was, back and hands against the wall as if she were bolted to it. Over the thunder of her heartbeat, she heard Jim hauling Mutt through the kitchen and out the door into the backyard.

She turned her head when she heard his footstep in the entryway, and her heart skipped a beat at the intent expression on his face. "Where was I?" he asked. "Oh, yes, I remember now."

He dropped to his knees in front of her. "You mentioned something about being horny."

"Oh," she said, her voice quavering.

"You've got three strikes against you at first sight with most people," he said, his eyes seeking out every curve and hollow. "You're a woman. You're short. You're Native. They have no idea who and what you are.

"But I do."

The buttons on her jeans popped open and they and her underwear were yanked down her hips. He left them to hang around her knees, shackling her in place, while he pushed her thighs apart and set his mouth on her.

"Ooohhhhh," Kate said, only this time it was a long, low growling moan that escalated into something like a scream. Her body arched as a blistering wave of pleasure rose up from his mouth to melt her spine. He wouldn't release her until the wave had receded, and then only to pull her down to the floor and settle in between her legs.

"There," he said, cradling her head in both hands. "Now that you're not in so much of a hurry, I've got time to play."

Much later, Kate, fresh out of the shower, pattered downstairs in an old white T-shirt of Jack's and nothing else. She went first to the back door. Mutt, napping in a corner of the postage stamp–sized yard, raised her head and regarded Kate with a sapient yellow eye. So, did the earth move?

"Yes," Kate said. "Now, you want to stay out here and crack wise or come inside with the rest of the grown-ups?"

Mutt sprang to her feet and galloped over to shove in between Kate and the door.

By the time Jim finished his own shower and came downstairs, Kate had assembled a chopped cucumber, a couple of tomatoes, half an onion, and cilantro into a shepherd salad, dressing it with olive oil and pomegranate molasses. The roast chicken was being reheated in the oven. She looked over her shoulder and smiled. "Five minutes."

"Good. I'm starving. I can't think why." He pulled out a chair and sat down, in the same movement pulling her in between his legs. He slid his hands under her T-shirt and over her ass. "Oh boy, commando."

She toyed with the open snap on his jeans, which was all he wore. "I'm all about easy access."

He laughed, a deep, satisfied sound. "Yeah, well, we'd better enjoy it while we can. Once the kids are in residence, there will be no more easy access to anything."

She smiled at him over her shoulder. "On the other hand, they'll be here. As in not in the Park." His eyes narrowed and slid down her body, as if he were speculating over just what position he could get it into in just what location on the homestead.

They took dinner into the living room and ate on the couch, sharing bits of chicken with Mutt, who tolerated the kissy-facing up to a point in exchange for protein. When easy access became more interesting than food, she moved into the kitchen with something of a flounce.

When Kate surfaced a little while later, she noticed Mutt had taken the remains of the chicken with her to assuage her hurt feelings, and gave a soft laugh.

Jim's voice rumbled in his chest. "What?"

"Look." He raised his head and she pointed.

"Ah." His head dropped back down on the couch. "Making a point."

"You snooze, you lose."

"Something like that." One hand toyed with the short strands of her hair, running them continuously between his fingers.

She figured it was safe, but played it cautiously anyway. "You were pretty wound up in Kuskulana this evening."

His hand paused for a beat. She kept her head down on his chest, and after a moment it rose and fell in a long sigh. "Yeah. Yeah, I was." He tugged at her hair so she would look at him. "Do you understand why?"

"I think so," she said, "but I want to hear it from you."

He sighed again, and levered them both upright and pulled her over to straddle his legs. He ran his hands over her skin, more in absent appreciation than with obvious intent. "The first case that brought me into the Park when I was stationed at Tok was the death of a bootlegger. His name was Pete Liverakos."

Her eyes widened a little. "I know the name," she said after a moment.

"Everybody does," he said, concentrating at a point somewhere over her shoulder. "He was flying booze into an old gold mining site, storing it in the adit, and moving it around the Park by ATV. Somebody found his cache and burned it, and somehow he wound up out there with broke-down transportation, in the middle of one of the longest cold spells during one of the coldest winters on record. People say he was probably dead before the wolves got to him."

"I hear tell," she said, her mouth dry.

"The point is," he said, looking at her directly for the first time since his story began, "is that he was a Kuskulaner. A cousin of Mitchell Halvorsen's, in fact."

"Yes," she said steadily.

"I was relatively new to the area then. People didn't have much to say to me, but one of the things I did hear about was the Kushtaka–Kuskulana feud. Everyone, and I mean everyone, just naturally assumed that a Kushtaker had something to do with Pete Liverakos winding up dead and savaged by wolves a stone's throw from five thousand dollars' worth of incinerated Windsor Canadian whiskey.

"I was never able to prove anything, of course. But I've been around for a while now, and I've heard a lot more stories, and what they tell me is that the Macks and the Christiansons could give lessons to the Kreugers and Jeppsens. Hell, they could give lessons to the Hatfields and the McCoys."

"You're not wrong," Kate said.

"By my count, over the last five years, there have been assorted vandalisms, thefts, assaults, you name it, in both villages. All perpetrated by a Kushtaker on a Kuskulaner or vice versa.

I've never been able to do anything about any of them. It's like watching a game of Ping-Pong with exploding balls, and then the players denying that their hands have been blown off when anyone can plainly see they have." He paused, and said, "Oh. I forgot to tell you. Somebody pulled the drain plug on Roger's skiff. Just before I climbed back into it to head upriver."

Her head snapped up. He nodded. "Yeah. It sank about a mile south of the Kuskulana landing. I made it to shore, but the skiff didn't. Had to hike up the river to the fish wheel, where I hitched a ride across."

"Who did it?" Kate's voice was very soft, but he was not deceived.

"I was leaving Kushtaka, so I'm guessing a Kushtakan."

She was vibrating like a strung wire in a high wind. "Simmer down, tiger," he said. "I'm fine. You want to be pissed, be pissed about Roger Christianson's brand-new skiff. He loaned it to me for the trip. Brand-new kicker, too. Both of which are now residing on the bottom of the Gruening River."

She closed her eyes, apparently to meditate on keeping her temper. Never one to waste an opportunity, he spent the intervening time in admiration of the velvet skin of her breasts, the sturdy strength of her waist, the lushness of her hips. Beauty, grace, and mystery in one compact package. He still had difficulty believing it was his.

She opened her eyes. "Okay."

"Really okay?" he said, with meaning.

"Have I killed Howie Katelnikof for shooting at me and hitting Mutt instead?" she said.

"No," he said. *Not yet,* he thought.

"Well, then. Have a little faith."

He eyed her doubtfully, and much against his natural instincts let it go, for now. He let his head rest against the back of the couch. "I get where it took a D6 Cat to smooth things over between the Kreugers and the Jeppsens, but at least it was smoothed over. Kushtaka and Kuskulana, nothing's ever smoothed over there. Nobody ever shakes hands and makes nice. Hell, Kate, George won't even fly low over that section of the river for fear he'll pick up a stray bullet from the Kushtakers and the Kuskulaners exchanging fire."

"So?" she said.

"So, fast forward. Now I've got a dead Mack in Kushtaka, which looks to have been predated by a dead Halvorsen in Kuskulana, which I have to say is ramping the feud up some."

When he didn't go on, she said, "I understand. But you've been in the middle of family feuds in the Park before. All cops have. DVs are our worst nightmare. What made you go off on this one in particular?" She thought she knew, but she also thought it would be better if he said it out loud. It was haunting her, too. It might even have been in part responsible for the most excellent sex enjoyed beneath this roof this evening. There was no better affirmation of life.

"Assume he went into the crawl space when he was supposed to have gone to Chignik for herring fishing back in May."

"Okay."

"You saw the holes. Someone nailed down the hatch cover after him."

"Yes," she said, unable to stop the shudder moving up her spine. She rested her forehead on his shoulder, relishing the smooth muscle, the warm skin.

He was silent again. At last he said, "I did my first probationary stint out of the academy in Anchorage. My first week, I was the responding officer on the Berta Young case."

She sat back and looked at him. "I did not know that."

"I don't talk about it. Doesn't mean I don't think about it. Way too often."

Berta Young was an eight-year-old girl whose stepfather had locked her in a closet for three years, where he visited her regularly for rape and abuse. After a while, like a child who became tired of a toy, he forgot to feed her, and after that forgot to give her water, and after that she died.

"The autopsy showed that at some point she must have tried to get out. The tips of her fingers were ripped and torn. There were corresponding scratches and blood and tissue remains on the inside of the closet door."

His voice was flat and unemotional. Just the facts, ma'am. She swallowed hard and tried to match him calm for calm. "Didn't a neighbor call it in because of the smell?"

"Yes."

Her brows pulled together. "Wasn't her mother in the house at the time?"

"Yes. Said she didn't smell anything. Swore to it in court. When they asked her what she thought had happened to her daughter, she said that her daughter was a temptress and a sinner and that the devil had taken her for his own. She was right about the last part." He paused again. "There were three other minor children in the house. All girls. One of them was already in her own closet. She survived, although I don't know what kind of life she was going to have afterwards. I've never tried to find out."

This story was way too close to the nightmares she still occasionally suffered from her years working as an investigator for the Anchorage DA. "The media circus surrounding that trial was—"

"Yes," he said. "It was. It was on Court TV and *Dateline* and, for all I know, *Judge Judy*. The reporters were worse than mosquitoes and way more resistant to deet. I hope like hell I'm never involved with that high-profile a case ever again. Happy to leave those to Liam."

"What made you think of it again?" she said, although again she was pretty sure she knew.

"I learned more than I really wanted to about what the average human being needs to survive," he said. "It turns out we can live a long time without food. Without water, not so much. If it's hot, dehydration can set in in an hour, and even a healthy person could be dead in three. Most you can live without water is six days."

She thought about that house. Mitchell Halvorsen had been building for the view. On the edge of the wedge, facing south, he would have been able to see damn near all the way to Prince William Sound, the Gruening River at the foot of the cliff beneath the house, with the Quilaks cutting a ragged outline into the sky on his left, the Park rolling slowly downhill all the way to the Chugach Mountains on his right, and the Kanuyaq River coiling back and forth across the landscape in between.

"And no food and no water in that crawl space. He might have had a candy bar or a pack of gum or some Tic Tacs in his pocket. But nothing else."

She swallowed, and suddenly felt very thirsty.

After a moment he said, seemingly at random, "That house is how far out of town, do you think?"

She thought. "A little under half a mile. Maybe a bit more, but not much. Can't get much farther from Kuskulana in that direction and not fall over the edge."

He nodded. "About what I figure, too," he said. "I'm hoping he was dead in three hours, Kate."

She met his eyes in sudden awareness.

"Because I'd hate to think he was nailed into that crawl space for six days, screaming for help the whole time, and nobody came."

He let his head fall back against the couch. "Sometimes," he told the ceiling, "sometimes I really, really hate this job."

She was looking at him, the strong throat, the broad shoulders, the six-pack abs, the slim hips, the triangle of hair and sex almost hidden by her own. His arms were roped with muscle, and his hands long-fingered and strong. He didn't look remotely harmless, even stark naked.

"Hey," she said, leaning forward to let her breasts brush against his chest.

He raised his head. "Hey, yourself," he said, well aware of what she was doing but sounding nonetheless a little halfhearted.

She put her fists on her hips and a glower on her face. "This is not the level of enthusiasm I have come to expect from you, Chopin."

His hands came up to cup her ass. They felt warm and solid against her skin. "Well, you kinda wore me out today, Shugak."

"You should talk," she said, and leaned forward.

Against her lips he said, "What about my beauty sleep?"

She nipped at his lower lip. "We can sleep when we're dead."

Act IV

Fifteen

FRIDAY, JULY 13, VERY EARLY IN THE MORNING

Kushtaka

IT WASN'T YOUR TYPICAL ELOPEMENT.

For one thing, there was no waiting until the dark of night to cover their movements, because at this time of year there was no dark of night.

For another, she wasn't climbing out from her bedroom window on a knotted sheet steadied by her lover below. There was no second floor on their house. For that matter, she didn't have her own bedroom, just an alcove she shared with Auntie Nan.

For a third, they were already married.

It took all her formidable self-control to conceal that joyous secret over the next twelve hours. Even then in an unguarded moment, when she reached inside her shirt to touch the ring on the chain round her neck, the expression on her face caused her mother to say sharply, "Jennifer, wake up! I told you to start the bread!"

Jennifer had woken from her trance and she had started the bread, but as she assembled the ingredients, a chant ran through her mind: *This is the last time I will heat the water. This is the last time I will dissolve the yeast. This is the last time I will measure out the flour. This is the last time I will knead the dough. This is the last time I will do any of these things in this house. In this village.*

It was already agreed between the two of them that they would leave the Park. No member of either family was going to accept their marriage. No member of either village would, for that matter.

Her mother, suspicious of happiness in any form but especially in faraway smiles on her daughter's face, had been keeping a beady eye on Jennifer ever since she came back from the woods. Jennifer, so close to being free of her mother's supervision forever, was tolerant, which only made her mother more suspicious. Her poor mother, who Jennifer was certain had never experienced a single happy moment in her own life, was only jealous, poor thing. Jealous of Jennifer's youth and beauty and determined that neither would help Jennifer escape her destiny, one very like her mother's own. She would marry a good boy from the village, very probably Rick Estes, and settle there and have babies and raise them and look after her parents when they got old. It was the way things were. It was the way things had always been. It was the way things would always be.

Her mother, poor thing, didn't know that Jennifer had already confounded one of those requirements, and was about to turn her back on the rest of them and not just walk but run away.

Every moment of Jennifer's life had been anchored by her parents' expectations. She was mature enough to realize that this was partly because she was an only child. More siblings would definitely have helped to share the load, but that was not to be, and she learned very early on that if she was to get anything she wanted then she would have to fight for it.

It did seem as if everything she wanted was forbidden to her. The first time she'd picked up her dad's rifle, it had felt natural and right, but by tradition she wasn't allowed to go after the big game, the caribou and the moose and the bear that might help feed her family and the whole village. She'd known instinctively how to bait and set a trap so that no trace smell of human on it would warn the mink and the beaver away. When she trapped her first wolf, she'd had to let her dad take the credit. A strip of it was on the hood of the parka her mother had made her, and every time she put it on, it reminded her of the joy she had felt in being out on the trail in winter, the crunch of snowshoes on the crusty snow, the bite of cold air in her nostrils, the bright glint of sun on the ice crystals that lined the creeks, the clear, clear water running between the ice growing out from the banks. The joy of finding that her traps, the traps she had baited and set with her own hands, had outsmarted even the wolverine. There was joy, too, at home, in the curing of the pelts, in the speculation around the fire of what they would bring at auction, in thinking of what she would buy with her share.

Not that she ever got her own share. Everything went into a communal treasury that supported the family. That didn't bother her. When you didn't have much, you had to share to survive, and she never went cold or hungry or was without a roof over her head. But it would have been nice to be given some of the credit for keeping herself that way, that her skill with rifle and trap and fishing net had contributed to the health and welfare of the family.

To his credit, her father didn't like it any more than she did, but she couldn't help but wonder if it was more about the son he didn't have than the daughter he did.

Other girls in other villages, she knew, were not forbidden these things. When the Kushtaka school had closed down and, with much misgiving, her parents had transferred her to the Kuskulana school, she had heard several of the Kuskulana girls talking about going hunting or fishing, usually with their fathers but sometimes with their mothers, too. Like everyone else, she'd heard the stories about the legendary Park rat Kate Shugak, upriver in Niniltna, who while not a hunter or a trapper or a fisherman by trade, per se, lived like a man, on her own terms, taking her own meat and her own fish and feeding herself with them through the winters.

A busybody, some people said. An avenging angel, said others. Whatever they called her, she waded into messes other people walked around and cleaned them up.

On Career Day, Sergeant Jim Chopin of the Niniltna trooper post had visited Kuskulana school and talked about being a trooper. The other girls swooned over his metaphysical product perfection, his blue eyes, his thick blond hair, his broad shoulders and narrow hips and long legs, the quick, easy grin that was beguiling without being flirtatious. Jennifer wasn't a nun, she appreciated all those things, too, but mostly she was curious to see up close and personal a man who would attract the attention of a Kate Shugak and not be found wanting. He was smart and funny and he didn't try to shine them on. "To be a cop is always to be other," he had said.

Jennifer got that. Of everyone in Kushtaka, she was the most other. Because of her looks and her gender she was watched more critically, and because she was a chief's daughter she was judged more harshly.

To be Kushtakan in the Park was always to be other, too.

And then she met Ryan. At Kuskulana she played guard on the girls' basketball team; he played guard on the boys'. Both teams went to a regional tournament at one of the high schools in Ahtna, where both teams slept on the gym floor in sleeping bags, guarded on every side by chaperones.

Not that well guarded, however. It had been Jennifer's first trip outside the Park, and she was not going to lose an opportunity to see the sights. Keeping her clothes on beneath her pajamas, she waited until everyone else was asleep before faking an old bathroom trick and ducking out a conveniently located back door.

Where, directly outside it, she literally ran into Ryan Christianson, who it turned out had his own escape plan.

That this was the very last person her family would want her associating with was only the icing on the cake. He was a boy. He was a Christianson. He was a Kuskulaner. Rebellion this sweet had never come her way before.

He'd been to Ahtna many times and he knew the quickest way downtown. On the way, they talked, and she discovered he knew how to read and he discovered that she knew who Robert Heinlein was. By the time they found the movie theater where, hallelujah, *The Avengers* was still playing, they were comfortable enough to share a bag of extortionately expensive popcorn. Afterwards, they found a video arcade where she clobbered him at *Asteroids*, and he had to defend himself when she accused him of letting her win. They found an open-all-night diner at a truck stop on the way back to the gym and spent the rest of the hours before dawn talking under the tired but benevolent eyes of a waitress who had been young once, too.

By the time they sneaked back into the gym, their chaperones none the wiser, they were both determined to further the relationship. It wasn't easy, which was part of the allure. She couldn't sit with him at lunch at school, because word would have beaten her back across the river, and her parents would have sent her to Chemawa the next day. He couldn't walk her from school to the landing, because word of that would have beaten him back up the hill, and while his parents wouldn't have sent him to a boarding school Outside, they might well have sent him to the boarding school in Galena.

So they met in secret, prearranged by notes passed discreetly from locker to locker, usually on the river, all that winter. He loved to hunt and fish and trap every bit as much as she did, which only strengthened the attraction between them. Those very few precious times when Jennifer managed to talk her father into letting her walk the trapline alone, she got word to Ryan and he met her and they walked it together.

They were young and madly in love and of course sex came into the mix early on. She would have, but he wouldn't. "I want to marry you, Jennifer," he had said. "I want us to build a cabin in the woods and spend the rest of our lives making our living there. Do you want kids?"

"I don't know," she said. "I hadn't thought about it."

"I don't know either," he said, "but between the two of us, however many of us there are, no one's going hungry."

She smiled.

And then Tyler was killed on the fish wheel in Kushtaka, and word had just come across the river that they found Mitch Halvorsen in Kuskulana, nailed into the crawl space of his own house. Her whole being was made for sunlight and fresh air and open spaces. The thought of spending her last moments imprisoned underground with no way out made her flesh creep, and in a way made her need to escape the ever-constricting limits of Kushtaka even more urgent.

They'd met at Kuskulana landing the morning of Tyler Mack's death.

"They'll never let us be together," she said.

"Then we run," he said. He looked older when he said that, and his voice sounded deeper. "I looked it up. We're both eighteen, so we're of age. I'll go up to Ahtna today and get a license."

The original plan had been to take a skiff and go downriver, get to Cordova and be married there, and then go to Kasilof, where Ryan had a friend with a set net site. "We'll have to work for our keep, but they'll never find us there," he had said. "When they get over it, we can come back, and build a cabin on the land my grandmother left to me."

She'd heard his message on Park Air that morning, and then the flying pastor had come for Tyler's service. Jennifer had sent Auntie Nan to Ryan. He had met her in the woods and Auntie Nan had brought the pastor to them, and she had married them there.

Jennifer had had to go back to Kushtaka until the fuss over Tyler's services died down and people went back to their own homes, or she would have been missed. Much better to get away by night. It was two o'clock before she was certain everyone was asleep and she felt able to leave the house. She grabbed a stuffed backpack from the hollow beneath a spruce tree where she had stashed it on a trip to the outhouse earlier that evening. She slung it over her shoulders as she walked, following the trail that ran down the river's edge.

It was a clear, cool night, the northern horizon rimmed with gold, the sky bleached of stars. She heard the hush of wings overhead and looked up to see a boreal owl backwing itself to a landing on a tree branch not far above her. She had heard their call before but had never seen one, and she considered it a good omen.

The river rippled and swirled and eddied on her right, a silver trail leading her to her lover and the life she had always wanted. Her heart grieved a little at what she left behind, at the same time that her footsteps quickened on the path.

By then she was almost running, her heart beating high up in her throat.

She burst out of the trees onto the tiny stretch of gravel at the river's edge. He was waiting for her. She dropped her daypack and hurled herself into his arms, her lips urgent on his.

She wanted him so badly, had for what now felt like forever, would have taken him down on the gravel in that moment, if a second person hadn't come crashing out of the trees right behind her. She didn't even hear him, her heart beat so loudly in her ears.

But Ryan jerked free of her arms and shoved her behind him.

"Jennifer?" The voice was disbelieving.

It was Rick Estes. Half dressed, out of breath, a red scratch on his cheek from a tree branch, Rick looked at her, glaring back at him over Ryan Christianson's shoulder, his expression one of revulsion crossed with horror, and despair. "Jennifer! What are you doing?"

She couldn't answer him, wouldn't. What right had he to interfere in her life? She knew he cared for her; she'd known that since she was thirteen and grew breasts. But Ryan had been there long before him, since the time as children their eyes first met across the river, her at the fish wheel, him at his skiff. She stared at Rick, inimical, unwelcoming, her lips a firm line that was in itself a rebuke.

"This is none of your business, Rick," Ryan said, steady, even stern.

"Jennifer," Rick said for the third time. This time it was a plea.

She would not answer.

"Go home, Rick," Ryan said.

Sixteen

FRIDAY, JULY 13

Anchorage

THEY ROSE LATE THE NEXT MORNING AND did justice to Snow City Cafe's Heart Attack on a Plate, and presented themselves at the crime lab at noon-oh-one.

Brillo looked like he'd been there all night, but then he always looked like that and frequently was. He accepted the twenty-ounce Americano and the bag of cream doughnuts as only his due.

They had to wait while he got on the outside of two of the doughnuts before he burped and said, "Where's Mutt? I got a steak bone with her name on it."

"In the car," Jim said. "Got anything for me?"

"I might have, if you'd'a let Mutt come in and say hi."

Jim looked at Kate. Kate looked at Brillo. Brillo paled a little and cleared his throat, spraying crumbs down the front of a shirt that looked like it hadn't been washed since Palin quit. "Your Kuskulana toe tag died of dehydration."

"Time of death?"

Brillo snorted. "Offhand? Late May, early June. A lot depends on the weather. How hot's it been in the Park lately? How dry?"

"Could he have been dead before he was put in the crawl space?" Jim said, and Kate could tell he was hoping.

"Was he right-handed?" Brillo said.

"Don't know."

"Cause his right clavicle was fractured, like he'd been using his right shoulder to run into something on purpose. Which he had. We found fibers from his Gaga T-shirt on the underside of the hatch, along with traces of his blood."

"Did you have a chance to look at his hands?"

"A look only, Sergeant, you didn't leave me time for anything more. So you know, everything I'm saying to you here today is subject to change without notice."

"Understood."

Brillo relaxed, or as much as he ever did. "Then, yes, from an extremely cursory examination of the vic's hands, it is my unsubstantiated opinion that he messed up his fingers trying to claw through that hatch. Which would indicate that he was alive when whoever nailed it down."

Kate had a momentary vision of that dark crawl space as she had seen it, devoid even of the small square of light provided by the open hatch. Roger Christianson was a good builder. She repressed a shudder.

"He wouldn't have just let them do that," Jim said, thinking out loud. "He would have been pushing up from below."

"If he was conscious," Brillo said.

"You saying he might not have been?"

Brillo shrugged. "He'd been in a dustup prior to his death."

"How prior?"

"Again with the guessing, but anywhere from a day to a week before he went into the crawl space. Something else."

Forensics techs were all about the call-and-response technique. "What?" Jim said patiently.

"If he hadn't died of dehydration, he might have died of alcohol poisoning. Were there any empty bottles where you found him?"

"No," Jim said.

"So," Brillo said, "if what we found left after this much time is any indication, he'd had a bunch to drink on his way out."

Jim looked at Kate and saw that her face was set and still. That much lack of expression was never a good thing.

"About that hatch," Brillo said, popping in the last bite of the last cream doughnut.

"What about it?"

"It had been nailed down twice."

"What?"

"What what, you got wax in your ears? It had been nailed down over the opening once, and then later the nails had been pulled out, I presume the hatch raised, and then nailed back down a second time."

"How much time elapsed between the two?"

"I can see under the lens where the nails went a little askew into the original holes," the ME said. "That's all I got time or equipment for."

"Any way of telling if the same person hammered the nails in both times?"

Brillo frowned some more. "Not by DNA. The nailed side of the hatch was exposed to wind and weather."

"How about if the first guy who nailed it down was right-handed and the second guy was left-handed?" Kate said.

Brillo's brows disappeared into the thicket of his hair. "I suppose, depending on which hand holds the hammer, it could affect how the nail went in." He meditated. "I'll have to see if there is any literature." He looked up. "You have a suspect?"

"I got two villages full," Jim said grimly.

"Oh. Ah. Well, then," Brillo said. "When you do—"

"Yeah," Jim said. "When I do. What about Tyler Mack?"

"The Kushtaka toe tag? He had water in his lungs matching the sample you gave me."

"So he was alive when he went into the water," Jim said.

"Alive, but not conscious," Brillo said. "That whack he took upside the head was, um, enthusiastically delivered. It might have killed him all by itself if he'd been left where he fell."

"What was the weapon?"

"Found flakes of rust in the wound," Brillo said.

"What kind of flakes?" Jim said.

There might have been a gleam of sympathy in Brillo's beady black eyes. "Unfinished tempered steel."

"Well, shit," Jim said with heartfelt sincerity.

"Rebar," Kate said with almost as much enthusiasm.

Brillo beamed at her. "Not just another pretty face."

Rebar was the abbreviation for reinforcing bar, ridged steel rods used to reinforce concrete and brick structures of every shape, size, and function. It came in various diameters, depending on the size of the structure, with the largest diameters commonly used as anchor rods for towers and signs. Jim remembered the pile of leftover construction materials stacked beneath the gangplank of the Kuskulana landing.

There were odd lengths of rebar on every construction site in the Park. Kate had seen rebar sticking up from derelict structures at the old Kanuyaq Copper Mine, and there was probably more rebar out at the Suulutaq Mine than in the rest of the Park put together.

One place you never found it was the dump. Park rats used found rebar for tree cages, garden fences, snow markers, signposts, clotheslines, doorstops, and animal pens, and anything else they could think of.

Like offensive weapons, far too often for the liking of any law enforcement professional whose patrol was in the Bush.

The only thing more ubiquitous than rebar in the Park was the fifty-five-gallon drum. "Any chance you can match the weapon with the rust flakes you found in the wound?" Jim said.

Brillo shrugged. "I can at least prove it was the same kind of rebar that inflicted the wound. You got it?"

"No," Jim said.

And they weren't likely to, Kate thought. It would be on the bottom of the river by now. Or tossed on any junk pile in the back of any cabin on the river, washed clean by the first good rain, its surface layer dissolved into rust by the first winter storm.

Brillo spread his hands and shrugged again. "When you do—"

"Time of death?" Jim said.

"He'd been in the water awhile, Jim. No way can I do exact."

"Damn," Jim said.

"What?" Kate said.

"I think Pat Mack lied to me about what time he sent Tyler up the river to the fish wheel."

"Why?"

"Habit," Jim said, and Brillo laughed. He subsided when Jim glanced at him. "Just generally wanted to confuse the evidence."

"Give the Kushtakans time to find whoever killed Tyler and deal with him themselves," Kate said.

Jim nodded. He didn't look happy.

"You done here?" Brillo said. " 'Cause I got a few other cases to tend to."

They got as far as the door when they heard his voice. "Oh, I almost forgot."

They turned. "What?"

Brillo smiled. "Both of them tested positive for cocaine."

"Use?" Jim said.

Brillo nodded. "Get this," he said, pausing to enjoy the dramatic buildup. "I won't be able to swear to it without further testing . . ."

Kate put her hands on her hips and glared.

". . . but I think it's the same cocaine," Brillo said in a rush.

In the lobby, Jim said, "I've gotta go upstairs, check in. Give me an hour or two?"

"I've got a few errands," she said. "Text me when you want me to pick you up."

She drove downtown and with unusually good parking karma found a space in front of the office building on Third Avenue. There was a sculpture of Moby Dick kicking Ishmael and Queequeq out of their whaling boat out front, and the usual amount of tourists wandering by in search of something to look at other than another T-shirt shop. "Excuse me, ma'am? Would you mind taking our picture?"

Kate looked around to see an elderly woman with short white hair, beautifully styled, holding out a camera.

Be a good host, she told herself, and took one and a spare to be sure. Handing it back to profuse thanks, she started to turn away.

"Are you all a—an Alaska Native?" the woman said hesitantly.

Kate's shoulders rose and fell in a soundless sigh. "Yes, I am."

The woman's accent sounded like Bobby's when he slipped back into Tennessese. "Could I take your photo?"

"I'm sorry, no," Kate said, trying to be cordial about it. There were already enough pictures of her floating around, never a good thing for someone whose job on occasion required strict anonymity. Which in this Internet age was a virtual impossibility anyway.

"Oh please, it won't take but a moment. It'd be so nice to have a photo of a real Alaska Native to show off at home."

Kate looked at her. Mutt, catching Kate's vibe, looked, too.

The woman stumbled back a step, bumping into her husband, who was also backing up.

Kate and Mutt went on their way without further molestation. Inside the lobby of the office building, Kate punched the elevator button and smiled down at Mutt. "We've still got it, girl."

"Wuff!" Mutt said, and the man stepping out of the elevator recoiled, reconnoitered, and finally sidled out, holding his elegant leather briefcase in front of him like a shield.

They emerged on the seventh floor and walked down the hall and through a door. Inside a neat, prim young woman sat behind a desk. She looked up. "Ms. Shugak," she said with composure. She ignored Mutt. Mutt ignored her right back.

"Agrifina," Kate said. "Is he in?"

"Let me check." This said when they both knew that the suite held only two rooms and that the second one was directly behind Agrifina Fancyboy's desk. She picked up the phone and pressed a button. "Mr. Pletnikof, Ms. Shugak is here." She listened. "Certainly."

She replaced the phone and rose to her feet to take all of the three steps from her chair to her boss's door, and opened it. "Ms. Shugak to see you, Mr. Pletnikof."

She held the door for Kate and Mutt with a polite smile.

Kate walked in. "I always feel like I'm entering the sanctum sanctorum when she ushers me in here."

Kurt Pletnikof was already around his own desk, arms outspread.

"Oof," Kate said, her voice muffled in his chest.

He beamed down at her. "I didn't know you were in town."

Her ribs appeared to be intact. "I didn't know I was going to be in town."

His gaze sharpened. "You on a case?"

"I'm with Jim, and he is."

"Ah. The usual, then. Want some coffee?"

"Just came from breakfast."

Kurt found half a stick of pepperoni for Mutt and the three of them retired to the seating area meant for privileged guests, or well-heeled clients.

The office, inner and outer, showed the hand of an interior decorator who worked for pay and not for love. A symphony in maroon and gray with teak grace notes, Kurt's corner office looked through adjacent windows onto Knik Arm, and summer mornings made it glow with an especially rich and tactile light. The desk was arranged across one corner, with the seating area in the opposite corner and sets of file drawers between. There were a few paintings perfectly spaced on the walls between the windows and the various pieces of furniture. "Aren't those new?" she said.

Kurt nodded. "Don't worry, we didn't buy them, they're on loan."

"Who from?"

He saw her expression and laughed. "I didn't take them in lieu of payment, if that's what you're worried about.

"Maybe a little."

"There's an art gallery a couple of blocks over. The owner and I have, ah, an arrangement."

Indicating that the paintings, unlike the interior decoration, might be there for love. Diplomatically, Kate refrained from comment but made a mental note to check out the gallery and the owner. There was a large art book on the coffee table featuring classical statuary. She opened to a page at random, and found a marble tear coursing down a marble cheek. "Quite a figure on Persephone there," she said. "No wonder Hades got a yen."

Kurt leaned back, linking his hands behind his head. "Most of my clients are wealthy men. Wealthy men like looking at pictures of naked women they think they might one day be able to afford to buy."

Kate closed the book and scanned the cover. "I doubt there are any Berninis on the market at present," she said.

"The illusion, then," Kurt said, shrugging.

Kate sat back in her turn and looked at him. Like her, Kurt Pletnikof was a Park rat, a second or maybe a third cousin by way of one of the aunties. Their first meaningful interaction had involved half a dozen gall bladders from poached Park grizzlies and a hatchet. That was, what, three, almost four years ago now.

She'd essentially blue-ticketed him out of the Park, and he wound up on the soup line at Bean's Cafe in Anchorage, where she'd found him again and hired him at minimum wage to do a little freelance investigatory work on an ongoing case.

It had been an action instigated, she admitted to herself, mostly by her own guilt. He was hungry and homeless and it was useless to tell herself that his own actions were responsible for putting him in that soup line. To the surprise of them both, he'd been good at investigative work. More, he liked it. When he got out of the hospital, she had bankrolled him as a silent partner and he had opened up his own one-man agency. He'd taken some computer courses at the University of Alaska Anchorage and discovered a real gift for cybercrime.

Pinkerton North, Jim called them, but even he was respectful of Kurt's results. The first year he'd done a great many background checks, divorce cases, and missing persons work, but the second year he'd scored a major coup by solving a commercial embezzlement case, and this year he'd helped the FBI's Cyber Crimes Task Force bust an Internet child pornography ring operating out of Wasilla. This had brought him to the attention of Alaska's major players, who so far as Kate could tell, appeared to spy on one another as a matter of standard business practice. They were also in constant need of discovering who among their own had leaked what to whom. The Native corporations were especially happy to be able to hire an Alaska Native for their PI work. Kate lived in daily expectation of hearing that Kurt had hired on anywhere from one to twenty associates and was building his own forensics lab.

The year before, he'd acquired Agrifina Fancyboy, a girl from Chuathbaluk, found on the same soup line at Bean's that Kate had found Kurt on. Agrifina displayed a dedicated professionalism, inspired by, Kate suspected, a terror of being forced back to the village. Sort of like Kate's cousin Axenia, who had married up and now resided in one of the nicer subdivisions in Anchorage, and who lived the determined life of the perfect suburban wife and mother with the same kind of motivated ferocity Agrifina projected on the job at Pletnikof Investigations.

Kate surveyed Kurt with no little satisfaction, and perhaps a little smugness, and maybe even a little gratitude. She'd been too much a student of the human condition for trust to come easy to her. Kurt Pletnikof had proved the exception to that rule.

So far.

"So," he said.

"So," she said. "Got your most recent report on Erland."

He nodded.

"Not a lot going on there."

He nodded.

"Which we both know is bullshit."

He nodded. "Indeed we do." Erland Bannister was the proximate cause of putting Kurt in the hospital after their first case together. "On the face of it, he's into rehabilitation and redemption, big time, starting with putting his money where his mouth is. He's investing locally, in everything from a photographer's book project on Kickstarter—five hundred dollars—to an A and P school in Kodiak—fifty thousand dollars—to a minority stake in a new natural gas project west of Beluga—five million dollars. He's bought into a local film production studio."

"Is Gabe McGuire a partner?" Kate said.

Kurt's eyes widened at her sharp tone. "Not that I know of. Why?"

"No reason," Kate said, and relented when Kurt raised an

eyebrow. “I met McGuire on that case in Newenham last winter. He knows Erland, and he’s in the film business.”

“Erland Bannister knows many people, Kate.”

She nodded, and made a come-along motion with her hand.

“He’s started a nonprofit foundation, the Bannister Foundation,” Kurt said, consulting his notes, “and is funding all sorts of charitable projects all over the state. He attends fund-raisers for the University of Alaska–Anchorage, Alaska public radio, Standing Together Against Rape, the YWCA, and the Kenai Classic, and he’s bidding often enough and high enough in their live auctions to win a ten-day cruise up the Inside Passage on someone’s private yacht. He’s managed to get himself on half a dozen boards, had his photo taken at Gore Point picking up Japanese tsunami debris, and—you’ll love this—he ran in the Heart Run in April, placed sixth in his age group, and raised thirteen thousand dollars for the American Heart Association from his sponsors.”

“He’s running competitively in three-mile races?” Kate said. “The guy’s as old as Bilbo Baggins.”

“I know. At this rate, he’ll be burying us all.”

She looked at him.

“Allow me to rephrase that,” he said.

“Never mind,” she said. “Any mention of the Bannister Foundation funding an airplane for the Flying Pastor in the Park?”

“Really?” Kurt said. “I hadn’t heard. They finally replaced Father Fred?”

“With Anne Flanagan, and financed her new plane while they were at it.”

“I’ll check, but it sounds like just the kind of project the Bannister Foundation is most fond of: small, local, and religious. Up, swish, score.”

"Anything else?"

He shrugged. "I did like you said, I haven't crowded him, or stepped over any lines. It hasn't been all that difficult."

"How's that?"

"This all-new and improved Erland Bannister evidently never met a reporter he didn't like. From what I hear, no journalist or blogger is able to get out of the way fast enough to avoid interviewing him. And," he added, "whenever the subject of his trial and conviction on conspiracy to murder comes up, he doesn't proclaim his innocence."

"No?"

"Heavens, no. He shakes his head and looks sad, and talks about bad choices and unfortunate coincidences. He never says a mean word about APD or the district attorney's office, and he always ends with a hymn to family values, especially his own, and a reference to his family's long residence in the state of Alaska."

"I bet his sister just loves that."

"She doesn't say anything one way or another. So far as I can tell, Victoria Muravieff regards herself as an only child."

Kate was silent, examining the middle distance with a slight frown.

"What," Kurt said.

She looked up. "Misdirection."

"Watch this hand," Kurt said, "so you don't see what this hand is doing."

She nodded.

"Okay," he said, "I'm with you. Just because you're paranoid about Erland Bannister doesn't mean he isn't out to get you."

"But?"

"But . . ." It was his turn to frown. "He's boxing you in, Kate."

"Look at me, says Erland," Kate said. "Look how squeaky clean I am now, what a good citizen I am. See all the good things I do, all the good causes I support."

Kurt nodded. "How could you possibly believe all those mean things that woman said about me?"

"She was uninformed, mistaken, confused," Kate said.

"Oh yeah," Kurt said, "she just didn't understand."

"Might even be a little crazy," Kate said.

"At the very least on the rag."

"If he's going to this much trouble to look this good," Kate said.

"Oh, hell yeah," Kurt said. "You want me to really get into it?"

She thought about it. "Wait," she said.

"For what?"

She met his eyes. "For when I really need you to."

He hesitated, and then let her turn the conversation to current cases being run by the firm. "One other thing," he said when she got up to leave.

"What?"

He went to a cabinet and extracted a plain buff file folder. "You wanted this."

She took it. He watched her open it and scan the contents.

She closed it again without surprise. "Thanks, Kurt."

"Did you know?" he said.

"I suspected. Why I had you check for me."

"You going to talk to him?"

"Probably not."

He was surprised and showed it.

"He's not breaking any laws, Kurt. The Supreme Court says money is speech."

She spoke evenly, without emphasis or anger. He looked at her closely but she had that impenetrable Shugak mask on, the same one that had made anyone who tried to cross her grandmother think twice and maybe three times. There was never any knowing what was going on behind it, until the wearer cared to communicate their feelings. And then you were left in no doubt, if you were left standing at all.

He looked at Mutt, who had stood up when Kate opened the folder. Her yellow eyes were intent on Kate, her tail motionless.

Kurt Pletnikof thought how grateful he was not to be Demetri Totemoff.

Seventeen

FRIDAY, JULY 13, EARLY AFTERNOON

Niniltna

THEY WERE WELL INTO THE PARK WHEN Jim banked left.

"Where we going?" Kate said.

"Want to show you something," he said.

She was silent until she realized they were coming up on the homestead. She smiled. "The scenic route home?"

"Partly," he said. They lost altitude until the tops of the remaining trees looked close enough to clean the gear. She saw the ridgeline of the house first, and the reflection of the sun off the windows nearly blinded her.

Mutt thrust a muzzle over Kate's shoulder and left a big wet nose print on the glass. She gave a long interrogatory whine. "Patience, girlfriend," Kate said. "No parachutes your size."

Jim flew past the house and the outbuildings, over the big,

flattened erratic at the top of the cliff, and banked right to follow Zoya Creek north. The ground rose and the Cessna rose with it. A few moments later, Kate saw the adit to the Lost Wife Mine and the rough zigzig trail that led up the cliff face to it. Jim banked right again and flew a wide circle, tilting the plane so that he and Kate could both look out his window. She leaned forward to see past him. "What?" she said.

"There's an old airstrip down there," he said.

"Yeah," she said. "When the mine was being worked, they used it to fly in supplies. I never maintained it, and so far as I know, neither did my father, so it's pretty overgrown now."

He straightened out the plane and headed back down the creek toward the homestead. "It's about half a mile from the homestead by air."

"A bit less," she said.

"And it's on the right side of the creek, so we wouldn't need a bridge."

She raised her eyebrows. "No."

He jerked his head at Mutt. "If we had our own airstrip, we could be home in fifteen minutes instead of a couple of hours. And I could respond from home a lot quicker."

She digested this. "It's an idea," she said finally, cautious as always with any suggested changes on her home ground.

"A good idea? A bad one?"

"Don't rush me." She pointed. "See that?"

He was content to have planted the seed and let her change the subject. He banked left and right again, serpentining. "Looks like an old trail. Really old. I never would have noticed it if you hadn't pointed it out."

"Cat trails never die in Alaska."

"What was it?"

She sat back. “An old prospector’s trail, or a federal surveyor’s, or maybe even an alternate route scoped out by the Kanuyaq Mine developers back in the day. Maybe all of the above, in sequence. Old Sam said it dead-ended somewhere up the other side of the Step.”

“Ever follow it?”

She chose to tell only part of the truth. “Ethan and I found it one summer and as I recall got about a hundred feet before we decided flying was a far more efficient means of locomotion.”

He laughed and banked right to find the Park road. He followed it into Niniltna, the river on their right, the rolling, descending foothills of the Quilaks on their left, and the blue-white fangs of the Quilaks before them. Jim raised Chugach Air Taxi’s office on the radio, speaking clearly and distinctly in hopes of alerting anyone else who might also be approaching Niniltna in an aircraft. Niniltna airstrip wasn’t exactly Merrill Field, not yet anyway, but good pilots were natural conservatives, as well as ever alive to the undeniable fact that not all pilots were created equal. He clicked back to headset audio. “You know my father left me some money.”

She knew, and she also knew that “some money” was an understatement. “You’re going to buy an airplane, aren’t you.”

He grinned. “You would pluck out the heart of my mystery, Shugak.”

“Promise me,” she said, not joking, “promise me you’ll stop at one.”

He looked at her in well-simulated surprise. “Why, what would I do with more than one airplane?”

“Exactly,” she said. “You can only fly one at a time.”

“Of course,” he said, wounded.

Right, Kate thought.

They approached the outskirts of the village. Herbie Topkok was in his driveway, bent over an ATV, and straightened up to wave at them. Jim waggled his wings in response. A few minutes later, they were on the ground and rolling to a stop. "No," he said as the prop slowed and stopped, "I don't want a second airplane. But I'm going to want my own hangar."

She unbuckled her seat belt and nodded across the runway at Chugach Air Taxi. "George is building another. Rent space from him."

"The state is going to, for this airplane."

"Oh," Kate said. "You mean you want a hangar out at the homestead strip, for your own."

"I hate getting in a cold airplane," Jim said, pulling off his headset and opening the door. Mutt squeezed between his shoulder and the airframe and took the distance to the ground in a single graceful leap.

Jim and Kate followed more sedately.

"Not only an airstrip, but an airplane, and a hangar, too." Kate handed him her headset and he pulled his pilot's bag from the back and tucked them inside.

"Think how much quicker we'd be home if we fly," he said.

Which would mean we wouldn't have to drive, Kate thought, except for bringing in the big stuff. She remembered Paul and Alice and the vision of herself at the controls of a Caterpillar D9 tractor, pushing up a mound of dirt to block the trail between her homestead and the Park road.

"Well," she said, helping him push the plane back to its tie-downs, "it's an idea."

He looked up to see the smile in her eyes. "What?"

"Back at HQ," she said, "did you go upstairs to ask for another trooper for Niniltna?"

They went to opposite wings. They would be in the air again shortly, but you never anticipated a calm day in Alaska staying that way for longer than five minutes. Jim was never going to be the guy who came out to check on his aircraft only to find it had flipped in a gust of wind because it hadn't been properly tied down. He paid more attention to the overhand knot than it perhaps deserved and chose his words with care. "Well, I don't want a VPSO."

She came around the tail. "You're dictating terms?"

He looked up to see that the smile in her eyes had moved to her lips.

"How much was it your father left you, again?"

⁂

At the post, Maggie, Jim's dispatcher, was looking no more harried than usual, fielding 911 calls about drunks, vandalism, and sexual harassment. "Boss," she said when they walked in, "we need help."

"I know," he said. "I talked to the Lord High Everything Else this morning. I think we'll be getting another trooper out of the next graduating class, and maybe even two."

"You're kidding," Maggie said, stunned.

"You're kidding," Kate said, stunned.

"If the price of gold stays up, and even if it doesn't, the Suulutaq Mine is looking like it's here to stay," Jim said, pulling off his cap. "Niniltna's transient population has already doubled, with the result that our caseload has tripled."

"Quadrupled," Maggie said.

"Someday, too soon," Jim said, "something big is going to blow up and something bad will go down because we just don't have the resources to deal with it."

Like Kushtaka and Kuskulana, Kate thought. Their eyes met and she knew he was thinking the same thing.

"One trooper and one dispatcher, however magnificent," he said, smiling at Maggie, who brightened right up, "are not sufficient to protect and to serve today's Park."

Kate applauded, discreetly.

"Thank you," Jim said, "thank you very much." To Maggie he said, "Anybody in the cells?"

"Probably should be," Maggie said, "but there wasn't anybody here to arrest 'em."

"Good enough," Jim said, and went into his office, followed by Kate and Mutt.

"You headed back to Kuskulana?" she said.

He nodded, booting up his computer to check his e-mail. "If Brillo is right and somebody pried up that hatch cover to find Mitch Halvorsen dead, that means somebody found him before yesterday. Which means there's a good chance Tyler's murder was retaliation. Just being there in uniform might help keep a lid on things."

"They won't talk to you," Kate said.

"I know," he said. "Kushtaka won't, either. Still have to try."

"Water on stone," she said.

He affected mock surprise. "You didn't know that was what most of police work is?"

There was too much e-mail and none of it worth reading. He opened a window into the state trooper dispatches from the previous twenty-four hours. A teenager had assaulted his mother and younger brother in Wasilla, a dozen fishermen were summonsed for fishing during a closed period along various parts of the Alaska coastline, a seventy-five-year-old man in Fairbanks shot at two troopers responding to a disturbance. The troopers returned fire, and no one was hurt in the subsequent shoot-out at the Midnight Sun Corral, which, Jim thought, would be drawing some unwelcome attention from the Lord High Everything Else. Troopers were supposed to hit what they aimed at.

Sexual assaults in Togiak and Tyonek (assholes); DUIs in Bethel, New Stuyahok, Girdwood, and Juneau (morons); three failures to log personal use shrimp on their permits in Whittier (idiots); and a bunch of misdemeanors that had much more to do with stupidity unleashed that it did an increase in lawlessness among the population. At any rate, there were no REDDIs or other alerts, which meant he could get on with the investigation in Kushtaka and Kuskulana.

"They won't talk to you," Kate said, and he realized it was for the second time.

He blanked his screen and sat back in his chair to look at her. "I'm not walking away from this, Kate."

"I know," she said. "I'm not saying you should. I'm just saying, absent a smoking gun, it won't be easy."

"Will they talk to you?" he said. "Kenny Halvorsen didn't seem all that happy to see you yesterday."

"Probably not. But there has to be someone with some sense down there. Someone who's tired of the communal warfare and is ready to help end it."

"Yeah," he said, unconvinced. "I'm not expecting cooperation, Kate. But I'll get it. However I have to."

"What, you going to run in the entire populations of both villages and sweat them under bright lights? You know it doesn't work like that, Jim."

He knew, but he was spared from answering when the door opened and Maggie poked her head in. He didn't like the expression on her face, and he really didn't like what she had to say.

"Got a call from Kushtaka."

He felt his shoulders start to droop and shored them up. "What?"

"Rick Estes is dead."

His eyes met Kate's. "Heart attack?" he said without much hope.

Eighteen

FRIDAY, JULY 13, AT THAT SAME MOMENT

Kushtaka

WHO CALLED THE TROOPER?"

"Tony Christianson, Roger's nephew, was on his way downriver. He got there about the same time we did. He had his phone out before he was out of sight."

"Always some fucking Kuskulaner around when you don't want them," Pat Mack said, not bothering to lower his voice.

The eldest was silent, his bright black eyes half-closed, his seamed face set in deep lines.

The daypack found on the beach next to Rick's body sat on the table in front of them, open and its contents arranged in neat piles. Lacy underpants, two bras, a pair of jeans, some T-shirts, a toiletries kit with toothbrush, toothpaste, a brush, hair gel.

When the marriage certificate had been found and spread out on the table for all to see, Dale's wife had shrieked, a raw sound of agonized denial that echoed far beyond their own walls and ripped fresh wounds in everyone present. Staggering back as though from a blow, when she hit the wall, her knees gave out and she slid to the floor, where she remained, keening into her arms.

Dale Mack was unable to tear his eyes from the document. No matter how many times he read it, there was no denying the names on the certificate, or the signature of the officiant. Or the date. His daughter, his only child, the heir to his flesh and his bone and his goods and his tradition, his precious Jennifer, that she could betray him, betray her raising, her village in this worst of all ways. To do it on the same day they were laying to rest one of their own . . . he shuddered, and finally raised his head to look around the room.

Only Pat Mack met his eyes, and Pat looked away again almost immediately. The younger men were straining at a leash that with every passing moment threatened to snap. The older men were just as angry, but they had more control.

Dale didn't know who he feared more.

The silence stretched on too long. A cough, a shuffle of feet, a whispered comment glared into silence, for the moment.

The eldest still said nothing. Either he could not think of a way forward, or he saw every way as bad, or he had grown too old to care.

"Everyone who has a skiff," Pat said, getting to his feet. "Come with me."

Nineteen

FRIDAY, JULY 13, TWO HOURS LATER

Kushtaka

"SON OF A BITCH," JIM SAID.

Kate couldn't recall ever seeing Jim quite this steamed. He never lost his temper at a scene and he was always careful of his use of language in any interaction with the public. Profanity offended a lot of people and could put an investigation on the wrong track from the get-go. In a place like the Park, whose instinct was always first to protect its own, a state trooper needed all the goodwill he could get.

In this case, the Park included Pat Mack, Dale Mack, and most of the rest of the male population of Kushtaka, who sat in skiffs nudged around the water's edge of the tiny beach a mile south of the village. None of them said a word, which was probably a good thing.

The beach was no more than a short, narrow shelf of smooth rocks between the earthen bank and the river's edge, almost completely hidden by the overhanging flora. As a trysting place, it was unparalleled.

Rick Estes dangled a foot above the gravel, wrapped in the less than loving embrace of Mother Alder. His face was bruised but not bloody, the skin white between contusions. His jaw hung open and a tooth was missing. Water dripped from his clothes and from the surrounding leaves and branches. Kate nudged a few rocks to one side with her foot. The rocks were a dryish gray where they were exposed to the air, dark with damp beneath.

It hadn't rained in three days.

The only marks on the beach were where the skiffs currently there had nosed in. There was nothing to be seen besides the body. Not an empty beer bottle or pop can, not a candy wrapper, not so much as a used condom. Which last, Kate thought, given the seclusion provided the little beach by the sharp downriver bend and the overhanging branches was at minimum unlikely and at maximum just plain unbelievable.

"Son of a bitch," Jim said again, this time with bitter emphasis. He was either incapable of or indifferent to hiding the fury that surrounded him like a fine, red mist, and even the most stoic among the Kushtaka males recoiled a little. Kate saw Jim realize it, saw him visibly bite back what else had been threatening to spill out from between his clenched teeth. After a long moment, pregnant with bile, he said curtly, "Who found the body?"

"I did," Pat Mack said. No one else so much as twitched.

The question had obviously been expected and the answer to it equally obviously rehearsed, which did not improve Jim's temper. "Finding murdered Kushtakans getting to be a hobby with you, Pat."

"Mr. Mack," Kate said, keeping her eyes lowered and her voice just high enough to be heard above the river. "I think what Sergeant Chopin meant to say was, Is this how you found Mr. Estes? Just like this?"

"No, I didn't mean to say that," Jim said.

Kate subsided into crushed silence, and the men of Kushtaka exchanged approving glances. Teach the woman to raise her voice in men's affairs.

"What I meant to say is exactly what I said," Jim said, destroying any goodwill he had generated by putting the uppity woman in her place. "This is the second dead Kushtakan you've found in a week, Pat, and from the looks of it, the second murdered Kushtakan as well."

"He fell out of his boat," Pat said.

Jim stared at him, and then he laughed—a sharp, mirthless crack. "Sure he did. And then the tide came in and tossed him up in the trees. That same tide that washed this little beach so sparkingly clean. Oh, wait. Except there is no tide this far up the river."

Pat Mack didn't blink. "Been warm, last couple days. Lotta meltoff from upstream glaciers."

For one fraught moment Kate thought Jim was going to belt the old man one right in the kisser.

He might have, too, if Mutt hadn't stopped it. Sniffing interestedly at the bushes, where a muskrat cowered in terror, she heard Jim's raised voice and trotted over. She plunked down on her butt in front of the trooper and barked once, sharp and severe.

He looked down at her. She looked up at him. Blue eyes met yellow, and blue eyes fell first.

In the meantime, there was a stirring among the Kushtakans.

Kate looked over to see them shifting uncomfortably in their skiffs and exchanging wary glances.

The wolf was an animal of great power in traditional Native culture. Okay by Kate if Mutt calling Jim to order frightened the living hell out of their archaic, misogynistic little hearts.

Mutt got up, turned around, and sat back down again, this time with her eyes fixed without favor on the men in the skiffs. There was some whispering, cut off by a fierce glance from Pat Mack.

"What time did you find him?" Jim said, his voice curt but no longer accusing.

"At noon," Pat Mack said.

"What brought you down here?"

"Looking for fish coming upriver," Pat Mack said. "There's a big run due, according to the fish hawks."

"And my cousin in Cordova," one of the other men said. "He fishes the flats. He said a big run of reds passed upriver in between periods."

"Uh-huh," Jim said. "Any idea what Estes was doing out here?"

"Maybe he was looking for the fish, too," Pat Mack said. "We all knew the run was due."

Jim struggled with himself again.

Mutt looked over her shoulder.

"Okay," Jim said, unclenching his teeth. "I want all of you out of here. Now."

His four-footed babysitter notwithstanding, he didn't say please.

⁂

He and Kate got the body into a bag and the bag into the skiff Jim had borrowed yet again from Roger Christianson, of necessity a different one this time. The two of them walked the area side by side, back and forth, and found precisely nothing. They found and followed the path that led from the little beach to Kushtaka all the way back to the village. There was some trash here and there, but nothing that hadn't been lying out in the weather for at least a year.

Jim stood at the edge of the forest, looking at the collection of tumbledown little buildings, at the closed school, at the overgrown moose trail that passed for a main street. It was difficult, Kate thought, not to draw a comparison between Kushtaka and Kuskulana, and to find Kushtaka wanting.

Without a word, Jim turned and walked back to the little beach and the skiff with the body bag in it.

The Kushtaka landing was deserted as they passed it going back. Jim faced upriver, his face grim. "You know what they did, don't you?"

Kate nodded. "They ran their skiffs up and down that section of river, using their wakes to wash off that little beach so you wouldn't be able to find any evidence other than the body. Probably washed off the body pretty good, too."

"Which means they know who did it. One of their own, or they wouldn't have bothered."

She said nothing, but her expression was eloquent.

"What?"

"Even if it wasn't one of their own, if they think it was someone from, oh, say Kuskulana, maybe? They would have done exactly the same thing."

"If they know who did it, then . . ."

"Yeah," Kate said. "They will."

He looked at the black body bag lying in the bow of the skiff and set his jaw. "Then I'll just have to get to whoever did it first."

Good luck with that, Kate was too kind to say out loud.

"I feel like the chorus in a five-act play," Jim said. "I can see everything that's going on, but I can't do fuck all about it."

"Exit, pursued by a bear," Kate said.

"Mitch Halvorsen died first," he said, thinking out loud. "Then someone found his body."

"Who the first time?"

"That I don't know yet, but someone in Kuskulana. Some kid, maybe, or a bunch of kids, screwing around."

It could have happened that way, Kate thought. "We're going with Kenny found him the second time."

"Yeah," Jim said, "two days after Tyler died. I want to know exactly when Kenny got home. Does he fly?"

"I don't think so," Kate said. She didn't say that his cousin, Pete Liverakos, had. She'd never thought to follow up on who had inherited Pete's airplane. A mistake, and not her first.

"Then we better pray he flew in on George. If he came upriver by boat, it'll be that much harder to track his movements."

"So he found Mitch on Tuesday, nailed the hatch back down, went across the river and killed Tyler, and then waited two days to 'discover' Mitch's body?"

"It's the explanation that makes the most sense."

"Why wait two days?"

"Two days be more convincing than one."

"Not to you."

"No." Jim's voice was grim. "Come on, Kate. You know as well as I do that a murderer is the biggest optimist there is. They've just killed someone and because nobody's noticed—yet—who did it, they think they can get away with everything else, too. If Kenny Halvorsen did kill Tyler Mack in revenge for Tyler killing his brother, he wasn't going to boggle at blowing smoke my way."

"If Tyler killed Mitch, and Kenny killed Tyler, who killed

Rick Estes? And why? The books would have been balanced with Tyler's death."

"Maybe Kenny thinks two Kushtakers equals one Kuskulaner."

Kate said nothing.

He knew that silence. "What?"

"Granted," she said, "things between Kushtaka and Kuskulana have been steadily deteriorating ever since ANCSA. But murder is one hell of an escalation from robbery, even assault."

"So?"

"So something started this particular chain of events," she said. "Let's go look at Mitch Halvorsen's crawl space again."

⁂

By contrast with Jim's last visit, when people had been if not welcoming then at least civil, this trip through the village, the Kuskulanans were out of sight. Kate thought she saw Carol Christianson peer out a window as they went by, but no one came out to say hello.

It could be the fact that they were carrying a black body bag between them.

Or it could be something else entirely.

They stowed the body in the back of the Cessna and walked to Mitch Halvorsen's half-built house. The hole Jim had cut in the floor gaped large beneath a blue tarp.

"What?" Kate said.

"I had that duct-taped to a fare-thee-well when we left yesterday."

It was up by three corners and flapping in the breeze. "Wind could have pulled it up," Kate said.

"Sure," Jim said.

The ladder was still in place. Before they went down, Jim pulled it up and looked at the treads. There was mud on them. Jim tested it with a finger. "Dry, but not that dry," he said.

"Someone's been down there since you pulled Mitch's body out?"

"Be my guess."

He replaced the ladder and they both descended. Last time Jim had only had his flashlight. This time Kate was carrying a six-volt LED lantern out of the plane that lit up the crawl space to the farthest corner. It was bright enough for him to see her expression. "What?"

"I don't like dark, enclosed spaces. Never have." She looked up, to see Mutt's head outlined against the rafters as she peered inquisitively over the edge. "It helps that you cut out the hatch."

"Be hard to nail us inside here like they did Mitch," Jim said.

He saw her swallow, and nod. He focused on the floor. "His body was sitting at the bottom of the ladder."

Her light swept the floor. Outlines of boxes were plain in the dust. She dropped to one knee. "A couple of pallets' worth of boxes moved in and out of here, and I'd say fairly recently, like maybe during the last two or three days."

He duck-walked to look over her shoulder. The dust was thick enough that there were outlines of boxes overlapping themselves, newer over older. "I should have done an inventory."

"Of the crawl space?"

"Yeah." He let his flashlight run over the boxes against the walls. "Because I think there are fewer boxes here than when I was down here last time."

"What was that Brillo said?" Kate said.

"About what?"

"That if Mitch hadn't died of dehydration, he would have died of alcohol poisoning?"

She pulled out a pocketknife.

⁂

An hour later, they were back outside, sitting on the edge of the house. The hole was again covered with the blue tarp and duct-taped to the floor. Jim uncapped a bottle of water and drank deeply. Kate finished it off. They were both sweaty and covered in dust. "So, no dope or booze on the premises," he said.

"Not now," she said. She looked down the road that led to the house. "Far enough out of town."

"And on the right side of it for a bootlegging operation," he said. "The airstrip's five minutes away, and the mine's, what, forty, fifty miles north-northeast. "

"Which doesn't prove anything," she said.

"Nope," he said. "And wouldn't, unless we caught them in the act."

She nodded, and stood up to walk around the perimeter of the building site. "Here," she said.

There was a track as wide as an ATV heading off into the bushes, concealed by a thick stand of alders.

"They fly it into Kuskulana," Jim said.

"They offload it into Mitch's basement," she said.

"And then they haul it up the trail," he said. "Just enough at a time to fill the trailer on a four-wheeler."

"Or a snow machine," Kate said. "You could fit, what, four, six cases of liquor and a lot more of beer into one trailer. Leaving plenty of room for a kilo or two of cocaine. Sell it fast and get out."

Jim pushed back a branch. "At some point, this track probably joins up with the track the village put into the mine."

She nodded. "No point in putting in a whole new trail when the village already did it for you."

"There will be a little turnout," he said. "Close to the mine."

"But under some kind of cover," she said. "So you can't see it from the air."

He nodded. "So, did somebody get greedy? One of the partners start cheating the others? Siphoning off some product, selling it on his own?"

She drummed her feet gently against the side of the house. "Bootlegging is a long tradition with the Halvorsens."

"That guy," he said. "Pete Liverakos. Cousin to the Halvorsens, right?"

She nodded. "He was originally from Outside. Lost his folks, some kind of car or plane wreck, I think. His nearest relatives lived here, Mitch and Kenny's parents, I think, and they took him in. He was fifteen or sixteen. Early teens."

"Rumors about him being a bootlegger true?"

She nodded.

"So we're not too upset over his tragic loss," Jim said.

"No," she said, meeting his eyes. "Not too upset."

"Not that it did any good in the long run," he said.

She nodded again. "Like a hydra," she said. "Chop off the head of one bootlegger, six more pop up in his place."

"Too lucrative," he said. "So how many Halvorsens left?"

"After Mitchell? Far as I know, Kenny is it. Not really the killing type, I would have said."

Jim looked at her. "Everybody's the killing type, Kate. Given the right motivation. You know that."

She looked away.

"I found a Brown Jug flyer in Tyler Mack's cabin," Jim said.

She frowned at her feet. "You think he was going into competition with the Halvorsens?"

"He ran with Boris Balluta."

Kate thought about that for a minute. "The new Howie and Willard? Only maybe just that little bit smarter."

"Not so much, as things turned out."

"No."

"If Boris or Tyler or both of them killed Mitch, and Kenny killed Tyler in retaliation . . ."

"And Rick Estes, too? Unlikely." She frowned. "For that matter, we don't know Rick was murdered."

"Somebody sure smacked him around."

"Smacking around and murder are two different things. The wake from all those skiffs could have bounced him around that beach pretty good." She added, "Did you see his hands? The knuckles were cut and bruised, like he'd held his own for a while, anyway."

"Why would the Kushtakers kill one of their own?"

The weird cluck of the sandhill crane sounded over the trees, and they both raised their heads to watch five of the graceful wide-winged birds sail overhead like kites. Mutt watched, too, with equal interest but from a far different motive.

"You know, Kate," he said, "every time Niniltna votes to go dry, my caseload drops by eighty percent."

"I know," she said.

"But I'm starting to wonder if I shouldn't try to talk Bernie into moving the Roadhouse into town."

"It'd about put the bootleggers out of business," she said. "Lot easier to just go in a bar and buy a drink. And no danger of the wrath of Jim falling on them when they did."

"Also," he said, "girls in bars."

"True," she said.

"And it'd be easier to control anyone who got out of hand," he said.

"And a lot shorter commute."

"Also true."

"I want to try something," she said. "Climb back down in the crawl space."

He returned to the house and disappeared down the hole in the floor. She walked ten paces from the house and stopped. "Can you hear me now?"

"Yes."

She walked another ten paces. "How about now?"

It wasn't a perfect experiment, because hatch and frame were two hundred miles away in Anchorage, but Kate was out of range of Jim's voice well before she got a hundred feet down the road to town. She was at least relieved to determine that Mitch Halvorsen hadn't died screaming for help within earshot of the entire population of Kuskulana.

Jim climbed out of the hatch and uncapped another bottle of water. They sat down next to each other on the edge of the house, legs dangling over the side. The sun was warm and a slight breeze stirred strands of her hair. He watched her drink, the movement of the strong muscles in her neck as she swallowed. The scar that bisected her throat from ear to ear, once an angry reminder of her life as an investigator for the Anchorage DA, had faded to a faint white line. Although it would never completely disappear, and she had never deliberately tried to cover it up with turtlenecks or buttoned collars. She wore it less as a badge of honor, he thought, than as a declaration of war. *Don't fuck with me.*

Smart people didn't. "Bernie would never go for it," he said.

"Neither would Annie Mike," she said.

"No," he said. "Crap."

She gestured in back of them. "This explains a lot."

He thought of the alcohol- and drug-related calls the trooper post had been receiving on a daily basis. Burglary. Robbery. Assault. DUIs. Spousal abuse. Child abuse. Murder. Daily acts of random violence. "How much of this is going to the mine workers," he said, "and how much to locals?"

She didn't answer, and he said, "You're pretty lukewarm about finding a bootlegging operation in your own backyard, Shugak. What, because their sales seem to be directed mostly toward Suulutaq miners, you don't have to give a damn?"

Stung, she said, "Not true." And then she remembered the young miner on overload in the Riverside Cafe, and never giving him a second thought after she'd relocated him to a cell at the post. Would she have followed up on a Park rat? "Not true," she repeated with less certainty.

"Yeah," he said, unconvinced.

She might have argued, but just then Kenny Halvorsen appeared, driving up on a beat-up Honda ATV. He pulled to a stop and let the engine idle, looking the two of them over, his gaze lingering on Kate. It wasn't friendly. "What are you doing up here?" he said.

"Investigating your brother's murder," Jim said.

Kenny grinned without humor. "You're on the wrong side of the river for that."

His eyes had dark circles under them, and his features were sunken, as if it had been a while since his last square meal. Mutt, lying on the ground next to Kate, sat up and fixed an unwavering yellow stare on his face. He gave her an indifferent glance and went back to looking at Kate. A steady growl rumbled out of Mutt's throat, stilled when Kate knotted a hand in her ruff.

Jim capped his water bottle and stood up, towering over the other man. "As it happens, I'm also investigating the murder of Tyler Mack. Where were you last Tuesday morning?"

"I was on my own side of the river," Kenny said.

"Anybody see you?"

Kenny smiled without humor. "Every man, woman, and child in Kuskulana."

The hell of it was, every single man, woman, and child in Kuskulana would swear to exactly that if Jim asked them.

To Kate, Kenny said, "Déjà vu all over again, huh?"

"I had nothing to do with your brother's death, Kenny," Kate said.

"No, you'd done enough already," Kenny said.

She said nothing.

"Hard not to notice, Kate," he said, needling her, "that I'm the last Halvorsen standing. How long have I got?"

She stood up. So did Mutt. "Well, Kenny, that would depend on you, now. Wouldn't it?"

His hands tightened on the handlebars. "Is that a threat?"

"Was yours?" she said. "Or was it just more of the same." She made a fist with thumb and fingers and mimed jerking off.

Kenny flushed a dull red. "Someday you and me are gonna have a conversation, Shugak."

"Yeah," Kate said, "I can hardly wait."

For a moment, Jim thought Kenny might put the ATV in gear and run Kate down. In the next, he gave a contemptuous laugh that sounded too close to tears for comfort, and put the four-wheeler into a 180 and headed down the track to the village at full throttle.

Jim thought about Kuskulanans and Christiansons and Halvorsens, and Kushtakans and Macks and Estes, all the way back to Niniltna.

Twenty

FRIDAY, JULY 13

Niniltna

IN NINILTNA, KATE WAITED UNTIL JIM TOOK off and then went into the post office. Bonnie put up her eyebrows in exaggerated surprise. "Three times in one week," she said. "Color me stunned."

"Yeah, yeah," Kate said, and went to check her box and then Jim's. Mixed in with the junk he had a personal letter, return address Medford, Oregon. She resisted the impulse—barely—to take a photo and text it to him. She didn't want him to wreck the plane.

When she came out again, she saw Demetri Totemoff with the same bunch of guys across the airstrip at George's. Curious, she watched from her pickup as he ushered them onto one of George's town-bound Otters. When it took off he looked across and saw her, and walked across the strip. "Hey, Kate," he said.

"Hey, Demetri." She nodded at the Otter climbing into the sky. "Clients?"

He braced his hands on either edge of the driver's-side window of her truck. "Not exactly."

"Didn't have the look," Kate said. She nodded and he stepped back out of the way and she got out.

Demetri Totemoff was in his fifties, dark and stocky and fit. He was Kate's second cousin a couple of times removed through one of the aunties, and they shared the high, flat cheekbones and the olive skin of the Alaskan Aleut. Her eyes were a changeable hazel, his a dark brown. They were both tanned a deep, golden brown from a life spent outdoors, and they both embraced taciturnity as a preferred mode of expression. "Something you want to tell me, Demetri?"

He looked at her, his expression as still as always. "I get the feeling I have," he said.

"You're funding Gaea," she said.

There was silence for a few moments. He stared over her shoulder while she stared over his.

"When did you find out?"

She snorted. "It wasn't all that hard. It probably took Kurt all of five minutes on his computer. If he didn't hand it off to Agrifina Fancyboy as beneath his skill set."

"Who?"

"Never mind. What I don't understand is, why the big secret? The Roberts court says all you're doing is exercising your right to free speech."

"You aren't pissed?" he said slowly, feeling his way.

She looked at him until he turned his head to meet her eyes. "When I am, you'll know it."

A little yellow and white aircraft appeared out of the southwest. They both watched in silence as it descended toward the far end of the runway.

"I don't get it," Demetri said. "I thought you were for the mine."

"Tell me why you're so against it," she said.

"Those earthen dams they want to put in to contain the tailings?" he said. "If they fail, the toxic outflow will kill every fish in every stream around my lodge."

"Will the dams fail?"

"One earthquake, Kate," he said.

She nodded. They watched the little yellow and white plane touch down, bounce once, twice, then settle down onto the asphalt. Not as smooth a landing as the last one Anne had made with Kate watching.

"We can't let it happen, Kate," he said.

"Then you better start praying," she said.

"For what?"

"For the price of gold to drop far and fast."

He looked at her. "I don't get it," he repeated. "It's not like you to take it up the ass just because there's no other option."

She smiled. "There are always other options, Demetri. They're just not all good ones."

The yellow and white plane kicked hard right rudder and buzzed onto their side of the strip.

Goaded, Demetri said, "I'll tell you someone else who's on the side of the angels, Kate, though you won't believe it."

"Who?" she said, indifferent.

"Erland Bannister." Her head snapped around, and he gave a thin smile. "That's right. Erland's writing us big checks. Keep the wilderness the wilderness, he says."

Later, Kate would date that moment as the beginning of her understanding of just how much Erland Bannister hated her. "But he's a partner in Suulutaq."

"I know."

"Don't you care that he has a foot in both camps?"

Demetri shrugged. "His checks clear the bank."

The yellow and white plane shut down its engine and Anne Flanagan hopped out. "Kate!"

"Think about it, Kate," Demetri said. "We shouldn't be on opposite sides on this." He nodded at Anne. "Reverend Flanagan."

"Mr. Totemoff," Anne said. Her face looked tight and drawn and she was making an obvious effort to be civil. "I hope I'll see you at services next Wednesday."

A faint smile creased Demetri's face. "I hope so, too." He nodded at her, looked at Kate, and walked away.

"Anne," Kate said. She looked over Anne's shoulder and noticed that Anne was carrying two passengers.

"I need to talk to you," Anne said. "Someplace private."

⚜

Kate drove them to the school, where she knew a back door that was always open, even in summer, and settled the three of them in the teachers' lounge. "Okay," she said, "what's going on?"

"This is Jennifer Mack," Anne said. "And Ryan Christianson."

"Jennifer Christianson," both young people said in unison.

"Oh," Kate said.

"They're eighteen, they had a license, they asked me to marry them when I went down to Kushtaka to officiate at the Tyler Mack service," Anne said. Anne looked at Jennifer and Ryan. "Tell her."

"All of it?" Ryan Christianson said.

Jennifer was a beautiful young woman, with long dark hair, a pure oval face, wide-spaced dark eyes, and a lovely, lissome figure. She would turn heads wherever she went, but it was also clear to Kate that her looks were not all or even most of what she had going for her. There was a fierce intelligence there, an indomitable self-possession, and an iron will.

"This is Kate Shugak," Jennifer said, and there was no gainsaying the certainty in that rock steady voice. "We tell it all."

They told it together, one picking up the story when the other stopped.

"You didn't mean to do it," Kate said at the end.

A vigorous shaking of heads, and real regret and sorrow on both faces. "No. It was an accident," Jennifer said. "He surprised us just as we were about to get in the skiff. He grabbed me and he hit Ryan."

A black eye and a split lip on Ryan's face supported their story.

"He was dead when you left him?" Kate said.

Ryan's face contorted. "Yes," he said, his voice husky.

Not depraved indifference, then, Kate thought. *Involuntary manslaughter at worst.*

Jennifer, too, was close to tears. "He thought he was in love with me, and he knew my father . . . but I wasn't going to let him force me back there," she said. "I won't go back now." She didn't say it defiantly. It was a simple statement of fact.

"Where have you been?" Kate said.

Ryan looked at Jennifer. "We didn't tell him anything."

"We don't want to get him in trouble," Jennifer said.

"Finish the damn story," Kate said.

Jennifer sighed, looking suddenly exhausted. Ryan put his arm around her and she leaned into his shoulder. He kissed her head and rested his cheek on her hair.. "The plan originally was that we would take the river up to Ahtna and take the bus to Anchorage and on down to the Kenai Peninsula. I've got a job waiting for me in Kasilof. We figured it would be a good place to hide out while the folks got over our getting married. And then—" He swallowed. Eighteen-year-olds were by definition immortal. It was difficult for them even to say the D-word in any kind of real-world context. "After Rick surprised us on the beach and it happened, we knew they'd be looking for us right away. At first we didn't know what to do. We couldn't go upriver, because we've both got too many nosy aunties in Niniltna and Ahtna. Same if we went downriver, because both our families and all our friends are fishing on Alaganik Bay. And then I remembered Scott Ukatish."

"Potlatch?" Kate said. "Why Potlatch?"

"He's sort of a relative," Ryan said. "I've stayed with him a couple of times before. I heard Bobby talking about him on Park Air, how Scott was dragging up, and I figured he'd be busy enough that he wouldn't be too worried about us. There would be a lot of coming and going to look at what he had for sale, and maybe we could bum a ride with somebody who couldn't care less about Kushtaka or Kuskulana." He looked down at the dark head on his shoulder. "When we got there, Jennifer saw that he had an airstrip, and got the idea to call Reverend Flanagan on Scott's shortwave."

"I flew up from Cordova and picked them up," Anne said. "They couldn't think of what to do next, so I suggested we talk to you. And here we are."

"If it was an accident, why didn't you stay and explain?" Kate said. Although she was depressingly aware she already knew the answer.

Ryan met her eyes straight on. There was nothing shifty about this young man. "It was an accident."

"So you said."

"We didn't stay, because there would have been no explaining," Jennifer said, looking up. "After Rick—after he—we were so scared, we just piled into the skiff and headed downriver as fast as we could go." She looked back at Kate. "If we'd gone to them, if we'd tried to explain, they wouldn't have listened. They would have torn Ryan to pieces on the spot."

"And they would have hurt Jennifer, too," Ryan said, his eyes bright. "Maybe not as bad as me, but . . ."

Kate looked at Anne, whose shoulders raised in a slight shrug. "I asked the same question. They gave the same answer. I don't have as much time served in the Park as you do, but from what I've seen so far, my guess is that Ryan now has the half-life of a gastrotrich if he's not out of the Park as in yesterday."

Kate got up and walked to the window. The view was a parking lot with a row of recycling Dumpsters. Behind them rose the cell phone tower, bristling with antennas and satellite dishes. Behind the tower the Quilaks rose from rolling green foothills to buttes with flattops leveled by glaciers to an impenetrable wall of jagged, blue white peaks.

Although not quite impenetrable, she thought.

If Kate turned Jennifer and Ryan over to Jim, Rick Estes's death would be squared away and off the books. She was certain that Jim wouldn't even file charges, but if he had to and it got as far as trial, she knew to a moral certainty that Judge Bobbie

Singh at the district court in Ahtna would never allow either one of these children to see the inside of a prison.

Jennifer and Ryan—and Anne—were right. Every extra moment they remained in the Park was hazardous to Ryan's health, and very probably to Jennifer's as well. It would, she realized with a sinking feeling, be even more hazardous to the health of the Park.

The advantages of being a Park rat were many. You knew your neighbor and your neighbor knew you. In the worst winter, there was help there for you when you needed it.

The disadvantages of being a Park rat were also many.

You knew your neighbor.

Your neighbor knew you.

The Suulutaq Mine was divisive enough, pitting parent against child, brother against sister, community against community. If the tensions between Kushtaka and Kuskulana were allowed to exacerbate an already incendiary situation, there was no telling where it would stop. Kushtakans and Kuskulaners were so far off the grid, they were used to doing and making for themselves. The law was at minimum half an hour away by plane, and if the weather socked in, it could be days before there was any kind of incident response.

The Kushtakers would not rest until Rick Estes was avenged. If they exacted that vengeance on the person of Ryan Christianson, the Kuskulanans would retaliate. Kate had a very real nightmare vision of landing in Kuskulana to find dead bodies littering the streets. This thing had already precipitated two murders and an involuntary manslaughter. Kate could not allow it to escalate to include collateral damage.

Okay, turning them over to Jim was out. However angry it made him, and she was sure he was going to be very pissed off.

But there was no possible way to guarantee either Ryan or even Jennifer's safety if they remained in the Park. Going home was not an option for either of them.

Putting them on a plane to Anchorage and getting them out of the state. Could that be done before the Kushtaka and Kuskulana jihadists found them? Like every other village, Kushtaka and Kuskulana had as many relatives living in town as they did at home, more probably.

Driving them out. There was one road out of the Park, and one road at Ahtna going one of two directions, south to Anchorage or north to Tok.

Again, Anchorage was not an option. She turned her head to look at the young couple. "What kind of identification are you carrying?"

They both had driver's licenses. No passports. Which meant, with the new 9/11-inspired border controls, they couldn't get through the Beaver Creek border crossing. So trying to get them out through Tok wasn't an option, either.

"Would our marriage certificate work?" Ryan said.

"It's in my daypack," Jennifer said, and reached for something that wasn't there. "Oh," she said, looking sick.

"What?" Ryan said.

"I forgot it." She looked at Ryan. "On the beach. After . . ." Her eyes filled with tears. "I'm sorry," she said, sounding like a frightened child ten years her junior.

"It's all right," Ryan said, trying to gather her close again. "It's all right, Jennifer."

"No," she said, pushing herself upright. "You don't understand. They'll have found the daypack. They'll have looked inside."

Ryan's eyes widened with dismay, and then he rallied. "We

were going to write to them anyway. They had to know sometime."

Jennifer looked at Kate. "You have to help us," she said, her voice maturing from one sentence to the next. "We have to get out of the Park, and we have to get out now."

What was the best possible outcome here? Kate thought, looking at the young couple, well aware their recent actions might be the spark that sent their villages up in flames, but in spite of their mutual terror, both of them determined to face whatever came together. What was best for them? What action would be most effective in averting all-out war between the two villages? What could she do to maintain the fragile peace of the Park?

Kate turned to look at Anne. "Get in your plane and go back to Cordova."

Anne looked at Ryan and Jennifer. "What about them?"

"If anybody asks, you can tell them the truth up to this point. After that, you don't know. Best all around."

Anne understood. She got to her feet and dusted her hands, unconscious of the irony. "Okay."

"Although if nobody asks, don't volunteer."

Anne's smile was strained. "Not a problem," she said.

Jennifer hugged her hard. "Thank you," she said, her voice muffled in Anne's shoulder. "Thank you."

Ryan hugged her, too. "We'll never forget what we owe you, Reverend Flanagan. Thank you."

"I'll walk you out," Kate said. "You guys wait here."

On the other side of the door, she said, "One more thing you have to do, Anne."

Kate kept her speed at a slow and sedate forty miles per hour, mindful of all posted signs, giving dutiful waves to everyone she passed, including even Iris Meganack, who was weeding strawberries in her garden and who wouldn't have pissed on Kate if she were on fire. Mutt sat up next to her, the tips of her ears brushing the ceiling whenever Kate wasn't quick enough to avoid a pothole. There was absolutely no reason for anyone to suspect that she was smuggling two fugitives out to her homestead beneath the blue tarp in the back of her pickup.

Ninety minutes later she parked outside the garage and twitched back the tarp. "Hop out. Jennifer, pull both four-wheelers out of the garage. Ryan, there's a fuel tank around the back of the shop. Top off both of the four-wheelers and fill up a couple of jerry cans. There's a trailer. Hook it up."

She didn't wait to see if they obeyed her, taking the steps to the house two at a time. On the back deck, there was a small, weatherproof shed where she kept her gear. She pulled out her backpack, Johnny's backpack, and an old army pack of her father's, one of the few things to survive the cabin fire. She took all three into the kitchen and filled them with packaged and canned goods, dried fruit and nuts and granola bars.

Jennifer came in. "Done. Where are we going?"

"There's a twenty-four-pack of bottled water on the back deck," Kate said. "Put it in the trailer."

Admirably, Jennifer didn't hesitate.

Kate went to the hall closet and started rooting through it.

Jennifer returned. "Done. What next?"

Kate tossed her a pair of XtraTufs. "Try these on."

Jennifer did. "Little loose."

"You would have Princess Ariel feet." Kate went upstairs and brought back two pair of heavy wool socks. "Try them on with these, one pair at a time, and then start trying on jackets from the closet." She grabbed Jim's boots and took them out on the deck. "Ryan! Catch." She dropped them into his hands. "Try them on."

He did so. "Little loose," he said.

Kate went back upstairs and returned with two pairs of Jim's wool socks.

She went back inside and found Jennifer zipping up Johnny's venerable Filson jacket. "It's the only one that fits," she said.

"It would be," Kate said. Maybe Johnny wouldn't miss it. Ha.

Spare T-shirts and socks. A first-aid pack, contents checked. Deet, 50 percent, a bottle in each pack. Sunscreen, 50 SPF. Kate bought both in bulk at Costco once a year. Toilet paper in ziplock bags, one roll per pack. More ziplock bags, freezer strength, gallon- and quart-sized. A ball of string, a coil of rope, bandannas, ball caps.

Each pack already had bear bells fastened to the outside. Kate could find only one whistle and stuck it in her own pocket.

She took down the .30-06, her father's and one of the other things to survive the cabin fire, and the relatively new double-barreled, pump-action 12 gauge from the rack over the door. She raided the closet again for ammunition. Jennifer had already started ferrying the packs outside, and Ryan appeared at the door. Kate pointed at the closet. "Find a jacket that fits."

She found her compass, took it over to the tattered map of the Park tacked to one wall, and lined up a route. She wasn't sure how far the compass on her phone would take her before they ran out of service area. She found a smaller-scale, plastic-coated map to carry with them.

"This okay?"

She looked up and saw Ryan zipped into Jim's Eddie Bauer

down jacket, no less venerable—or favorite—an item than Johnny's Filson. It was a little big on him, but he wouldn't have fit into anything of Johnny's or Kate's. "Fine."

She stood there, thinking. What had she forgotten? Something.

Matches. Fire starters. If she had had time, she would have smacked herself in the forehead. She found both and a couple of Bic lighters and leaped down the steps into the yard to distribute them among the packs.

"Everybody have a knife?" They nodded. "Show me." They did without protest. They were both Swiss Army knives, Ryan's the big one with all the tools. "Good."

Heading into the Bush in a hurry resulted mainly in injury and death. She felt at her belt for the sheath of her Buck knife. Whetstone. There was one in her pack; she had checked. Water filter. Again, in her pack.

She looked out the window and saw that the sun had sunk low into the sky. They wouldn't be able to go far this evening without stopping, but the upside was at this time of year they wouldn't have to wait long before it got light enough to see their way again.

She closed all the kitchen cupboard doors and the closet door and the door of the house. She went down the steps at a more decorous pace this time, and halted in front of the young couple. "I have something to say, and I need both of you to listen to me very carefully as I say it."

They moved instinctively to stand closer together, and looked at Kate with sober faces.

"It's not too late to change your minds," she said. "From what I saw and from what you told me, I don't think anyone is going to jail over Rick Estes's death."

She saw a flash of sorrow cross Jennifer's face, and regret on both their faces. "Right now, this minute, we can put all this stuff away, drive back into town, and go to the trooper post and surrender to Sergeant Chopin. He's not there right now, but he'll be back tonight or tomorrow morning. He's a smart guy and a reasonable man. I can't speak for him, but as long as you're telling me the truth—"

"We are," Ryan said, as if he were taking a vow.

"We are," Jennifer said at the same time, and with a little more attitude.

"—then at best you'll be charged with leaving the scene, at worst involuntary manslaughter. You're first offenders, I doubt very much there will be any jail time. Probation, probably some community service."

"But we'll have to stay in the Park," Jennifer said.

Kate nodded. "Be my guess. Judges like to know where you are."

"We do that, Ryan's dead," Jennifer said flatly.

Kate looked at Ryan. "Her, too, maybe," he said.

A shadow passed over the clearing, and Kate looked up to watch a golden eagle soar overhead, brown feathers gilded to bronze by the sun. "Okay," she said. "But know this: There's no coming back. You run, you're automatically guilty of something. They find you, the law will make sure you pay for making them go to all the trouble of catching you."

"We understand," Jennifer said, and Ryan nodded.

No, you don't, Kate thought, and made one more try. "You do this, you're dead. Do you understand? You're dead, you're gone, you're never coming back. You can't tell your families where you are. You can't even let them know you're safe and well, because there are no secrets in the Park. It will get out, and then someone will come for you. Maybe the law. Worse, maybe not."

They stood with their arms around each other, eyes red. With difficulty, Ryan said, "Better to be dead now than dead later."

Jennifer looked up at him and nodded, a tear spilling down her cheek.

Beyond the clearing the golden eagle went into an abrupt dive, disappearing behind the brush, reappearing again almost immediately with an arctic hare in its talons. The hare wriggled at first and then went still.

"All right," Kate said slowly, and much against her better judgment. "Let's go."

Act V

Twenty-one

FRIDAY, JULY 13, ANCHORAGE
SATURDAY, JULY 14, THE PARK

BRILLO LOOKED FROM JIM TO THE BODY BAG and back at Jim. "You're killing me here, Chopin."

Jim patted the air with one hand. "Just . . . tell me if you think he was deliberately murdered or if he died of injuries after he got beat up."

"So, what, now I'm a medium?"

"Just do it, okay, Brillo? I've got a civil war brewing in the Park."

Brillo scowled. "Great, more bodies." He brightened. "Maybe new kinds of wounds, though."

Jim looked at him.

Brillo heaved a sigh. "Just trying to lighten the load, Chopin." He unzipped the bag and extracted the body with unexpectedly gentle hands. "Now, sir, what have you to tell me?"

Kate had closed Rick Estes's eyes, but he still looked dreadful, bloated and leached of color, except for the bruises.

"What position was he in when you found him?"

"On his right side, sort of."

Brillo looked up, eyebrow raised.

Jim hesitated, and then spoke with care, choosing his words. "Water had washed him to the side of the river. He was tangled up in the trees."

"Mmm. Well, he died on his back. Lividity shows us that much."

"I saw that."

"Then what do you need me for?" The question was asked absently and without pugnacity. Brillo explored Estes's head and body with gentle fingers and a detached scientific curiosity that nevertheless gave the impression that he still knew he was dealing with a man, a human being who had once walked the earth, who had had a life and family and friends. He unbuttoned the shirt, miraculously intact, inspected the chest, and rolled the body up to one side to examine the back. He pressed here and there, to the crackling sound of bones rubbing together and the squishy sound of interior damage done. He opened the mouth and peered in with the aid of a penlight. He inspected the nostrils and the ears and the eyes.

"Hmm." Brillo straightened. "Yes. Well."

"Well what?"

"He'd been in a fight, all right."

"Thank you for that insightful diagnosis," Jim said with awful sarcasm. "I'd never have known."

"No need to get snippy," Brillo said. "And the answer is, I don't know if he was just in a fight or in a fight to the death. If you made me guess—" He looked at Jim over the tops of his black-rimmed glasses.

"I made you," Jim said.

Brillo sighed and stepped back from the table. "Then I'd say he was in a fight, a rib broke and punctured a lung, and he drowned in his own blood." He held up an admonitory finger. "I won't know if any of that is true until I open him up."

Jim was already pulling on his cap. "Thanks, Brillo. I appreciate it."

"He coulda just had a heart attack!" Brillo yelled after him as he left the lab.

"He coulda," Jim said without breaking stride.

It was late and he knew better than to get back into the air before he'd had some rest. He spent the night in Anchorage, breakfasted well, and was at five thousand feet on an easterly heading half an hour later. Two plus hours after that, he was landing in Niniltna.

First order of business was finding Boris Balluta. Jim was going to find him and if necessary beat some answers out of him. Whether it resulted in a "heart attack" or not.

Easier said than done, however. Boris wasn't in the tiny cabin at the edge of the village that he'd fallen heir to when his brother Albert married Dulcey Kineen and moved to Cordova, as far away from Boris and Albert's other brother Nathan as he could get and still be almost in the Park. Jim drove the fifty miles to the Roadhouse, where Boris wasn't, either.

"Probably working his fish wheel," Bernie said. "He makes the best smoked fish I ever ate." He made a face. "Must be making a mint, the price he charges for it."

Jim looked for answers in the bottom of his Coke and found none. "What do you hear about this feud between Kushtaka and Kuskulana, Bernie?"

Bernie, a thin man with a hairline receding all the way back to a graying ponytail that reached his waist, moved a damp rag up and down the already shining surface of the bar. The big square room, the floor filled with mismatched tables and chairs and the walls and ceiling decorated with gill net, glass floats, moose racks, and women's underwear, was quiet at this time of day. "I know what everybody knows," he said. "They hate each other's guts." He meditated. "The Kuskulana kids show up here from time to time, trying to pass themselves off as legal." He smiled. "Doesn't get 'em far."

Jim smiled, too. Bernie Koslowski had an encyclopedic memory of every child born in the Park since he'd arrived in it. "I'm told Boris hung with Tyler Mack," he said.

Bernie nodded.

"Tyler's dead," Jim said. "Murdered. Why I'm looking for Boris."

Bernie's face was grim. "Man, it just doesn't get any better down there." He topped up Jim's drink.

"They ever bring any of that here?"

"No," Bernie said definitely. "They know better. Well."

"What?" Jim said.

"The Kuskulana chief's son, what's his name?"

"Ryan?"

"That's him. He and his buddies showed up here one night last winter on snow machines and tried to talk their way in the door. Kenny and Mitch Halvorsen, some kinda Christianson cousins, I think, were here. They booted the boys out the door, none too gently, either."

"Kuskulana on Kuskulana," Jim said.

Bernie shrugged. "I remember Mitch was especially enthusiastic with Ryan. Although Ryan got in a few good licks. Mitch came back in looking like he'd been through the wars, and Kenny gave him a pretty hard time for taking such a beating from a teenager."

⁂

Jim drove grimly back to Niniltna and down the Park road to the turnoff to Boris's fishing hole, where Boris put up his fish wheel every year. It was invisible to passersby on the road, and the only reason Jim knew where it was was because he was the perfect trooper. Also because Kate had once showed it to him. If he'd had a brain in his head, he would have started there.

He bumped carefully down the rudimentary road to the side of the river, branches scraping at the trooper seals on the doors. Alas, the fish wheel was there but Boris wasn't. A Honda Rancher, the Park's default ATV, was hidden in a thick stand of alder. No keys. There were a few reds in the holding pen, which indicated that either the fishing was really bad or that Boris had just been there.

Across the river a black head poked out of the underbrush. As if on cue in front of a Disney camera, three much smaller heads poked out of the leaves beneath her. A black bear sow with triplets. Maybe they'd been feeding out of the holding pen. Bears were nature's most dedicated opportunists.

Jim climbed back in his vehicle and drummed his fingers on the steering wheel. If Boris wasn't sleeping, and he wasn't drinking, and he wasn't fishing, where the hell was he? It was July. No Park rat got that far from the water in July.

The only other place he could think to look for him was at Howie Katelnikof's. There was a variety of reasons Jim hated going out there, not least of which the shooting of Bernie's late wife and who had really killed her. Not to mention the risk of catching weasel cooties from Howie.

But go he would if go he must. He sighed and reached for the key. A movement caught the corner of his eye and he looked around just in time to see the terrified look on Boris's face as he vanished back into the alders. Jim was out of the cab and after him in a moment, shoving through the bushes and getting slapped in the face by vengeful spruce trees. His eyes stinging, his skin smarting, he crashed through to a small clearing that held a pop-up tent and a fire pit made of river rocks. Jim was just in time to snag the collar of Boris's shirt before Boris hit the trees on the other side.

The fabric twisted around his neck and Boris choked, hands going to his collar to try to pull it free. Jim hauled him up on his toes, not trying to help. "Boris Balluta, as I live and breathe," he said, "how nice to see you again."

"Gug, ack, gah," Boris said, clawing at his collar.

"Oh," Jim said, "I'm so sorry, Boris, are you having trouble speaking?" He released the tension on Boris's collar a minuscule amount.

"They'll kill me," Boris managed to gasp. "They'll kill me, too!"

"Interesting," Jim said. "Tell me who they are, who else they've killed, and why they want to kill you." He smiled, which could be a terrifying sight when he wanted it to be. "And why I shouldn't let them."

It turned out Boris wasn't into reticence. Or loyalty. When the frantic babble of words finally abated, Jim said, "Okay, let me see if I've got this straight."

They were in his vehicle, Boris behind the screen in the back, and the black sow and her three cubs sniffing interestedly at his tires. He rolled down the window a couple of inches. "Hey! Hey! Get away from there!" He honked the horn a couple of times. "Scat!"

Momma got up on her hind legs and gave him a look that gave him to understand that this was her territory, not his, but one of her cubs squawked and lit out into the brush, followed by his siblings. Momma seemed to sigh and might even have rolled her eyes. She dropped back down on all fours and lumbered after them.

Down the bank, Boris's fish wheel creaked as it turned, water dripping from it and sparking in the sun, and there was the occasional splash from a salmon jumping. Across the river a couple of eagles roosted in a scrag, one immature and looking very skinny. The mature one, probably one of its parents, launched forth, did a strafing run over the surface of the water, and scooped up an unwary salmon in its claws. Returning to the scrag, it tore into the salmon without bothering to share.

"You and Tyler notice that Mitch and Kenny got a good thing going for them in their bootlegger business, and you decide they need some competition." He paused, more out of incredulity than because he had to collect his thoughts. "However, you don't have any money to buy stock, so you decide to steal from their stash to get your own business going. That right?"

He looked over the back of the seat. Boris, who looked like a teddy bear someone had ripped all the stuffing out of, gave a miserable nod.

"Mitch showed up and caught you in the act. There was a fight, and Mitch went down. That about it?"

"I didn't hit him," Boris said, repeating the words for the fourth or maybe the fortieth time. Jim had lost count. "It was

Tyler. Mitch was pretty pissed. Him and Tyler got into this big-ass fight. I didn't want no part of it. I was up the ladder by the time Tyler yelled that Mitch was dead."

"Uh-huh," Jim said. "Why did you nail down the hatch cover?"

"It was Tyler's idea," Boris said. "Like I told you. He saw the toolbox and found the hammer and nails. He didn't want the body to be found too soon. Give us time to get away from there and get our alibis straight."

Jim wondered if Boris could even spell "alibi." *CSI* really did have a lot to answer for. "Boris?" He met Boris's eyes in the rear-view mirror. "Mitch was alive when you left him."

Boris gaped at him. "What?" he said, his voice little more than a croak.

"Oh yeah." Jim nodded. "And eventually conscious. He broke a collarbone trying to get out of that crawl space."

"Oh man," Boris said, now turning an interesting shade of puce.

"The two of you left him in that crawl space alive. Tyler might have knocked him out, but Mitch woke up later, nailed up inside what would become his tomb."

"Man," Boris said, bent over, groaning. "Don't say that, man. Don't. He was dead, man. He was dead! Tyler said he hit his head on something."

"He might have died from alcohol poisoning from drinking the stock you were trying to steal while he waited for someone to find him and get him out of there." Jim watched Boris's reaction in the rearview with an entirely clinical eye. He was afraid Boris was going to puke in his vehicle. He hated when that happened. "Although his body was so desiccated when Kenny finally found it that we might never know for sure."

"Oh man," Boris said, rocking back and forth. "Oh man, don't tell me that, man."

"When was the last time you saw Tyler, Boris?" Jim said.

Boris stared at him. "I told you, man!"

"Tell me again," Jim said.

"That was the last time I saw Tyler!"

"Uh-huh," Jim said.

"It's the truth! I don't want nothing to do with him after that! I came out here to the fish wheel and I been out here ever since!"

"Uh-huh," Jim said.

"You have to believe me, man, you have to!"

Jim probably did have to, given that of the three men in the crawl space that night, the only one left alive was sitting in the backseat of his vehicle, trying not to spew.

"You ask Tyler," Boris said desperately, "he'll tell you!"

"Tyler's dead, Boris," he said.

Boris went white. "What!"

"Tyler's dead," Jim said again. "Murdered." He looked at Boris's fish wheel circulating steadily with the flow of water downriver.

There was a short, electric silence from the backseat, followed by something that approximated a shriek. "They'll be coming for me next, man! You have to protect me! You have to protect me, man!" he sputtered. "Witness protection! You have to!"

"Uh-huh," Jim said, and turned the key in the ignition.

⁂

As they were coming up on the turnoff to Mandy's, her truck nosed up onto the road and turned toward Ahtna. She waved and he braked and rolled down the window, closed against the dust of the road. "Hey, Mandy."

"Hey, Jim," she said. She looked at the backseat, where Boris Balluta sat, white-faced and subdued. "What's up?"

"You know, serving and protecting. The usual. How about you?"

She nodded at the road. "Got a community meeting in Ahtna."

Mandy, championship musher, retired, was the new community representative for the Suulutaq Mine. "Lucky you," Jim said.

She shrugged. "People have questions. They live here, they deserve answers."

Depends on how true those answers are, Jim thought.

"What's Kate up to?" Mandy said, by the change of subject leading him to believe that he might have to work on his stone face. "Chick and I were cutting dead wood on the north edge of my property yesterday. We saw her headed out on her ATV."

"Oh?" he said. "Out where?"

Mandy hooked a thumb over her shoulder in a generally eastward direction. "She waved but she didn't stop to talk. Van and Johnny were with her, on Johnny's four-wheeler."

"Johnny and Van?" Jim said.

"They were at the top of that ridge, you know, the one that backs both our homesteads?"

He remembered very vividly, having surveyed the area from the air not two days before.

A slight but distinct uneasiness ran beneath Jim's skin as they headed off in their respective directions, although he couldn't have said precisely why. It wasn't as if Kate had to clear her activities with him.

He laughed suddenly.

Which was a good thing, because it would never occur to her ever to do so.

He deposited Boris in a cell at the Niniltna post, checked in briefly with Maggie, and on impulse called Johnny's cell. It rang three times before picking up.

"Hey, Jim," Johnny said.

"Hey," Jim said. There was noise in the background. "You in the middle of a riot or what?"

"Kind of a party," Johnny said. "Pipe down, you guys!" To Jim he said, "Somebody got hold of some booze, and, you know."

"I know," Jim said. "Which you are not drinking?"

Johnny's grin was almost visible. "Who, me?"

"So you're at the mine?"

"Yeah," Johnny said.

"You and Van both?"

"Yeah," Johnny said. "We're on shift for another week, and maybe more if somebody calls in sick."

"It's all about the money with you, you filthy little capitalist."

Johnny laughed. "Damn straight it is. Why'd you call? Something up?" His voice changed. "Kate okay?"

"She's fine," Jim said. "Just checking in."

He was back in the air shortly thereafter. It was a gray day with a stiff, chill breeze out of the southwest, and some trick of the atmosphere made the Quilaks feel taller and more menacing on his left. When he lifted off the Niniltna strip, he knew a momentary urge to turn north and east to try to find Kate. As numerous as airstrips were in rural Alaska, he couldn't be guaranteed she would be anywhere near one, or that she would be in cell range, or that she would even be visible in the overabundant summer undergrowth.

Not to mention his sworn duty. He put his curiosity about

whom she was with and what she was up to resolutely in the "Later" file and headed south-southeast.

When he landed in Kuskulana, he tied down the Cessna and headed straight for Roger Christianson's house. Carol answered the door, looking a lot older than the last time she'd seen him. "Jim," she said, and didn't step back.

"Let him in, Carol," Roger said behind her. If anything, he'd gained a couple of decades on Carol in the time since Jim had seen him last.

They settled into the kitchen as before, although this time there was no offer of coffee and cake. Jim dispensed with the preliminaries. "Here's what I know," he said. *Or think I do,* he thought.

"Mitchell and Kenny Halvorsen were running a bootlegger operation, alcohol and I'm guessing drugs, too, out of the crawl space of the house Mitch was building. They'd fly it in from Anchorage or wherever, offload it and store it in the crawl space, and then transport it a load at a time up the trail to the Suulutaq Mine, where they'd sell it to the miners."

He waited. Roger and Carol studied their hands and said nothing.

There is no way in a community this size you couldn't have known, he thought. "Tyler Mack and Boris Balluta saw what was going on and decided there were enough McMiners to support two bootlegging operations in the Park. Since neither of them had a pot to piss in, and since Mitch chose to build his house in such a nice private spot at such a nice convenient distance from Kuskulana, why not acquire seed stock from their competition?"

Roger opened his mouth, and closed it again when Carol gripped his wrist.

"So, late one night last May, Tyler and Boris came upriver and started lifting cases of booze out of Mitch's crawl space. Mitch caught them in the act. There was a fight, and Mitch died. I don't imagine for a moment they meant to kill him, but Tyler and Boris, in a spectacularly intelligent move you might expect from a couple of guys with a combined IQ of, oh, I don't know, twenty-two, nailed the hatch down over him and ran for it.

"Then two months later, Kenny came back from Alaganik, went to the stash in the crawl space of Mitch's house, probably looking to fill up an ATV trailer with product and sell it at Suulutaq for walking-around money. He found the hatch nailed down, thought what the hell, pried it up, and found Mitch's body. He jumped to the same conclusion anyone who'd ever spent five minutes in either village would jump to, nailed the hatch back down, made himself visible in the village while he laid his plans. After which, he headed across the river looking for payback, which he satisfied by whacking Tyler over the head with a piece of rebar—"

Jim paused for a moment, a memory tickling at the back of his mind.

"—a piece of rebar," he repeated slowly, and then said, "Son of a bitch!"

And he didn't apologize that time, either. "Kenny whacked Tyler upside the head with a piece of rebar," he continued in a grimmer voice, "and stuffed his body into a bucket on the Kushtaka fish wheel, either to finish the job or try to make it look like an accident, or maybe even both, because that's the kind of rocket scientists I'm dealing with here." He looked at Roger and Carol. "How am I doing so far?"

The answer, when it came, was unexpected. "What the hell else was Mitch supposed to do?" Roger said. "He was the sole support of his brother after his cousin died."

"That'd be Pete Liverakos?" Jim said after a moment. He didn't know what this had to do with the subject under discussion, but at least they were talking to him.

"Ask your girlfriend," Carol said in a cold voice.

"Carol," Roger said.

She looked at him, eyes bright, and folded her lips into a tight line.

Roger turned back to Jim. "Okay, yeah, Kenny and Mitch were running a bootlegging operation."

"Roger!"

"Carol," Roger said in exasperation, "three men are dead. How many more before this is over?" He turned back to Jim and held up an admonitory hand. "Understand, we only heard things, we never saw them."

Uh-huh, Jim thought, and looked at Carol, chief of Kuskulana village. "Did you know Mitch's body was lying up there in the crawl space of his half-built house?"

"No," Roger said with force.

"You didn't hear him yelling and trying to get out?" A shot in the dark, this, after he and Kate had tested the theory. But there was every reason for his relatives to wander up to the house now and then to make sure it hadn't been messed with.

Especially any relatives who might be involved in the family business.

Roger looked appalled. "No!"

"You didn't just let him sit there and die in the dark, because you knew what he was up to, and you figured he deserved it?"

Both Christiansons surged to their feet, shouting. In turn, Jim stood. He didn't place his hand on the butt of his weapon, but just by raising it into view he lowered the decibel level.

"He was ours," Carol said, her voice choked. "He was ours,"

she said again, thumping her breast with one fierce fist. "Do you understand?"

"Yes," Jim said, "I think I do." He let the silence gather for a moment. "That fight Ryan got into with Mitch Halvorsen, last winter over at the Roadhouse."

Both Christiansons froze. After a moment Roger said stiffly, "What about it?"

"You can see how it looks," Jim said. "They fight, and later Mitch winds up dead."

"Ryan did not kill Mitch," Carol said, her voice high and strung very tight.

"Yeah, I know," Jim said. "He's yours, too. Where is he?"

There followed a silence that lasted just that bit too long. "You don't know," Jim said.

"He's fishing down on the Alaganik," Carol said. Her hand reached blindly for Roger's.

"Sure he is," Jim said.

Twenty-two

SATURDAY, JULY 14
SUNDAY, JULY 15

The Park

THE NEXT TWO DAYS BROUGHT KATE TO an appreciation of air travel as she'd never had it before.

Their journey was only a hundred miles as the crow flew, but they were on the ground. The first day was the easiest, beginning with the old track she had pointed out to Jim from the air two days before. In spite of what she told him then, Kate had grown up in the Park and there were few if any roads and tracks and game trails she didn't know. Overgrown roads to defunct gold and silver mines, bushwhacked trails into abandoned homesteads, timber trails crumbling on the sides of clear-cut hills whose old-growth forest was only now slowly coming back, Kate knew them all and displayed an uncanny ability to connect one to the other in a track that however meandering in execution took them steadily toward the Quilaks and kept them mostly under the radar of Park rats. Mandy and Chick were cutting wood at the north edge of Mandy's homestead and stopped to wave when the two ATVs came up over the ridge.

"Do you know them?" Kate said, waving back but keeping any invitation out of the gesture.

"She came to our school to talk about the mine," Ryan said. "I didn't meet her personally." Jennifer nodded.

"Good," Kate said, and put the ATV back in gear and headed down the ridge and out of sight of the musher and her partner.

They were lucky in the weather, which was cloudy and cool. The mosquitoes provided an incentive to forward motion because they swarmed to attack every time they stopped. Ryan was the worst off, and by the evening of the first day his eyes were very nearly swollen shut.

They lost count of the moose they saw. The bears were like mice, everywhere they looked, on the edge of every creek, stream, and rill; asleep on the gravel or under a bush; batting fish out of the swift-running water, ripping them apart, fish eggs flying everywhere. The salmon had hit fresh water by now, thankfully, and none of the bears were hungry enough to do more than snap their teeth in warning, even the sows with cubs.

The first night, she pushed the three of them until they crossed the Step Road and into the foothills, stopping a little after midnight to make camp. Jennifer proved adept at camp cooking and made a hearty meal of prepackaged chicken stew with dumplings made from Bisquick. They cleaned up, packed all the food away in the trailer, and tarped it. "We'll have to stand watch," Kate said. "Too many bears."

Ryan nodded. "I'll go first."

"Both of you go first," Kate said. "I'm an early riser, and I'm not going to let us sleep that long anyway." She gave them a stern look. "I don't want to hear any noises."

Her admonition produced two wan smiles, but when she woke herself three hours later, they were still fully clothed and, what surprised her even more, still awake. A honeymoon to remember, she thought as she watched them roll into their sleeping bags. They were both asleep almost instantly. Jennifer snored.

Kate sat with her back against a tree, her sleeping bag beneath her, her .30-06 across her knees, and Mutt warm and solid by her side. The moon was a pale, last-quarter crescent. If she squinted, she could imagine that she saw a star or two, although it would be another month before it got dark enough at night to be sure.

The lack of vehicle noise, by land, air, or water, allowed the Park at night to come alive around her. The rustle of spruce branches teased by a midnight zephyr, the white shadow of the outspread wings of a great snowy owl, the contented gurgle of the tiny stream at the foot of their campsite. A coyote's howl, followed by a hare's scream abruptly cut off. A porcupine rattled out of the underbrush and through their campsite, taking no notice of the puny intruders into her realm. There was nothing as impervious as a porcupine.

A bear or some other large mammal—*not a wolverine,* Kate thought, *please, not a wolverine*—passed through some thick brush to the north. She had deliberately picked a campsite next to a stream too small for salmon, but her hands tightened on the rifle anyway. The sound faded, and she relaxed again to listen to the music of the forest.

After a while, not greatly to her surprise, the ghosts began to appear.

Her father, Stephan, short, stocky, a Park rat to his fingertips, he fished, he hunted, he trapped, he lived a subsistence lifestyle because he knew no other and no complaints. Her mother, short, slender, softer but as competent in her own skills of homemaking and skin sewing, beautiful before the drink took her looks and eventually her life and her husband's soon after. Their ghosts came into the clearing hand in hand and smiled at her, young again, healthy again, eternal.

Kate smiled back at them, unafraid.

After them came first Emaa, solid and stately and stern, and Old Sam, thin and sharp as a razor blade, wearing his iconic shit-eating grin.

Jack. Tall, homely, rumpled, looking slightly pissed off, as if he was still irritated that his time with her had been cut so short.

We had almost ten years together, she thought. *In the end you saved my life. And you gave me Johnny. No regrets.*

She closed her eyes against sudden tears. When she opened them again, the ghosts were gone.

A wolf howled, another responded, a third. Mutt didn't wake, but her ears twitched.

The sky was lightening. She roused Ryan and Jennifer at four o'clock, and noted with approval and not a little relief that there was no whining. They ate a quick breakfast of peanut butter spread on apple slices, packed up the camp, and left, Kate again in the lead.

This day the landscape was a lot steeper and the undergrowth a lot thicker. Kate had packed the chain saw and had it out half a dozen times when a too-large spruce had fallen in a way impossible to go around. Three times one of the ATVs got stuck in a bog and had to be pulled out by the other. The mosquitoes were even fiercer than the day before, to the point that they were beginning to bother even Kate, and they soaked bandannas in deet and tied them round their necks, wiping their skin with them as they sweated off the last application. Even Mutt looked a little sullen, although her thick fur was a better deterrent than their thin skin.

Now and then they would find a clearing and on a few heavenly occasions a bald knoll high enough for Kate to eyeball local landmarks and figure out where they were. The first time she'd gone back to Canyon Hot Springs after an absence of some years, she'd taken two wrong turnings before she'd found the right one. That was in winter on a snowmobile on thick snow that had covered most of their present obstacles, resulting in much easier going. Making the same mistake on this trip would involve a lot more manual labor, which she was determined to avoid if at all possible. She consulted map and compass frequently.

As the day wore on, she had more cause to respect her companions. If somebody got stuck, they both got out and pushed without being asked. When the young cow moose crashed out of a stand of willow, on the run from some unidentified predator and prepared to take out everything in her path to get her two calves out of danger, Ryan had the shotgun up and had fired a discouraging blast in her direction before Kate had her rifle out. Jennifer spotted the lynx before Kate did, and twice was able to find a better way around a bog.

There was little conversation and no complaining about fatigue or hunger and no stopping to spoon, either. Kate witnessed the occasional glance, but it seemed the young people were able to encompass the notion of delayed gratification. Life now, love later. She could only respect their choices, and the maturity it took to make them.

The higher they climbed, the thinner the vegetation and the

fewer the mosquitoes. By nine o'clock that night, they had found the entrance to the canyon. The 60 percent grade on the doglegs made it slow and tedious, but they made the springs before midnight.

Kate had never been to the canyon in summer before. In winter, the sharp, V-shaped notch in the Quilaks was blunted by a white, smooth, easily navigable surface. In summer, not so much. The summer growth of grass and shrubs was so enthusiastically prolific that, even from the seat of an ATV, about all that could be seen of the cabin Old Sam had built so many years before was the moss-covered roof. Even then, it kind of blended in.

Only the pools looked the same, creating a steamy string of black pearls draped along the notch of the vee.

She pulled to a halt in front of the cabin and dismounted wearily. Her butt hurt from sitting on it for seventeen hours straight. Her thighs ached from straddling the vehicle. Her hands were numb from gripping the handles. Jennifer and Ryan weren't in much better shape, and even Mutt looked tired.

The cabin was built of logs and chinked with moss that had long since fallen out. Kate pushed open the door and went in.

The interior was much the same as she had left it the previous winter. The blue tarps remained tacked to the walls. The woodstove made from an oil drum stood against the wall, next to a pile of firewood.

She looked up into the corner, and only because she knew it was there saw the faint outline of the hidey-hole Old Sam had put there for her to find. She smiled.

She felt Ryan and Jennifer come in behind her. "We'll camp here tonight," she said.

"Tomorrow?" Ryan said.

"Tomorrow," Kate said, "we leave the four-wheelers behind."

They went outside to unpack without further question or comment.

Really, she was liking the two of them more and more.

She let them sleep in all the way to eight o'clock, waking them to the smell of coffee and enormous bowls of instant oatmeal with a handful of raisins each, heavily doctored with brown sugar and canned milk. Afterwards, she stood over them as they jammed everything into their packs that would fit, including the rest of the deet and the sunblock and the lion's share of the first-aid supplies. She made sure they took the water filter, the whetstone, all the matches, both lighters and all but one of the fire starters, and she gave them the map and the compass.

For herself, she packed two bottles of water, a can of mixed nuts, and a bag of sweetened dried mixed fruit into her pack, picked up her rifle, and said, "All set? Okay, let's go."

This time the direction was easy. They followed the bottom of the canyon up. When it doglegged right, they went right. Because of the altitude, the vegetation was thinner and lower to the ground, which made the walking easier, which was good because they quickly grew short of breath in the thin mountain air.

It was high noon before they toiled to the top of the little saddle that bridged the two sharp peaks to the north and south. For a while all they could do was drink water and catch their breath. Kate insisted they eat something, although no one was very hungry and no one could taste anything, either.

The view made up for it all. It felt as though if they stood on tiptoe they could scrape their fingernails on the roof of the world. The mountains, which looked like an impenetrable wall from the Park, here parted to reveal the tiniest of passes between two tall massifs, the width necessary to take one pair of feet and no more. It began in the west from Canyon Hot Springs and ended . . . "I don't know," Kate said when Ryan asked. "I haven't hiked it. Canada, I can tell you that much."

They had almost enough energy to smile.

She packed their trash into her pack. "Take my shotgun," she said. "You'll need a firearm for basic protection, and not just from the wildlife. Many people get themselves lost in the woods on purpose, so they can do whatever they want." She thought of Crazy Emmett, and Father Smith, and Liam Campbell's chilling stories about Clayton Gheen. "Be careful. Don't just blindly trust the first person you meet. Or the second."

They gave sober nods. They were so damn young.

"Canadians have strict laws about firearms, but you'll be in the YT. They're good people there. Almost Alaskans. Find a place that feels friendly, with as large a population as you can stand because it's always easier to hide in a crowd, and settle in. Work for cash. Stay off the grid as long as you can, and when you've absolutely positively got to get that driver's license, make sure the paperwork will stand up."

She pulled out an envelope full of twenties and fifties she'd brought from her stash at home. "Take it," she said when Ryan would have waved it off. "American cash works everywhere, and no matter how self-sufficient you are, there will be some situations where only cash will do."

"We'll pay you back," Jennifer said.

"No," Kate said. "You won't." She nodded at the envelope. "There's a name and a phone number in there, too. Make sure the first two words you say are my name or he'll hang up. He can set you up with documents. He won't be cheap, so hold off on that until you've got some money saved."

"Will he barter?" Ryan said.

Kate shrugged. "You can ask. He's pretty capable his own self, and a mean, nasty, suspicious bastard besides. He doesn't put it past you or anyone else to hide a black helicopter under his woodpile."

She rose to her feet. They followed and shouldered into their packs, fastening chest and waist belts and pulling ball caps down over their eyes.

"We'll pay you back," Jennifer said. "Someday, somehow, we'll pay you back."

"No," Kate said with more force this time. "No, you won't. Don't call, don't write, don't e-mail, don't wire money, don't mail it. Most of all, don't get caught. If you get caught, you're on your own. I've just aided and abetted in a felony escape. I'm trusting you not to bring that home with you."

"It was an accident," Ryan said.

"I believe you," Kate said, and she mostly did. "But Rick Estes's death is the third in a row, and Jim Chopin is not going to stop until he finds out why those three men died, and how. He can't. He swore an oath." Her expression was stern and inflexible. "And your villages need some sense shook into them anyway."

"Good luck with that," Ryan said.

Jennifer nodded, her eyes shadowed. "Kushtaka is dying, Kate. You know how, when you land the fish, it beats itself against the beach, trying to get back in the water? It doesn't go peacefully. That's Kushtaka."

"And Kuskulana . . ." Ryan looked despairing. "My folks won't be happy until there's cable TV in every house."

"And a liquor warehouse on every corner?" Kate said.

Jennifer looked at Ryan.

"Mitch and Kenny Halvorsen," Kate said. "They were running a bootlegging operation out of Mitch's crawl space."

Ryan's eyes met Kate's and fell. He gave a reluctant nod.

"Who killed Mitch?"

"We all thought he was fishing down Alaganik," Ryan said, choosing an oblique answer. "Dad went up to check on his house while he was gone, and he saw that the hatch on the crawl space was nailed down. He thought that was odd, so he pulled it up."

"Why did he leave Mitch there?"

"He had to talk to Mom. She's the chief."

"And what did the chief decide?" Kate said in a very dry voice.

"Mom said Chopper Jim could tell if we moved the body, and that before we called him, we had to get all that booze out of there."

Kate remembered the marks of multiple boxes in the dust.

"Before we could, Kenny came home from Bristol Bay. It's where he has his permit. He went to Cordova first, looking for Mitch. When he couldn't find him, he came home. And then when he found Mitch, before anybody could stop him, he called Chopper Jim."

"Who killed Tyler Mack? Kenny?"

A short silence fell. "Tell her," Jennifer said.

"He's my cousin, Jennifer," Ryan said.

She held his eyes. "No," she said gently. "That's what she's been trying to tell us. He isn't your cousin anymore."

They stared at each other while Kate waited.

"Tell her," Jennifer said again.

Ryan swallowed hard. Kate appreciated how much a betrayal

this was, given the years Kuskulana had invested in him keeping his mouth shut, so she didn't push.

"We met that morning at the landing," he said in a low voice.

"I came up the river in my father's skiff," Jennifer said. "Tyler came up the river right behind me."

"Did he see you?" Kate said.

"I don't think so," Jennifer said, "but I don't know for sure."

"He didn't yell or anything?"

"He wouldn't," Jennifer said. "He would have held it over me, used it to get something he wanted."

Kate stared at her, not hiding her suspicion.

"No," Jennifer said. "No, Kate."

"What?" Ryan said.

"We did not kill Tyler," Jennifer said.

"Huh?" Ryan said. "No, we sure as hell did not! We beached Jennifer's boat and we went to a little clearing around the point, on Cataract Creek side. That's when we saw him."

"Saw who?"

Even then, it was hard for him to get the words out. "Kenny."

"What was he doing?"

"He was in his skiff, floating down the creek toward the river. He must have hidden it there."

"Did he see you?"

"No. We didn't know what he was going to do, so we kept quiet. If we'd known . . ." He hesitated, and Jennifer took his hand and held it in a firm grip. He gave her a grateful glance and looked back at Kate. "He beached his skiff way down at the end of that gravel bar the Kushtaka fish wheel is on. He snuck up on Tyler when Tyler was pitching fish out of the holding pen. He had a piece of rebar." He stopped.

"Tyler didn't hear him?"

"I wish," Ryan said, his face gray. "If we'd known, we could have done something, anything—"

"It happened so fast," Jennifer said. "We didn't even have time to shout."

Kate looked at her, and she wondered. If Tyler Mack had seen Jennifer meeting Ryan, and if Jennifer knew Tyler had seen them, then Tyler Mack dead might have been more desirable to Jennifer than Tyler Mack alive.

"This shit has to stop," she said, more to herself than to them. She looked up. "In the meantime, you two need to get down the trail. Do not be in a hurry. Down is always the most dangerous part of a hike."

"Kate," Ryan said.

"Get going," she said.

Jennifer walked a few steps, and turned. "Can I at least call my dad? Someday?"

Kate took two giant strides forward and grabbed Jennifer by the straps on her pack. "And what happens when he knows you're alive? If they've found your daypack and seen the marriage certificate, he already knows you're married to Ryan, a Christianson from across the river, a Kuskulaner, a tribe he's been raised to hate. And how long before he finds out what really happened on the beach that night, and what happens then?"

"It was an accident," Ryan said.

"What happens when they find out what happened at Kuskulana?" Kate said. "When Roger and Carol find out their precious only child married one of those backward Macks from the wrong side of the river, the village where they won't let the women hunt and fish and where they let the school die because they couldn't keep their young people home?"

"But—"

"Open warfare," Kate said. "The Kuskulanans will blame you for this elopement, Jennifer. The Kushtakers will blame Ryan. Don't you think they already hate each other enough?"

Jennifer's eyes were full of tears.

Kate released the girl and stepped back. "I told Anne to stop at Scott's on her way back to Cordova. He'll sink Ryan's skiff with your belongings on board somewhere on the river it's sure to be found. If you're lucky, if everybody's lucky, they'll think you drowned."

Jennifer leaned her head on Ryan's shoulder, and, again, he rested his cheek on her hair.

"You're gone," Kate said. "You can't call. You can't write. You can't e-mail, you can't text, you can't IM, you can't post a comment on the Kushtaka homepage, always assuming they ever put one up. You can't ever come back."

She looked at Ryan. "Unless you want to come back with me now and surrender to Sergeant Chopin."

Tears ran unchecked down Jennifer's cheeks, and Ryan looked ten years older than he had the moment before.

"Running now means running forever," Kate said.

"Decide."

Twenty-three

SUNDAY, JULY 15

Kushtaka

JIM TOOK ROGER'S NEWLY RE-SURFACED SKIFF downriver without asking, noting only that Roger had already bought a new outboard, a twin of the first. No money problems for the Christiansons, that was for sure.

Kushtaka looked as harmless as ever, a tumbledown little Alaskan village eroding quietly into its own past.

Appearances could be deceiving.

Jim thumped on the door of Pat Mack's cabin. "Pat! It's Jim Chopin."

He felt the sensation of thirty pairs of eyes on his back.

"Pat, open up. I've got some questions that need answers."

Dale Mack came out of his cabin and stood there, his hands on his hips, glaring at Jim. At least he wasn't carrying a weapon.

The door creaked open and Jim turned to see Pat Mack standing there. He looked tired. "Got some questions, Pat," Jim said.

"You can let me in or I can take you to the trooper post in Niniltna. Your choice."

It was a big gun to bring out on a village elder. Jim had worked hard to forge relationships with Park rats so that if they didn't feel friendly toward him at least they were tolerant of his presence.

Today, he really didn't give a shit.

Pat hesitated for what felt like a long time, before stepping back and allowing Jim to enter.

Inside, the cabin was divided by a wall. A door in the middle of it looked into a small bedroom with a bed consisting of a mattress and box springs on the floor and a dresser built of Blazo boxes, open ends out. The outer room was where Pat lived. It resembled Tyler Mack's tar paper shack in nearly every detail, except Jim was pretty sure there was insulation in these walls. The woodstove was lit and the room was stiflingly hot. Jim removed his cap.

Pat sat down in the room's only chair, an old wooden rocker pulled up close to the stove. He picked up a mug and used it to gesture to the dented old coffeepot on the stove. "Help yourself, if you've a mind to."

"Thanks." Jim looked around and found a step stool and hauled it over to sit down. One was not blunt with elders, unless one had a wish to be summarily and comprehensively ignored, but the last three days had rendered Jim beyond common Park politeness. "Tyler drowned in that fish basket, Pat," he said, "but he went into it alive. Unconscious, but alive."

He watched Pat's face carefully. One of the rockers squeaked as Pat shifted in his chair, but that was all the reaction he got.

"His killer hit him first, in the back of the head, using a piece of rebar."

Squeak.

"I saw that piece of rebar in Tyler's skiff, Pat."

Squeak.

"Was it the murder weapon?"

Squeak.

Jim could feel his temper fray at the edges. "Was the rebar what jammed the fish wheel so the basket Tyler was in would stay underwater? Did you wash it off and put it in the skiff? To wash away any evidence I might find? Like all those skiffs washed the beach clean where Rick Estes was killed?"

Squeak.

"Goddammit, Pat!" Jim said. He could hear his voice rising and fought to bring himself under control. "I know all you Kushtakers think you're living out the moral precepts as set forth by Don Corleone, but this shit has to stop. Three men are dead. You and I both know more will die if we don't stop this now."

The door opened behind them. "That's enough," Dale Mack's voice said. "You come on outta there, Sergeant Chopin."

Not Chopper Jim, not Jim, not even the more casual Trooper, but Sergeant Chopin. Jim looked down at the mug turning between his hands and resisted the impulse to look around to see if Dale Mack had gone for his rifle. "Why don't you come in here instead, Dale," he said to his mug.

There was a long silence, broken only by the squeak of Pat Mack's rocking chair.

But Dale Mack did come in. He stood next to Pat Mack, arms folded, face set. "Got nothing to say to you."

"Got something to say to you, however," Jim said, setting the mug on the floor and rising to his feet. "I've just been up to Kuskulana. I know the Halvorsens were bootlegging booze and dope out of Mitch's crawl space. I've talked to Boris Balluta and I know he and Tyler were going into competition with them, and that Mitch caught them thieving his stock and that he got killed in the fight that followed. For whatever reason, Kenny didn't find his body for two months. My guess is when he did, he came across the river and killed Tyler in revenge."

The round black-and-white clock on the wall had a minute hand with a hushed click as it moved from second to second. In the silence of the room that followed, each click sounded like a rifle shot.

The sectarian nature of life along this part of the river had hardened its inhabitants into a silence that would not be broken. Boris had talked only because he was from Niniltna, where family feuds were settled by the aunties before they ever really got started. There were advantages on occasion to having the might and majesty of the law seconded by four tough old birds who knew where all the bodies in the Park were buried, and who weren't afraid to remember the burial locations when it was necessary.

Kushtaka and Kuskulana had no such human brake pedals, unfortunately, and worse, they had raised their children to believe that vengeance was theirs.

"Okay," Jim said heavily. "I didn't expect to get any answers by coming here, and I wasn't disappointed. What the hell, maybe I just wanted you to know I'm not so stupid as to not notice all the non-clues you were so determined to leave behind."

He went to the door and paused with his hand on the latch. "Was Rick Estes in on it with Boris and Tyler? Is that why he was killed, too?"

"No!" Dale Mack said, exploding. "Rick was a good man! He didn't have anything to do with that shit!"

Pat put his hand on Dale's arm. Jim watched him do it. Carol had put her hand on Roger's arm in that same restraining way. And Jim watched Dale master his anger in a way that, had he but known it, mirrored the same emotions and actions as the chief's husband across the river.

"You go on now, Jim," Pat said, looking suddenly weary, as Roger and Carol had looked weary. "You just go."

He went.

Dale Mack's wife was standing in the door of her cabin, watching, expressionless. He didn't see the beautiful daughter or anyone else in the village on his way down to the landing.

He untied the bowline and pushed the skiff back into the river.

"Sergeant Jim! Sergeant!"

He looked around, the rancor at Pat Mack's cabin still with him enough that he dropped his hand to his weapon. When he saw who it was, he relaxed. "Auntie Nan," he said, perking up. Was here a Kushtakan who would talk to him?

But no. "You give me a ride?" she said. She was carrying plastic grocery bags in both hands, both of which looked full of clothing.

"To Kuskulana?" he said, surprised.

"To Niniltna," she said.

The Cessna was a state-owned aircraft, with its fuel paid for by the Department of Public Safety, and as such not to be used to give joyrides at the state-paid pilot's whim.

On the other hand, Auntie Nan had been a witness to all the goings-on in Kuskulana for longer than he'd been the Park rats' personal trooper. Simple though she might be, she was bound to know things he didn't.

"I'd be happy to, Auntie Nan," he said, and handed her into the skiff.

Twenty-four

SUNDAY, JULY 15, CANYON HOT SPRINGS

Monday, July 16, Kate's homestead

KATE CAME DOWN FROM THE PASS FULLY intending to pack up and head back to the homestead that afternoon. Instead, she spent the rest of the day and that night at Old Sam's cabin. If there were questions you didn't want to answer, you couldn't do better than stay out of cell phone range, and Canyon Hot Springs was as far out of cell phone range as she could get.

She unpacked and set up camp in the cabin and then stripped down to bare skin and jumped into the largest pool feetfirst. Mutt climbed to a small ledge halfway up the side of the canyon. Kate watched her curl up in a fugitive ray of sunshine. Canyon Hot Springs was where she and Kate had had their come-to-Jesus meeting last October, when Mutt had stated in no uncertain terms that she was either a full partner in the firm, entitled to all the same benefits and especially risks that Kate was, or she wasn't. And if Kate had decided that Mutt wasn't, Kate was pretty sure Mutt would have vanished out of her life for good.

"Of all the homesteads in all the Parks in all the world," Kate said, "you had to walk into mine."

Mutt's ear twitched, but she didn't bother opening her eyes. So far as she was concerned, their argument had ended when she demanded and got an unconditional surrender.

When Kate had soaked all the weariness out of her bones, she left the pool and dressed. She spent the rest of the day making a leisurely survey of the cabin and its surroundings. Astonishingly, the outhouse was still upright. The cabin needed a few nails here and there, a few holes made by inquisitive mammalian and avian creatures needed plugging, and she gave it a thorough cleaning while she was at it.

She'd sent all the food and cookware over the mountain, and that night dined sumptuously on an overlooked package of Top Ramen noodles cooked in an empty tin can she had found and boiled clean.

She slept outside. For the slice of open sky over her head, for the sound of the wind in the spruce trees, for the smell of their sap in her nostrils, it was a risk she was willing to take. With Mutt beside her as her own personal hostile wildlife DEW Line, it wasn't all that risky.

Nothing disturbed them. Not bear, not wolf, not moose, not ghosts, not dreams.

The next morning she rose early and breakfasted on dried mango slices and tamari almonds, topped off with one of the new Starbucks instant coffees, which weren't bad after you added three packets of Coffee-mate and a couple of cane sugars.

Fortified for whatever the day might throw at her, she packed up and scoured the area for any trash. She spent some quality time in the outhouse and left behind a liberal layer of lime.

She left Johnny's ATV behind at the cabin, tarped and roped like a mummy in the vain hope it would keep the porcupines from getting into the engine and eating the belts. When Johnny got back from Suulutaq, she'd bring him up here and they could drive out together. Be a nice sendoff before he went to college, a trip for just the two of them.

Three of them. No way would Mutt allow herself to be left behind.

The trailer she left hitched to hers. She had a full tank and a full jerry can, which should more than see her home.

The doglegs were a little more exhilarating on the way down, especially since she geared down instead of using the brakes. Mutt galloped alongside, her tongue flopping out of one side of her mouth. The need for stealth gone, she turned onto the Step Road just down the bluff from Park HQ. The only people she saw were Keith and Oscar, stooped over in their extensive commercial herb gardens. They stood to wave as she and Mutt went by.

She was in Niniltna by eight o'clock that evening and passed through without stopping, taking the Park road home and not sparing the horses. At a little after nine she rolled into the clearing and dismounted, weary but calm.

That calmness evaporated when she looked up and saw the expression on Jim's face.

"Hey," she said warily.

"Where have you been?" It was very much the trooper speaking.

In every good lie, it was always best to include as much of the truth as possible. "Up to the springs."

He nodded, and came down the stairs. "You go up there alone?"

She stared at him. "You know I didn't. How?"

"Mandy."

"Of course." More and more crowded every day.

"She thought you had Johnny and Van with you."

"Oh," she said.

"But I called Johnny, and he and Van were still at the mine."

"Oh," she said again.

"So who was with you?"

His tone was inflexible. He wasn't going to let this go.

She looked past him, at the house the Park had built, the house he had moved into with her, one clean shirt at a time. It had taken two years of both of them ignoring the fact that his toothbrush had taken up permanent residence next to hers in the bathroom, that he had an equal share of drawers and closet space, that he'd forged a relationship with her adopted son that looked a lot like foster father.

So, if she wanted this to continue, lying was probably not her best option. "Jennifer Mack and Ryan Christianson."

His brows snapped together. "You took Jennifer Mack and Ryan Christianson up to the springs?"

She nodded.

He was groping to make some sense of her revelation. "You're going to leave them up there for the summer?"

Mutt hopped down from the back of the ATV and stood looking from Kate to Jim, scenting the tension in the air.

Kate unstrapped her backpack from the rack behind the four-wheeler's seat. "No," she said. "They're not there anymore."

"Where are they?"

She fiddled with the backpack, killing time, and then looked up to meet his eyes. "I took them up to the pass."

"What pass?"

She looked away. "Something I didn't tell you about Canyon Hot Springs."

"Yes?" he said, his voice dangerous.

She almost squirmed, and caught herself in time. "The canyon takes a right turn, way back up, past all the mines Old Sam's dad dug into the cliffs. You remember?"

He nodded, grim-faced.

"I didn't take you all the way up when we went to get the Cross of Gold."

"What did I miss?" he said in a tone that would brook no evasion. If she but knew it, she was paying for all the hours he'd spent being lied to in Kushtaka and Kuskulana this week.

"When you get to the top, there's a pass through the Quilaks. About one person wide. Goes down the other side."

"Into the YT," he said.

She nodded.

"So you took them up there and turned them loose."

She nodded again.

"Interesting," he said, "when I'm pretty sure you know Ryan Christianson murdered Rick Estes."

"I don't know that," she said, her voice steady.

"I flew down to Alaganik this afternoon," he said. "Ryan's friends were there, but Ryan wasn't with them. And his parents are worried. I thought it was because Ryan might have killed Tyler, or Rick, or both of them. I already know Tyler and Boris killed Mitch. And now you're telling me Ryan ran off with Jennifer? Kuskulana's heir apparent absconded with Kushtaka's darling?" He laughed. He didn't sound even remotely amused. "Oh, that's great, that's just, that's . . . Jesus. I'll definitely be wearing Kevlar the next time I fly down to Kuskulana."

"No," she said, "listen. Anne Flanagan married them secretly four days ago. Jennifer snuck out of her house that night and met Ryan on the river. Rick Estes saw her and followed her there. They told me he just appeared out of the brush, seconds after she met Ryan. He tried to stop her going with Ryan—no, Jim, he actually laid hands on her. Ryan tried to stop him, and they started fighting. Rick had time and pounds on Ryan and he might have won, if . . ."

"If?"

"If Jennifer hadn't hit him from behind."

"What with?"

"She said one of the oars out of Ryan's skiff."

"Which is now where?"

"In Potlatch." She thought she wouldn't mention the fact that the skiff and all its contents would have been sunk in the river by now. "They knew they couldn't get much farther without being seen by some relative or other, so they stopped at Potlatch and got Scott Ukatish to call Anne Flanagan in Cordova. He's got a small strip. She picked them up and brought them to me in Niniltna." She paused. "For what it's worth, I believed them when they said it was an accident. Jennifer says that Rick had a crush on her and that her father wanted her to marry him. It sounds like he thought he had the right to stop her."

"You'd better hope the autopsy bears them out," he said.

She did, most fervently.

He hadn't changed out of his uniform, and with his hands on his belt he looked like a recruiting poster for the Alaska Department of Public Safety. Badass trooper about to clean house.

"You're not as surprised at any of this as I thought you'd be," she said.

"I went back out to Kuskulana and Kushtaka," he said. "I talked to the Christiansons, and then I went over the river and talked to the Macks."

"They tell you anything?"

"No, but before I went, I found Boris Balluta. He told me his side of it. Pretty much like we'd thought, Tyler figured he'd start his own bootlegging business on the Halvorsen's stock. Boris was his partner. Mitch caught them at it, and from what Boris says, killed himself staggering around in the dark trying to beat on Tyler and Boris. They nailed the hatch down—you saw the toolbox—and ran for it. Boris, naturally, says it's all Tyler's fault."

"Fortuitous, since Tyler's too dead to contradict him."

"Two months later, Kenny Halvorsen notices Mitch isn't fishing. He comes home to find the hatch nailed shut. He pulls it up and finds Mitch, but he can't call the cops until he gets all the contraband out of the crawl space."

"And Boris— "Kate said.

"And poor Boris is petrified that both villages are going to come after him."

"He's not wrong," Kate said.

"No," Jim said. "I can't believe he was still in the Park when I found him."

"Ryan . . ." Kate said.

Jim's head came up. "Ryan what?"

"Ryan says Roger found Mitch first."

"Oh hell no," Jim said.

She spread her hands. "Don't shoot the messenger. Ryan says Roger nailed the hatch back down while the council figured out what to do with the contraband before calling you. Before they could, Kenny came home and found Mitch."

They frowned at each other. "Which one's telling the truth?" Jim said.

"Who has more to lose?" she said. "So far as anyone knows except you and me and Anne Flanagan, Ryan Christianson is dead, and he knew that when he told me his story. Roger Christianson, on the other hand, is very much alive and well and still living in the Park. Plus Kenny is only a low-rent Kuskulaner at that. If anyone gets thrown to the wolves, it'll be him."

Jim nodded. "I've been looking for Kenny. I haven't found him yet. I banged on every door in Kuskulana on my way home, but no one admits to seeing hide nor hair of him, although one or two of them were willing to swear that he'd moved Outside."

"When?"

"Oh, they weren't sure, but last week some time, they thought."

"Was this before or after they swore on their mothers that he'd been in their sight every minute of the day Tyler Mack was murdered?"

"The very same, or close enough as to make no never mind. Not like any of them would have a different story." The stern lines of his face eased a trifle, and he looked less angry than tired. "Oh, and Auntie Nan hitched a ride with me to Niniltna."

"What did she tell you?"

"Not a goddamn thing. Although I don't think she's as dumb as she pretends to be."

"Anne Flanagan says it was Auntie Nan who made the wedding possible. She pulled Anne out of Tyler's services and took her to the two kids."

"Definitely not as dumb as she pretends to be,."

"Never underestimate an auntie," Kate said.

"You know, Kate," Jim said, shoving his cap back on his head, "I used to be a pretty good law enforcement officer. I could serve and protect with the best of them." A surge of rage flooded up over his face. "If fucking people would just fucking let me!"

"Where is Auntie Nan now?"

The rage ebbed. "With Auntie Edna, who if I understood correctly is by way of being a shirttail relative to everybody named Mack in Kushtaka." He thought it over and added, "Better them than me."

Kate almost smiled. "So," she said. "We've got three deaths. Best guess is, two were accidental, one deliberate. You figure Kenny for Tyler?"

"Course I killed him," a voice said, and they looked up to see Kenny Halvorsen emerge out of the trees, the business end of a .30-30 pointed their way.

Jim unsnapped his weapon and pulled it out. "Put the rifle down, Kenny," he said.

Bolt action, Kate thought, looking at Kenny's rifle. *Take some time to get off more than one shot.*

Next to her, Mutt went up on all fours, a menacing snarl ripping out of her throat that could have been heard in Niniltna.

"He killed my brother," Kenny said, his face congested with rage. "What'd you expect me to do?"

"Drop it, Kenny," Jim said. "Drop it. Now!"

"Like you said, Kenny," Kate said in a steady voice, hands up and palms out, "I didn't kill Mitch."

"No," he said bitterly, "but you killed Pete."

"What?" Jim said.

Kenny ignored him. "What the hell else were we supposed to do to support ourselves? We're the poor relations in Kuskulana. It was what we knew how to do. Pete came from Outside, and when Dad died he took over. He showed us how to move the booze. It was the only thing we knew, the only way we could put food on the table. And then you." He looked at her with bottomless hatred. "Did you think we didn't know? Did you think we'd never pay our debt? Pete's dead. Now Mitch is dead, too. I'm the only one left. And what the fuck does it matter?"

From a standing start at Kate's side, Mutt went airborne, launching herself at him with teeth bared.

He shot her, more in reaction than with malice aforethought.

Jim fired at the same moment.

Kate saw Kenny's left shoulder jerk back and red bloom below.

Mutt seemed to stop in midair, and then fell heavily to the ground.

Somebody screamed. After what seemed like forever, Kate realized it was her. She took a step forward, so slowly, as if she were waist-deep in one of the bogs they'd been caught in going up to Canyon Hot Springs, pushing her way through the water and mud toward Mutt, who seemed somehow to be receding into the distance.

Kenny's rifle swung back toward her, and Kenny and Jim fired at the same moment a second time.

Kate felt as if she'd been punched hard in the chest. She looked down in surprise and saw a small dark hole, replaced by a rapidly spreading stain. The strength drained from her limbs as if someone had pulled a plug. She sat down hard on the seat of the four-wheeler.

Across the clearing, Kenny grunted and staggered back, nearly dropping his rifle, but not quite. The barrel began to rise again.

Behind her, Jim's gun boomed a third time.

This time Kenny Halvorsen went down.

Kate blinked at him, her vision starting to blur.

A tiny songbird with a golden crest lit high up in the branches of a spruce tree, and sang a mournful three-note descant that echoed beyond the clearing, down the river, and off the peaks of the very Quilaks themselves.

Acknowledgments

Heartfelt thanks go to my editor, Kelley Ragland, whose comments made this a much better book. You would think that by now I wouldn't need to be told to show, not tell. Yeah, you'd think that.

Thanks go to my friend Pati Crofut, whose travels around Alaska have provided me with so many great story ideas, including the entire plot for this novel.

My thanks to Der Plotmeister, who came through yet again with an all! new! and improved! method for murder. This guy really shouldn't be allowed out without supervision.

And my thanks to Carl Marrs, for giving me a great, true line, without even knowing he was doing so. All writers are thieves, especially when you don't know we're robbing you.

Many of the minor crimes passingly referenced in my novels come straight from the trooper dispatch page on the Alaska Department of Public Safety Web site. It makes for very entertaining reading, although not as entertaining as Sergeant Jennifer

Shockley's Unalaska police blotter, which has also provided much grist for my crime fiction mill, not to mention Facebook posts.

A long time ago in an Alaskan village not that far away, I babysat for Darlene Kasheverof Crawford. Darlene had three kids and full-cast recordings of all of Shakespeare's plays. I'd make Crystal, Kim, and Don go to bed early so I could listen to the plays. It is Darlene's fault that the first place I went on my first trip to Europe was Stratford-upon-Avon, England, and saw there at the Royal Shakespeare Theatre my first Shakespearean production, *Romeo and Juliet*, starring Timothy Dalton as Romeo, no less.

I thought then and I think now that *Romeo and Juliet* is less about the lovers than it is about their families, and that their elopement could have been much better managed. Forgive me, Will.